KISS ME HARD
A NOVEL
BEFORE YOU GO

Shannon McCrimmon

THE HEARTS OF HAINES SERIES

Book 1 - *Kiss Me Hard Before You Go*

Book 2 - *Like All Things Beautiful*

Book 3 - *This is Where We Begin*

Published by Shannon McCrimmon
www.shannonmccrimmon.com
www.facebook.com/shannonmccrimmonauthor

Cover Design: Popcorn Initiative • www.popcorninitiative.com

For the Lee family

CHAPTER 1

JUNE, 1978

The front door slammed shut downstairs. Evie opened her eyes wide and jolted up off of her pillow. Her heart hammered against her chest. Someone clomped around on her front porch, and the wood creaked with each and every step. She could hear shouting, but it was pouring buckets. The rain pelted against her house's tin roof, muffling their conversation.

Her three-legged dog, Tripod, howled; his raspy bark echoed into the thick night air. Thunder rattled the loose glass windows, and lightning dashed across the sky like the crack of a whip.

She was too scared to move. Her mind told her to get her cowardly butt out of bed, but the rest of her body wouldn't cooperate. She lay frozen stiff and her limbs wouldn't budge an inch.

A beam of light quickly flashed into her room, and she knew that the warm glow wasn't coming from the lone dim light on her porch. It was bright, and she swore she heard the roar of a truck engine.

She pulled her thin blanket over her head, feeling the warmth of her breath. Her body slightly shook, and her heart continued to beat wildly. She knew she couldn't stay in that position forever.

The sound of a gun shot pierced the humid night air, and a bullet flew through her window. Glass shattered everywhere.

"What the hell!" she cried out, fearing the worst.

She quickly jumped off of the bed and hid underneath it. Her cool, damp skin stuck to the cold hardwood floors. She crouched, wrapping her arms around her legs and moving as close to the wall as she could. She breathed heavy and hard, wondering what had just happened and where the heck her dad was.

The door downstairs flew open, crashing against the wall. Loud, booming footsteps bolted up the stair case in a hurry.

He shoved the door open and turned the light switch on. She could see his wet boots. A puddle was forming, and water flowed toward her on the old house's slanted wooden floor.

"Evie," he said breathlessly.

"Down here," she whispered to him.

Her dad, Gray, peered under the bed. He breathed a sigh of relief. His lips curled up just a tinge. "You all right?"

"No," she said, answering him as if it should have been obvious.

"You can come out." He motioned to her, nodding his head encouragingly.

She crawled out from under the bed. Her pulse was still haywire.

"What happened?" Her eyes darted to the broken window and then to the floor now covered in glass.

"We'll fix it tomorrow," he said.

"What happened?" she asked again.

He took off his red baseball cap and scratched at his scalp of bushy brown hair. He was drenched, and his sopping shirt clung to his big belly. "I heard a loud noise and went out to see what it was. When I got outside, all I could see were a few shadows moving around and a truck parked on our grass near the end of the drive. It was real dark, and their lights were blinding me. Don't know what they were up to but makes me wonder if they're the same jack holes that messed with our fence."

"You shouldn't have gone out there by yourself." *If only I had been awake*, she thought. She would have gone out there with him and given a few strong choice words to these hooligans. It took a couple of days to repair the fence, and wrangling in the two cows that had escaped wasn't much fun, either.

He placed his hand on her shoulder and gave her a warm, appreciative smile. "Ain't nothing but some dumb teenaged kids. When they saw I had a rifle, they got scared."

Evie looked at the broken window again and then at him. "But...?"

He sighed and tightened his lips. "It don't matter," he said.

She gave him a look.

He huffed. "I had my finger on the trigger and tripped over a dern rock."

"You." She laughed. "Tripped." She laughed. "Over a rock," she said and then placed her hand in front of mouth to silence her laughs.

"This ain't funny," he said. "You could've gotten hurt."

"Yeah, well, I guess first thing tomorrow morning I better scoop up all the pebbles out of our driveway since they're a hazard now," she said and chuckled again. "So that's why it was like the Battle of Gettysburg in here because you tripped over a stupid rock?" She shook her head in disbelief and smiled, thinking of the fact that she had crawled under her bed and crouched on the floor because she was frightened. "A rock," she thought to herself.

She could see a hint of a smile forming on his lips.

She grew serious and said, "Daddy, I thought the worst."

"Me too." He touched her cheek with his damp palm and gave her a tired smile. "Go on back to sleep, Punkin. We're gonna have to get up early tomorrow."

"Oh, there's no way. I can't sleep now," she said and headed out of her room.

"Where are you going?" he asked as he followed her.

She grabbed her sweater and put it on. "Downstairs for a Coke. You want one?"

"Guess so. I can't right sleep either. Too stirred up. My heart's still racing a mile a minute," he said.

She turned to face him, a look of concern filled her face. "Maybe you should sit down."

"I ain't the one who had a bullet fly at them," he said. "Lawd have mercy, I nearly soiled my britches when I heard that bullet crash through your window. Fastest I've run since my football playing days in high school."

"I know," she said. "I heard you coming up the steps."

A trail of water and mud followed her father as they made their way downstairs. The front door was still wide open, and the rain continued to gush from the sky. Tripod sat in front of the door, wagging his tail, acting as if nothing had happened.

"Looks like he's recovered," Evie said. "Must be nice living in the land of oblivion."

"He's still a good watch dog, ain't you boy?" Gray patted him on the head before closing the door.

Evie turned on the kitchen light and opened the refrigerator, taking out two glass bottles of Coke. She picked up a bottle opener and peeled off the caps, handing a bottle to her dad. She took a swig as she sat down across from him.

"It's getting worse," she finally said.

"What's that?" he asked, feigning ignorance, but she knew he knew exactly what she was talking about.

She raised her eyebrow.

"Like I say, they're just some dumb kids messing around is all."

"They must be really dumb because they've come back more than once. Think we should call the Sheriff?"

"Nah. Ain't nothing to call about. Winton wouldn't do nothing no how," he said. "Don't you worry. They ain't gonna come back."

"They might, since they saw you can't shoot straight," she said with a smile. Deep down she tried to believe him but suspected this might not be the last time they showed up on their land.

CHAPTER 2

The rooster crowed, waking Evie. She stretched her arms above her head and let out a long-winded yawn. It had been one hell of a night, and the few hours of sleep she managed to get weren't enough. She forced herself out of bed and shuffled to her dresser, pulling out a pair of denim overalls and a faded green John Deere Tractor t-shirt.

She glanced around the room, the puddle of watery mud had been cleaned, and the shattered glass had been scooped. A piece of cardboard was taped over the window. She tiptoed carefully, knowing that she could have missed a few sharp pieces of glass in her haste to get back to sleep. After slipping into a pair of stark white, over bleached socks, she dragged herself downstairs.

The hardwood floors moaned as Gray moved around in the kitchen. The scent of bacon and burnt toast filled the room. The bitter aroma went straight into Evie's nose and stuck to the top of her tongue. Gray had tried his hand at cooking but had failed miserably. Once again. Evie never understood why he even bothered to try. It wasn't his specialty, and as much as he tried, it never would be. She appreciated the effort but hated the aftermath – dirty dishes that needed to be scrubbed clean and ridden of crusty attached food.

She scrunched her face at the blackened toast and peered over at the bacon, thankful it wasn't scorched too.

"Morning, Punkin," Gray said, kissing her lightly on the forehead. "I thought I'd make breakfast today."

Evie gave him a grateful smile and said, "That's okay, Daddy. I've got it. How about I make us some new toast?"

She placed two fresh slices into their toaster and grabbed the other charred pieces of bread, throwing them in the trash. She glanced at the coffee in the coffee pot, noticing it was light brown, looking almost like iced tea and not the usual dark brown color. "How many grounds did you add?"

"A few teaspoons," he answered.

"That's not enough," she said and poured the full pot down the sink. It baffled her how a 45 year-old man could go through his whole life without ever learning how to make a simple pot of coffee.

"I thought it tasted like water," he said, laughing at his ineptness.

"What kind of water have you been drinking?" she teased as she added several heaps of coffee grounds to the empty coffee filter and poured water into the machine, starting it up again. "It'll be a few minutes." She motioned to the pot and turned off the stove, so the frying bacon wouldn't burn.

The toast popped up and she placed the slices on plates, slathering butter liberally on all of them. She grabbed a few pieces of bacon and plopped them down on the plates. "Here," she said, sliding a plate in front of him. He looked down at it and back up at her, giving her an appreciative smile—the kind of smile that spoke the words "what would I do without you," at least that's how Evie read it.

"Is everything okay?" she asked, gesturing with her head to the outside of their house.

He nodded. "Seems to be. I think they were just some drunk kids trying to have a roll in the hay." He snickered at his humor.

"In the rain?" Evie pointed out.

"Not in the literal sense. There's plenty of 'Inspiration Points' around here," he said and raised his eyebrows up and down.

Evie ignored his last comment and asked, "What was all that shouting I heard?"

He sighed in annoyance. "I was yelling at them to get off our land."

"Dumb kids would've left the minute you came out with a rifle. From what I heard upstairs, they didn't leave until you pulled on the trigger and tripped over that pebble."

"It was a rock, a really big rock, Smarty Pants," he said.

Evie didn't respond and tried to force a serious expression, but the more she fought it, her lips curled up into a wide grin. Gray was a notorious exaggerator. She knew that if she found the rock he tripped over, it would probably fit in the palm of her hand.

He changed the subject, "We're gonna have a busy day today. That's why I thought I'd cook for us."

"We know how that always works out." She smiled. She knew he was done discussing the matter so there was no need to bring it up again. "Busier than usual?" she asked.

Every single morning of her current adult life was filled with things to do. Since she graduated from high school just a couple of weeks before, her days were set: get up at the crack of dawn, make breakfast, work the farm, fix dinner, and then go to bed. Every day was routine, and she had a sinking feeling that her life would be like that for a very long time, possibly forever. This was the thought that kept her awake at night; it was also the thought that woke her in the mornings.

He shook his head while chewing on the bacon. He swallowed and then said, "The carnival is coming today."

Evie sat back against the chair and let out a sigh. The carnival.

Ugh. She knew it was coming, but just hearing him say it made her groan. She hated it when the carnival came— filling their farm with loads of tourists and out-of-towners, cigarette butts littering the grass for her to clean up, and the disgusting aroma of funnel cake and cotton candy. How could someone loathe such a sweet smell? Well, Evie could, because after smelling it summer after summer for ten straight years, she couldn't stand the sight of it, much less the scent. To her it was a putrid mix of all the things she hated about the carnival. Why couldn't her dad stick to farming like everyone else in town? That was a question she had asked herself most of her life, but Gray Barnes had the spirit of an entrepreneur.

He was raised to be a dairy farmer, just like his daddy was, and his daddy before him. And that's what he was for a while. The Barnes Dairy Farm was a thriving business, but when the economy took a hit and big competitors dropped their prices to a point that Gray couldn't compete, he settled on raising cattle, fattening them up before they could produce milk. It was a task he enjoyed doing – working with the heifers – and it was the one way he could continue to do what he knew best without losing his shirt. Gray had a strong head for business and dabbled in ventures any time he saw an opportunity. The carnival was one example of Gray's flair for creativity when it came to using what was his biggest asset – his property.

In a town as small as Haines, South Carolina, Gray owned a majority of the land. Last count was five hundred acres of sprawling, fertile, precious land – the most picturesque and scenic in the entire area. Nestled near the interstate with views of the peaks and valleys of the foothills of the Blue Ridge Mountains, Gray's land was prime for development – for a shopping center or one of those neighborhoods with identical, cookie cutter style homes complete with a community pool. He had been solicited more than once by Nate McDaniels, the only other person in Haines who owned as much property as Gray, if not more. Some speculated that his records were flubbed with the county, and Gray in fact owned two acres more than the greedy tycoon, but according to public record, McDaniels owned five hundred and two acres of land. His wasn't in an ideal location like Gray's, and the views weren't as majestic. Rumor had it that more than half of Nate's land couldn't even grow grass good enough to graze cattle on.

No way was Gray Barnes ever going to sell his land. It had been in the family for generations, and he wanted his only child, Evie, to inherit it. He just wasn't so sure she was too keen on working with cattle; this was evident to him that at this point in her life, she wasn't.

At the age of eighteen, the last thought on Evie Barnes' mind was running her dad's farm. She couldn't think about her future – it was too mind boggling trying to decide what she wanted to do with her life. Not that she had very many choices in 1978. She could become a teacher, but only if she could scrounge enough money to go to college. She knew that was an impossible feat in their household. Gray earned enough to take care of them but not so much that he could afford an extravagance such as a college education. That left her with the choice of working as a secretary or running the farm with her dad until she got married and had kids. Having her fate sealed at such a young age scared the bejesus out of her.

This conversation had never been brought up with her father. He just assumed, everyone assumed, that she'd take over the family business once she settled down. Any man within the four adjoining counties would be so lucky – at least that's what the people of Haines thought. For one, Evie wasn't a sad sack of potatoes. She had golden sun-kissed hair, the kind seen in suntan lotion ads or hair commercials. California blond – the same color her mother had. And her eyes. She had her daddy's sky blue eyes. When the light hit them just right, it was like looking into a clear mountain lake—a place anyone wouldn't mind spending the rest of their life. Blond hair and blue eyes already made her seem more attractive than she really was. But Evie wasn't ugly. She was a pretty girl – attractive enough for an Army guy to show all his pals a photo of her boasting that she was his girl. "Ain't she a beauty?" he'd say, and they'd all agree because any doofus who wasn't blind would in fact agree, Evie was easy on the eyes.

She knew it. A girl couldn't go through life unaware that she was good looking if she was indeed good looking. But being pretty didn't stop people from teasing her and treating her like she was a social outcast.

It didn't help that she had a father who claimed to be a dairy farmer and opened his land up to carnival folk year after year. Whispers and shushes became more apparent each year. She noticed that when she'd walk into a room, voices would grow low, hushed tones were more evident. She knew what they were saying. Being pretty wasn't going to stop them from talking about her or her dad. She'd just have to deal. She was the expert at dealing. She'd been dealt a bad hand in life and learned to handle that, so all the nasty gossip spread about her and her dad was easy in comparison to what she went through when she was a child.

She poured their coffee and proceeded to add cream and sugar to their mugs. They sipped and sat quietly while they ate their breakfast. The smell from the burnt toast still permeated the room. Evie got up to turn on the ceiling fan, hoping it'd help kill the odor.

"So, the carnival..." she started, trying not to sound like an angst-ridden teen while saying it. This was his deal – his baby, and it had been a part of their summer since she was eight years of age. Gray swore up and down that the carnival made them money. Evie knew there had to be some truth to that, otherwise, a smart business man like him wouldn't allow it to continue. It brought in extra income, but never enough, not so much that they could take it easy and relax a little. That was simply out of the question.

Evie had never gone on a vacation. Sure she had traveled to North Carolina to visit Gray's aunt, an older taciturn woman who wasn't much for company, but that was the extent of her travels – one neighboring state and that was that. It was always a thought in the back of her mind – would she ever get to go anywhere in her life or was North Carolina the extent of her adventures?

"They're coming later on this morning and setting up," he said, taking a big gulp of his coffee. He patted his belly and smiled. "Good breakfast."

"Thanks," she said.

"It's gonna be a good summer," he said. He always said that – promising the moon and more without an inkling of how things were really going to go. The glass was always full in his eyes.

"Sure," she agreed halfheartedly. How did she know if it was going to be good? Last time she checked, she'd be working the entire summer from dawn to dusk without a break.

They finished their breakfast, and Evie cleaned up. Gray was outside and had already begun to wrangle the cattle to the barn for feeding. It was time to get to work. She slipped into her muddy boots and shot out the door, ready for another day of hard labor.

CHAPTER 3

The window was rolled all the way down. A soft billowy breeze blew through the truck, and Finch took a whiff, smelling a fine-tuned bouquet of manure and flowers—a strange mix— but one common to the area. Cattle farms were prominent in this part of the country, and the scent of manure was just a part of everyday life in Haines. The truck meandered up and down the hills, taking them out of the valley and up into the mountains. He liked the crispness in the air – the lack of humidity and cleanness of it. The air did have a freshness about it – different from the thick, sweltering heat he was so accustomed to in Gibsonton, Florida.

Gibsonton. There wasn't much to the odd town, and Florida was only known for Miami, and more recently, Orlando, due to the recent development of Walt Disney World. Every time he told someone he lived in Gibsonton, they'd give him a strange look as if he'd just told them he lived on the Moon. It was the quintessential town of oddities, of carnies and circus folk, of former circus freaks who had decided to retire in a place with their own kind. It was what he called home and was all he ever knew.

Finch Mills was a lifer. A carny since he was born. His mother had given birth to him while the carnival was in a small town outside of Des Moines, Iowa, and Finch was named for the state's bird. It seemed like a practical idea at the time, but in the years following, having that name and working the carnival made him an instant weirdo in many peoples eyes. He didn't care. Winning the adoration of strangers and others who he thought were vacuous asshats with the IQ of a beetle didn't concern him. He had nothing to prove to anyone.

The radio was on, and Bruce Springsteen's "Born to Run" played. Finch stopped staring out the window and peered over at his friend, Stoney. A cigarette hung from Stoney's mouth as he drove with one hand on the steering wheel, the other on his thermos. He let out a puff of cigarette smoke and took a swig of his black coffee. It was all Stoney ever drank, that and beer. He wasn't known for having pleasant breath.

"Sun's out early," he said to Finch. He took a drag off his cigarette.

"Yup," Finch answered.

"Gonna be hotter than a two dollar pistol today," Stoney said. "That'll be a pisser when we're setting up. Hate the heat."

"And you chose to live in the pit of hell," Finch said, referring to Gibsonton.

"Where else could an old carny like me fit in? I've learned a lot of things in my life, but one of the most important is you don't belong where you don't fit."

"True," Finch said and looked back out the window. They were almost there. He could see the big white house on top of the hill. It was his favorite place on the circuit. He liked the old farm house and thought if he had been given a different life to live, he'd call a place like that home.

"Look at all them cattle." Stoney pointed to the long line of cattle walking into the barn. Finch could see Evie riding on her ATV, yelling at the stubborn creatures who were either too dumb or too obstinate to move. Finch never paid much attention to her, but he could see that she had definitely grown up since he last saw her. Well, at least since he last noticed her. He shook the thought away, and turned his gaze in the opposite direction.

"Don't know how they get 'em in there," Stoney remarked.

"If someone was shouting at you to move and promised you food, you'd bust ass too," Finch said.

"I bet they eat better than we do."

"Aww come one, funnel cakes are good for you. They'll put hair on your chest."

"Don't need more of that." Stoney laughed and hacked a horrific sounding cough. He cleared his throat and took a sip of his hot coffee.

The truck came to a stand still behind several other trucks. "Gonna sit here till someone opens the gate," he said and lit another cigarette.

Finch got out to stretch. He bent over and jolted up, cracking his back while he did so. He raked his fingers through his shaggy, long dark hair and shook it. It was damp from the heat, and he could feel the sweat trickle down his forehead. The sun beat down on him. His dark clothes were like magnets for the sun's rays.

He got a whiff of cow manure and brought his hand up to his nose, trying to quell the stench. The smell was overpowering on this hot summer's day. His friends in the carnival said he had the sense of smell of a comic book hero. That he could smell things no one else could. He argued that it was because they all smoked for so long their sense of smell was gone.

Finch hopped on the bottom rail of the fence and leaned forward, propping his arms on the top rail. He watched the massive beasts trickle into the barn. A few loner heifers grazed on a bail of hay, ignoring the commotion around them.

"Sug! Sug!" Gray shouted. Finch thought it was an odd thing to say, but the cows seemed to respond and moved in a hurry.

Finch noticed that the barn needed repairs and that the grass was overgrown in certain areas, that the wood on the fence was wearing thin and in need of a good overhaul. He thought if things were different, he'd stay put for a while and offer to fix everything that was broken at the farm. That's what he was good at, or at least what he was always told. "If it's broke, Finch is your guy."

Wildflowers added pops of color throughout the land. The cattle mooed, and he could still hear Gray yelling at the them. Evie drove next to him, shouting along with him. Finch could see her golden locks flying up like wildfire. She didn't seem skittish or too afraid to get her ATV close to a heifer. The last of the heifers made their way into the barn, and she sped off in the opposite direction.

"Better get back in," Stoney called from the truck. "Looks like we're moving."

Finch opened the truck door and plopped down against the vinyl seat. "We'll be drenched within an hour." He could feel the sweat pouring down his body. His denim jeans stuck to his legs, and his shirt clung to his wet back.

"Told ya," Stoney said and put the truck in first gear. "'Course you were the idiot that stood out in it. Ain't nothing interesting about a bunch of dumb cows. All they do is poop and eat."

"Sounds like you," Finch retorted. Stoney smacked his gums and took a sip of his coffee.

They moved slowly, at a turtle's pace, but thankfully they were toward the front of the line. Their truck harbored a cotton candy machine, as well as other various odds and ends, and the semis that carried the rides were in the back of the long caravan.

They veered right and turned onto the dirt path that led to Gray's farm. This was just one of three entrances to his property.

Evie stood near the gate; her ATV was turned off and parked adjacent to the drive in the grass. She looked annoyed, and Finch couldn't tell if she was glaring at him purposely or just mad at the world. He smirked, which seemed to tick her off even more.

He vaguely remembered her from the summers before – he'd see her working the farm with her father, just like she was on this day, but he had never interacted with her. Not even once.

Gray had given a set of rules for the carnies to follow, and a spit with a handshake from Kip, the carnival's owner, made him certain that the rules would be adhered to. If Kip shook a man's hand and spat to boot, then his word was as good as gold. One of the rules, and it was the most sacred, was that no carnies have contact with Evie. She was off limits. They respected what was asked of them and left the girl alone. What'd they care about a young girl anyway? They had business to attend to, and a distraction like her wasn't part of their daily routine. Besides, she didn't get near them or the carnival for that matter.

Finch had met plenty of girls on the circuit. Not so many that he was a ladies man, and not so little that he wasn't experienced in the ways of love. Hook-ups along the circuit were common. He tried to steer clear of getting together with anyone he worked with. That was senseless drama, and he had witnessed too many fights and squabbles because of illicit love affairs gone bad. He only formed relationships with girls he met in the towns they visited along the circuit. Meet a girl, make-out or take it a step further, then move on to the next place. That was his mantra. His mom tried to teach him how to treat a girl, but buying flowers and chocolates wasn't who he was. He wasn't into dispersing worthless compliments or kissing ass. He wanted things real and honest, not fake and full of unkept promises. A part of him wanted a long-term relationship – the kind where he could fully open up with a girl. The other part told him to keep things as they were and enjoy the ride. Life was short, and he didn't need unnecessary complications like having a steady girlfriend.

Stoney parked the truck, and they got out. Truck after truck trudged through, driving onto the grassy knoll. Finch moved to the back of the truck and lowered the bed. He jumped up into the truck bed and got behind the cotton candy machine – it was tethered to the truck and tightly bound. He pulled on the rope. "Jesus, Stoney, this is tight." He grimaced, knowing he'd have blisters once he was finished.

"Tighter than a virgin gnat," Stoney said and smiled. Stoney wasn't known for being tactful. "Gotta be, kid, otherwise she'll move." He patted his hand against the truck proud of his work.

Finch huffed and grabbed hold of the braided burlap rope, trying to untie the knot. Out of frustration, he took his knife and cut the rope in half.

"Jesus, kid, we can't use that rope now," Stoney complained.

"Well... if you hadn't tied it so damn tight, I wouldn't have had to cut it," Finch replied.

"Wasteful," he spat.

"Since when do you care if we're wasting Kip's money?" Finch said, leaning his body against the machine.

"Since he started counting every single penny. I'll never hear the end of this," Stoney said, a few wrinkles covered his forehead. "He's been riding us all real hard."

"It's a rope. He won't notice," Finch retorted. He pushed the machine in one failed attempt.

"You could help," Finch said in between breaths.

"Old man like me ain't 'spose to exert himself," he said and took another drag off his cigarette.

Finch stood upright and folded his arms against his chest, his eyebrow cocked.

"What?" Stoney asked, trying to feign confusion.

"You know *what*. I'm not moving an inch until you get up here to help me."

Stoney stomped his cigarette out on the ground and heaved himself up into the truck. "You happy, kid?"

"Yup," Finch answered and they worked together to move the machine off of the truck. "I'll go grab a dolly," Finch said.

He scoured the area searching for an unused dolly. All of the trucks had made their way into the farm. The rides weren't set up yet, and Finch knew he'd be in the middle of it, setting them up until the sun went down, possibly later. It'd take hours to unload it all and get everything ready. That was the part he detested – setting it all up only to take it all down within a matter of a week.

That was another thing he enjoyed about this farm. They stayed five weeks, instead of their normal one week stint. They never stayed anywhere that long. But after a successful summer, Kip saw the benefit of sitting tight longer and found that he could compromise with Gray who had originally proposed the idea. The area thrived with customers who never tired of the rides and spending money on food and shows.

Finch grabbed a dolly and wheeled it with him toward Stoney's faded red truck. The old man was smoking again. This was the norm. Most of the carnies smoked, even Finch's mother had. He hated the stench and, after smoking one cigarette when he was thirteen, saw that there was nothing interesting about it. Since then, he'd sworn them off and was glad he hadn't inherited the nasty hacking cough that so many of the carnies had.

"Hey," a voice called. "Excuse me."

Finch turned to see who was calling him. It was Evie, and she didn't look happy.

"Yeah," Finch said, waiting for her to get on with it.

"Could you tell your friend to put his cigarette butts up in his truck bed? He's got a pile higher than a moon pie and guess who's gonna have to clean it up?"

"Mother Theresa?" Finch quipped.

She scowled at him. "You're a riot."

"Thanks." He flashed a sardonic grin. "If you look around, you'll see he isn't the only one smoking."

She glared at him. "I've got enough shit to clean up. I don't need to clean up after y'all too," she explained with a stressed expression almost evoking the word "please" with her eyes.

"I'll tell him, Laura Ingalls," he teased and sauntered away. He could hear her breathing heavy and muttering to herself. He tried not to laugh, but she had some nerve. Coming up to him and bossing him around like she owned the place. Okay, so she kinda owned the place, but that wasn't the point. He had been there less than one hour and she took it upon herself to tell him where to stick Stoney's cigarette butts. He was libel to turn around and tell her where she could stick the cigarette butts. He knew just the place, but when he peered over his shoulder, he saw her golden hair blowing from the breeze and lost his train of thought.

Fine, she was cute. Really cute. He could admit that. But man could she give a mean look – the kind that'd send anyone running.

Not him though. He could handle an irate female. And the attitude? She talked to him like he was a nuisance. Didn't she know that they were doing her dad and her a favor? They were helping them make money. There was no way those cows put out that much income, not in five weeks anyway. He figured she'd at least show a little bit of gratitude.

"Spoiled little brat," he muttered under his breath. He turned around and rolled the dolly toward Stoney.

"Saw the girl talking to you." Stoney was annoyingly observant.

"More like talking at me," Finch said and shrugged her off. He was tempted to light up a cigarette and drop it to the ground just to tick her off. He knew that'd be immature, but so help him, he wanted to irritate her.

"Ready?" Finch gestured to the cotton candy machine. They lifted it slightly and placed it on top of the dolly. Finch pushed the dolly – the machine was heavy – while Stoney walked in front of him directing traffic. He had the easy job. Finch figured he'd cut the old man some slack.

"Almost there," Stoney said, a cigarette hung from his lips. "Right here will do." He pointed.

Finch set it down, and rubbed his sore muscles. He moved his hair away from his brown eyes. It was going to be a long day.

CHAPTER 4

They had been there less than an hour and already she was livid. Cigarette butts were all over the place, and she'd be the one who'd have to clean up the mess. That's the way it was each year. Her bent over, picking them up, and tossing them into large garbage sacks. For days and days and days.

The guy had some nerve, smirking at her and calling her "Laura Ingalls." And his walk, he sauntered about in an arrogant sort of way. Like he thought his shit didn't stink. She knew the kind; there were tons just like him in Haines. Rednecks with big trucks who went muddin' and tried to prove themselves when they didn't have anything worth bragging about.

"Cocky son of a bitch," she mumbled. If her dad heard her, he'd threaten to wash her mouth out with soap. Cursing was not allowed in the Barnes' home, and any time she used an expletive, she had to drop a dollar of her hard earned cash into the cursing jar – a mason jar labeled *Potty Mouth Fees*. Gray was no better, and Evie enjoyed the times she'd caught him, pointing to the jar for him to make an offering. At last count, there were thirty-three one dollar bills in it, and that was just from the beginning of the year.

All of the cattle were fed and made their way out of the barn and onto the land to graze the rest of the day until meal time came again. Some of the heifers were more stubborn than others they'd had in the past. It took a few strong words and empty threats from Evie to get them to the barn that morning. Thank goodness for her three wheeler. Gray used to ride a horse to wrangle them into the barn, but that was years ago and Evie refused to get near any horse for that matter. At the age of nine, she fell off of one and broke her leg as a result. Since then, she was scared of them, and every single one she encountered sensed her fear. He bought two ATVs for that one reason, and they used them to get around the farm since that time.

She saw her dad talking with the carnival owner, Kip. She recognized his slicked back silver hair and thin, gaunt face. Both of them looked pleased with their little venture, watching as the trucks were being unloaded and all of the carnies were hard at work. Of course they were happy: they were supervising while everyone else did all the work.

But Gray wasn't a lazy man. He worked hard. Really hard. And Evie couldn't fault him for taking a break to watch everything unfold. His eyes lit up, and his grin grew wide when the carnival came to town. Like a little kid almost. Evie thought her dad loved the carnival because of nostalgia. There was nothing nostalgic about it for her. She was trying to put on a happier, more content face. Her dad didn't need to see her lack of enthusiasm and pissed off nature. But that was what she was – pissed off.

***

Evie sat on top of their wooden fence. It needed a paint job, and she knew what that meant. She and her dad would be laboring away with paint brushes in their hands for days come fall. Her feet dangled and kicked against the bottom rail.

It was getting dark out. The sun was slowing fading, and a crescent moon glowed in the sky. She could hear the carnies chattering and moving about; the circus tent flapped in the wind, and an odd array of sounds came from the rides. Music and the hum of motors created an odd harmony that Evie hoped to become immune to in the days to come. Then there was the smell of cigarettes and motor oil that lingered in the air from the crew's hard day's work.

Miles, Evie's pet ox, stood near her and mooed every now and again, begging for her attention. She patted him on the head and cooed at him. His big brown eyes blinked in recognition. She swore he understood her.

On one of their trips to a cattle auction, Evie first laid eyes on the little fellow. "Aww, isn't he cute?" she had said to her dad who didn't seem as impressed by the bundle of brown fur. A bull was a bull. Big deal. They didn't do much. A donkey would be more useful. At least it would haul something. But a bull?

Evie knew how to reel Gray in hook, line and sinker. He'd lasso the moon for her if she asked. And staring into her bright blue eyes and seeing her face all giddy with excitement over the calf, well, he could give in.

He was mocked. A bull calf? For what purpose? Other than to please his daughter so she could go out each day, pet him, and treat him like she would a cat or a dog. But she hadn't ever asked for a cat or a dog, or anything else. He felt the need to make her happy, and if the bull did just that, then he'd buy ten of them if he had to. Gray was called a fool behind his back. Wasting dollars on a bull just so his daughter could have a pet. Seeing the twinkle in Evie's eyes every time she approached Miles made it all worth it. He was willing to endure mocking. If his daughter was happy, then that was all that mattered.

Miles was just one week old when she got him. With no mama in sight, Evie was the substitute, staying awake all hours to bottle feed the hungry bull. He was so needy, whining for attention. She ended up sleeping in his calf hutch with him the first week he arrived on the farm. Gray warned Evie that he'd turn mean as a snake if he wasn't turned into a steer before he grew too old. The thought of it made Evie squeamish, but she understood the laws of nature. It had to be done, and within a few months, Miles was castrated and became a steer.

He had been Evie's pet for six years. He wasn't shy about people and would nuzzle up to anyone and start chewing on their clothes. He liked to be petted and talked to. Baby talk suited him just fine. And he was the laziest animal Gray had ever had. Sleep and eat. That was what he did. He had free reign of the property and was known to wander about, graze in one spot for a while, or stand near the barn when Evie was working, and then move on. Gray was often asked if he was worried about Miles wandering off the property, but Gray would just shrug and say, "Nah. He's too smart for that."

Gray interrupted Evie's thoughts. "They're starting to test some of the rides out. Wanna ride one?" he asked, a gleam in his eye.

"That's okay," she said. She was content sitting there on that fence, away from the spectacle. She'd be fine never riding any of the rides for the entire five weeks.

"I may try a few out," he said, and for a brief second she could picture her dad as a little boy riding every single ride, screaming at the top of his lungs with his hands high up in the air. "Sure you don't want to ride one with me?" He nudged her while flashing a goofy grin.

He might as well have begged. "Just one, and it has to be that thing." She pointed to The Super Slide. It seemed like the safest bet as far as rides went. She wasn't into being jostled or having the sensation to vomit, and with the exception of the kiddie rides, the slide was the most tame of rides the carnival offered. It was new to the carnival; she hadn't noticed it the previous summers.

"Sure." He beamed. Any ride suited him just fine.

Evie jumped off the fence and followed him. A rainbow colored sign flashing *Super Slide* illuminated the darkening vanilla sky. Red triangles with yellow bulbs flashed on both sides of the three lane slide. Each lane was a different color: light green; aqua blue; and sky blue. She and Gray walked up the metal ramp to the top.

Finch stood at the top, tightening one of the bolts with a wrench. He turned his gaze in their direction. Evie shot him a dirty look. He responded with an arrogant smirk and stifled a laugh.

"Is this one ready to ride?" Gray asked Finch.

"She is, but this is a kiddie ride," he said to Gray.

"It is?" Gray said.

"Yeah. There's a weight and height limit," he said and peered over at Evie. "She should be okay, though."

Evie tried ignoring his snide comment. She hated being petite, and he had just pointed out the obvious – that she was small enough to ride a kid's ride. Just what every eighteen- year-old girl wants to hear.

Gray gave a look of disappointment and frowned.

"We don't have to ride this. I'll ride that spinny thing over there." She pointed to The Whirly Twirl. She gulped loudly and hoped her dad didn't notice. Finch heard her loud and clear. It was the last thing she wanted to get on, but she'd make this one exception for her dad. Five minutes of pure hell and the aftermath of throwing up would be the penance for trying to make her dad happy, but she'd do it. She'd do it for him.

"Nah. You go on ahead and ride this. It'll be fun," he said and nudged her on the arm.

"That's okay." She shook her head slowly, spun on her heels and started down the ramp.

"If she's scared, I can promise you this is one of the safest rides we have." Finch stood up and placed the wrench in his jeans pocket.

She turned around quickly and glared at him. "I'm not scared," she said defensively. She was high up off the ground, but frightened of a stupid slide? He made her sound like a timid weakling. Who was afraid to ride a slide? Toddlers rode slides. She was an adult. She could glide down a slide. No problem. She jerked the sack from his hand and plopped down, pushing herself off.

She slid down and reached the bottom before Gray had walked down the ramp.

"How was it?" Gray called down to her.

"Great. I had so much fun, I think I'll ride it again," she said, looking up at Finch. His arms were folded against his chest, and his eyebrow was cocked. She wanted to punch that cocky look off his face.

"Have fun. I'm gonna go ride some of these rides." Gray rubbed his hands together excitedly. "Can't wait to get on the ferris wheel."

Evie stormed up the ramp scowling at Finch the entire time. She had no idea why she was so irritated and why she felt so compelled to prove a point to him. He was under her skin.

"You're back?" he said, teasing her.

"Humph," she mumbled. A sassy response escaped her. "I had so much fun I wanted to ride it again," she lied. Okay, so the slide wasn't scary, but fun? No. Entertaining to toddlers and six-year-olds maybe but definitely not worth another trip.

"Well if you liked all the excitement this ride offers, Laura

Ingalls, you should probably go on that one." He pointed to the compact fire trucks that were bolted down to a rotating platform moving as fast as a turtle. "I hear it's a thrill of a ride." He flashed a sarcastic smile.

She glowered at him. "My name is Evie, not Laura Ingalls. How would you like it if I called you Jerk Face?" She quickly plopped down and pushed herself off, hearing him laugh her entire way down.

CHAPTER 5

Evie was counting down, waiting for the arrival of the thirty-fifth day so she could move on with her life. The carnival would consume her entire being for five entire weeks, and she'd be exhausted by the end of it.

It was early in the afternoon, and in less than twenty-four hours, hordes of locals would invade her land (at least that was how she saw it) to enjoy the carnival. Even though the carnival was set up on the far end of Gray's property, she knew that the air would soon be filled with whiny organ music emanating from the carrousel layered with rock tunes blasting from the speakers of one of the faster rides. There would also be the nonstop sound of people screaming at the top of their lungs, thrilled that they were going so fast they'd surely puke once their ride came to an abrupt end. The sweet scent of cotton candy and funnel cakes would drift with the wind and eventually find its way to Evie. She had no doubt that her body would revolt and send the acidic taste of bile up the back of her throat into her mouth. None of this was appealing to her. None of it.

The grumble of her stomach and the position of the sun told her it was time to eat. Gray was on the other side of the pasture. She could see the speck of his large body far off in the distance. She jumped on her ATV and rode in his direction.

The rumbling engine got his attention. Deep in dirt, he was on his knees repairing a part of their wooden board fence. Just one of the many things that needed to be fixed around the deteriorating farm.

He peered over his shoulder.

"It's time to eat," she shouted so he'd hear. He nodded in recognition, and she turned the wheel, driving back toward the house.

She noticed Katie's brown Toyota Corolla parked in her drive way and opened the screen door. "Katie!" she called as she marched through the house and headed to the kitchen.

Katie's face was more pink than usual, and her hazel eyes were blood shot. Evie took a closer look at her best friend. It was a clear sign that she had been crying. She moved toward her and touched her gently on the arm. "You okay?" she asked.

Katie nodded, sniffling. Her eyes watered, and a few tears trickled down her face. She shook her head no and then started to sob.

Evie wasn't sure what to do. She pulled Katie to sit down and made a concerned face. "What's wrong?" She knew something bad had to have happened. Katie was usually bubbly and cheerful and definitely not one to cry unless it was for sentimental reasons. Katie was the only person Evie knew who cried at the end of *Star Wars'* cheesy, happy over-the-top ending where Luke, Han and the rest of the bunch stood on stage facing the audience after receiving medals from Leia.

"They're all together, and the Death Star was destroyed," she had said to Evie.

Evie grabbed a bulk of napkins and handed them to Katie. She dabbed her damp eyes and took a shaky breath. "I'm pregnant, Eves," she said, causing a stunned Evie to sit down.

***

Evie and Katie McDaniels had been best friends since kindergarten. It wasn't a friendship anyone expected would form or last as long as it had. Katie was Nate McDaniels' daughter, the one man in town who Gray didn't get along with.

It was during their first day of kindergarten—out in the playground during recess— that their friendship began. Katie had sat at the wrong place at the wrong time. A group of clumsy, amateur boys who were trying to dribble a basketball and shoot hoops way too high for their four foot frames, bounced the ball beyond their reach, and it found its way to the back of Katie's head.

The sound of the high-pitched cry got Evie's attention. Evie went over to her, staring at her peculiarly and poked her in the arm.

"Are you okay?" Evie had asked, and at the time, she had a very prominent lisp thanks to her two front teeth missing.

"No," Katie had sniffled.

"Do you wanna play with me?"

Katie lifted her head and smiled. "Okay."

They sat side-by-side swinging back and forth, competing to see who could go the highest, who could reach the white puffy clouds up in the sky. It was a harmless competition, and neither of them cared who won. It was more about the thrill. After spending a few minutes on the swing, their friendship was sealed. When one is five years of age, the list of reasons to become friends is short. Often times, the simple question of "Will you be my friend?" is asked and then a friendship blossoms. In the case of Evie and Katie, the question wasn't even needed.

***

"What? How?" Evie said, still shocked by Katie's admission.

Katie raised an eyebrow at Evie's question, giving her a "bless your heart" look. In the south, saying "bless your heart" was as bad as saying, "I'm sorry you're too dumb to get it. Or, I'm sorry that you're just so naïve."

"Okay, I know how," Evie said. "How far along are you?"

"About twelve weeks," Katie answered. She unconsciously touched the small bump in her stomach. Katie had always been voluptuous, so if she was showing it wasn't noticeable yet.

"Does Todd know?"

Katie shook her head, indicating she hadn't told him.

Evie leaned forward. "What? You haven't told him yet? You've gotta tell him."

"I know," Katie said, looking down at her fidgety hands. "I just need time to think."

"Think about what? Do your parents know?"

"Not yet," Katie said. "I'm scared to tell them. You know my dad. He's libel to shoot Todd."

"That wouldn't be too bad would it?" Evie said, trying to sound like she was joking. Truthfully, she had never liked Todd. He was arrogant, and she had heard one too many stories about him cheating on Katie. Katie refused to believe the rumors, but Evie knew better. She had seen his wandering eye, how he flirted with any girl that passed in his direction.

"That's not funny. He's the father of my baby," Katie said.

"Sorry," Evie lied. She was sorry the schmuck got her best friend pregnant but not remorseful for saying what she said. "What are you going to do?"

"I have to tell my parents and Todd. I just don't know when the time will be right," she said. "Todd's so excited about going to Wake Forest. I hate to ruin it for *him*."

"Ruin it for him? It takes two to make a baby. He was just as much a part of this equation as you were. You've gotta tell him,"

Evie said.

"I will..." she started and then abruptly stopped talking. She gestured with her eyes toward the door.

Gray swung the screen door open; it slammed into the wall. Gray could never just open a door like normal people. There was plenty of evidence of his strong armed pushes. Dents and chipped paint were scattered throughout their old home.

"Well, hey there, Katie," he said with a smile on his face. He liked Katie even if she was Nate's daughter. His ball cap hung low against his sweaty forehead, and he wiped his dirty hands against his denim jeans.

"Hi Mr. Gray," Katie said. She didn't call him by his last name and refused to call him by his first name without adding the "Mr." In the south, it was considered disrespectful otherwise.

She got up and headed toward the door. Evie followed.

"You leavin' so soon?" Gray asked, making a face. "We're fixin' to eat lunch. Evie made pimento cheese."

"That's okay. I already ate. Thank you," Katie said, offering him a plastered grin.

"Call me later," Evie whispered.

"I will," she said. She closed the door and walked toward her car.

"What was wrong with her?" Gray asked, opening the refrigerator. He grabbed the pitcher of sweet tea and poured it into his cup, gulping it down within seconds.

"Nothing," Evie lied. She slathered pimento cheese on a two slices of bread.

"She looked like she was crying," he said.

"She and Todd had an argument, that's all." Evie placed a pimento cheese sandwich on his plate.

He pursed his lips. "He's a no good for nothing."

"You're preaching to the choir." She handed him his plate.

He grinned at her. "Glad you're not dumb about boys."

"I can't be dumb about them if I don't date them," she said. She poured the rest of the sweet tea into two glasses, fixed her sandwich and sat them down at the table.

Gray frowned and sat across from her. He said, "You know any boy in town would love to date you."

"That doesn't offer me any consolation. The pickings are pretty slim, and most of the boys around here are either dumb as doorknobs or are as slimy as Todd."

He took off his cap and wiped the sweat off his sunburned face. "Well, it's a good thing you're not dating any of them then." He grinned and playfully nudged her on the arm. "The rink's gonna be busy tonight."

The roller rink—it was such a novel idea. A few years before, Gray had a huge slab of concrete poured. He figured if he offered it, people would come. They'd pay to skate under a moon lit sky, with white lights and music in the background. A long pole was dead center in the rink and on it hung a huge glittery disco ball that captured the light from the moon's glow. White lights were strung at the nearby concession stand. A roller rink wasn't a roller rink without sustenance and music. And he was right. They did come. Roller skating had become a favorite way to spend wonderful summer nights for both young and old. Little kids, big kids, adults, and the elderly paid a few dollars to skate on Gray's concrete slab and snack on popcorn and Cokes afterward.

Evie, with the help of Cooper, an old friend of Gray's from his high school football days, managed the rink. She ran the concession stand, and he took their money and gave them their pair of skates. Gray, with his deep southern drawl, was the disc jockey. Many swore that he was born to be a radio announcer. Gray would shrug the compliment off and tell them he could never give up his cattle. "I'm one of the great many that feed this country, and I'm proud of it."

His music selection left much to be desired, and Evie begged him to play some newer tunes – music that she and her friends were listening to – Fleetwood Mac, the Eagles, Led Zeppelin – these were just a few bands she asked him to play, to liven the place up. Kids her age didn't want to hear Patsy Cline or Mel Torme. They wanted rock and roll, music with an upbeat tempo that spoke to them. As much as she wouldn't admit it aloud, disco would've been better than most of the classics he would dish out night after night. Gray decided a compromise was in order and told Evie she could have free reign and choose the last song of the evening this year. Since the rink had been open, the last song of the evening had always been the same: Patsy Cline's "Crazy" blared through the speakers. Knowing the song's relevance to her father and what it meant to him, Evie began to despise the beautiful tune. It was her parents' song – their song, and she couldn't fathom how he could torture himself by playing it every single weekend night. Evie decided she'd steer as far away from Cline as she could – her first choice, and only choice for that matter, was Fleetwood Mac's "Dreams." To her nothing could compare to the poetic lyrics of Stevie Nicks.

He bit into the pimento cheese sandwich. The creamy filling oozed out of the bread as he chomped into it. A clump fell onto the table, and he scooped it up with his hand, sticking it into his mouth. He then proceeded to lick the remnants off of his fingers.

"Daddy," Evie groaned. "That's gross." She wondered why she even bothered.

"Can't let it go to waste," he said, chewing with his mouth open. "We could use the extra money," he added, searching for her reaction.

She looked up at him and swallowed her food. "Are we okay?"

He nodded while giving a tight lipped expression. "We're okay. Just try and be friendlier to people. If you act like you want to be there, they'll want to be there too."

"I'm nice to them," Evie said.

"Nice and friendly ain't the same. Just smile a little. Be your charming self," he said.

Evie wasn't all that hungry. Her worry for Katie made her lose her appetite. She took another bite of her sandwich, and set it down on her plate, resting her elbows on the table.

"You gonna eat that?" he asked. His plate was empty.

She shook her head no and slid the plate in his direction.

***

Evie took a quick shower, rinsing the grime and stench off of her. No matter how much she scrubbed her hands, the orange South Carolina clay still stuck beneath her finger nails.

In a matter of minutes, the roller rink would be open. She could hear her dad and Cooper talking down stairs. They were both so loud. Cooper was losing his hearing and spoke ten decibels above everyone else.

She headed down the stairs wearing a pair of bell bottom jeans that tightly clung to her hips and thighs and a plaid shirt tied at her waist. The bottom of her jeans swiveled against the top of her leather platform sandals.

"Hey Evie," Cooper shouted. He gave her a big grin and pulled her toward him and hugged her.

"You're gonna burn up in that sweat shirt," she said, pulling on the heavy cotton fabric.

He patted his stomach. "I'm cold, and it gets colder than a witch's tit once the sun's down anyhow." Cooper's fashion sense consisted of wearing sweatshirts and shorts throughout each season. He held onto an old soup can, the label was completely worn off, and spit chewing tobacco into it. His bottom lip was full and protruded outward, and when he smiled at Evie, brown tobacco covered most of his crooked teeth.

"You're wearing those clod hoppers again. You're feet are gonna be sore by the end of the night," Gray said, gesturing to her feet.

Evie shrugged. "I'll be fine." She looked down at Cooper's feet and saw that he was wearing knee-high socks—each with a different color stripe—and an old pair of tennis shoes.

"Starting tomorrow this place is gonna be buzzing with people," Gray said with a hint of excitement.

Evie didn't say anything. She grabbed the zipped up pouch off the table and opened it, counting the bills inside. "This should be enough."

"I'm hoping that bag is full by the end of the night," he said and handed the other pouch to Cooper. "Here's yours."

"Thanks. I'm thinking we're gonna have an interesting group of skaters tonight. When I drove up, I saw some of them carny folk. They're a strange bunch if you ask me," he whispered loudly to Evie.

"No one asked you," Gray said. "They mean no harm, just some of them are odd to look at."

"You reckon that tattooed man has anywhere left on his body to tattoo?" Cooper asked.

"Probably not. He's covered in 'em," Gray answered.

Cooper shuddered. "When I got this one," he pointed to the *Semper Fi* tattoo on his forearm, "it hurt something awful. I can't imagine doing that over and over again until my body was covered."

"That's why you're not a side show freak," Gray said. "Well...a freak maybe."

"You see the abuse I get from your daddy," he said to Evie. "Not like I get paid much either."

"What else are you gonna do on your weekend nights?" Gray said.

"Not get harassed by the likes of you," he retorted.

Evie looked up at the kitchen clock and interrupted them. "If y'all keep going at it, the sun's gonna set and rise before you get your fat butts outside."

"She just called us fat," Cooper said, trying to feign offense.

"She sure did," Gray said. "Like we ain't got any feelings." He guffawed as he opened the door. "Enough horsing around, let's get going."

CHAPTER 6

Finch massaged the back of his sweaty neck. Setting up the carnival was work. Real work. He wanted to call it a night and crash until morning came.

His cot wasn't the most comfortable place to rest his head, but after working hard for two days straight, it was heaven on earth and it'd do just fine. He couldn't complain. He heard stories of other carnivals where workers slept under trailers in the mud and took showers with a cold watering hose. These were the carnivals run by crooks. With people who had no scruples and didn't mind cheating other people and taking all their money. Kip refused to be associated with that type. This type, that type. There was a difference, and Finch was thankful he at least worked for *this* type. The type that had some ethics and earned money the good ole fashioned way, the honest way. He didn't trust Kip completely, but he knew the man had enough of a conscience that he wouldn't cheat someone, and although their sleeping accommodations weren't the best, they at least had four walls with a roof and a cot to lay on.

He lay down and rested his palms against his shaggy dark brown hair. He looked up at the top of the tent; it flapped a little from the wind. Even if it was summer time, the weather in Haines was decent, better than Gibsonton's brutal heat.

His eyes shut, and he could feel himself slipping into sleep. "Finch," a deep, heavily accented voice said. "Finch," he repeated.

"Uh huh," Finch said, his voice low and groggy.

"We're headed to Mr. Barnes' skating rink. Do you want to come?"

"No," Finch said.

"You're going to lay here all night? That is not healthy for a young man your age."

Finch could hear the concern in his old friend's voice. "Friedrich," he said with a sigh. "I'm tired. Roller skating doesn't sound like a lot of fun."

"There will be ladies there your age. A handsome man such as yourself should not be holed up in a tent."

Finch sometimes had to remind himself that Friedrich was a lot older and European and calling a guy "handsome" wasn't strange in his eyes. "I'm dead tired man, but thanks."

He rolled over on his side ready to fall asleep and suddenly felt Friedrich's big hand grip his arm. Friedrich yanked him up off of the cot. "What the hell," Finch said in a huff. He felt his sore arm and scowled at Friedrich.

"You will come with us," Friedrich said and nodded his head in confidence.

Finch glared at him and sighed heavily. "Okay. Okay," he said with frustration. "I'll go, but I'm not staying long."

Friedrich gave him a smug look. His long black mustache curled up at the ends, and his face was a spectrum of colors completely adorned in an array of tattoos. His dark and silvery hair was greased down and slick but brittle to the touch.

Finch yawned and stretched. "Next time you wanna take a nap, I'll be sure to return the favor."

"I would like to see that." Friedrich was at least a half a foot taller than he was. "My arm is the size of your thigh." He let out a loud, bellowing laugh and flexed his bicep. Even if Finch was muscular, Friedrich's physique made him seem small in comparison. He patted Finch on the top of his head and laughed again.

As they walked out of the tent, they were met by Doris and Mouse. Besides Friedrich, they were the only remaining side show freaks left in Kip's carnival. Most "freaks" had retired or were close to retirement, and as time progressed, carnival owners saw that they weren't the star attraction like they had been in the past. They didn't have the same mysticism or appeal that they used to. And this didn't make carnival owners like Kip happy. He wanted to make money, and taking care of three people was costing him more than he was making. They all three knew that it was only a matter of time until they were tossed out. Things had already begun to change.

Standing only slightly higher than Doris' chubby knees, Mouse, whose real name was Hugo, was thirty-two inches tall. The carnival bragged that Mouse was "The World's Smallest Man" which was not a fact and no where near being the truth. There were a few other carnivals in the US with men much smaller than Mouse, but most townies didn't know the difference.

Doris' wide body was triple the size of everyone in the carnival. Known as "The World's Fattest Woman," Doris swore that no other female was as fat as her, and no one disputed her either. Doris was huge, and that was putting it mildly. At last count, she weighed over four hundred pounds and was continuing to expand. At any given time of the day, she was known to have a turkey leg in one hand and a soft drink in the other.

"About time you got out here," Doris said. Her voice was loud, and she had a slight southern drawl influenced by her Texas upbringing. Her hair was teased and set in tight wound curls. A huge pink bow was clipped to the left side of her head. She rarely wore anything other than the color pink, and those pink frocks were long night shirts, sheer and fit tight against her rolls of fat.

Bright red lipstick was painted on her plump lips, and her pudgy face was powdered white, almost as if she had used talcum powder instead of regular make-up.

"Friedrich didn't give me a choice," Finch said.

"A young lad like you shouldn't be laying around in bed anyway," Friedrich said, and Doris and Mouse nodded their heads in agreement.

Mouse pulled on his suspender straps and yanked up his britches. "It's our only night to play." His voice was higher pitched and his lips twitched to the side when he spoke in tic like fashion. A gray fedora sat back on his head, exposing his high brow. Underneath the felted hat was thinning red hair showing more freckle covered scalp than anything.

"We only get to enjoy a few quiet nights when we're on the circuit. We should make the most of it," Doris said. She licked a huge rainbow colored lollipop that had caused her tongue to turn blue and purple.

"All right. All right," Finch said with exasperation. "I get it," he tried to sound annoyed, but he couldn't be mad at them.

They headed toward the skating rink. Because it was located on the other side of the farm, it wasn't an easy trek over the rolling hills. Doris came to a stop and fanned herself. "It's hotter than the Devil's armpit," she said.

Mouse's petite hand touched the side of his left hip, grimacing as he did so.

"How about a lift?" Friedrich said and picked him up, sitting him on top of his broad shoulders.

"Thanks. View's much better from up here," Mouse said.

By the time they reached the rink, Doris' pink satin dress was covered in her sweat, and she carried her special pink satin slippers in her hands.

"We should've drove," Finch said, noticing Doris' red face.

"Too late now," Doris said with a heavy breath. "That popcorn smells real good." She licked her lips. "Let's get some." She meandered toward the concession stand before they had time to answer her.

Evie stood behind the counter in a weathered wooden shed. An aged sign with the painted word "Concession" was nailed to the top left corner of the battered station. The nails had rusted, some of the wood was rotted, and most of the paint had chipped from the Concession sign.

Evie wore the same annoyed look on her face that she had given Finch when they arrived on the property the day before. Two guys leaned against the counter obviously trying to flirt with her, but Finch could see she wasn't biting.

"What can I get you?" Evie asked Doris, ignoring the two drooling guys.

"I'd like a large popcorn and Coke, please," Doris said.

The two boys snickered. "She'll need a feed sack of popcorn to satisfy her appetite," one of them said.

Doris ignored them and gave Evie two one dollar bills.

"She's so fat she wears two watches for both time zones she's in," the same guy said to his friend, loud enough for Doris to hear.

"Is that all you got?" she said with exasperation. "Listen. I've heard them all, and on the scale of insults, yours is piss-ant poor. You're gonna have to do better than that if you want to upset me." She took the bag from Evie, grabbed a handful of popcorn and placed it into her mouth, chewing with her mouth wide open.

"Yum," she said.

"I'm gonna be sick," the guy said, making gagging sounds.

"Todd," Evie said, glaring at him. "You are proof that evolution can go in reverse. Go loiter somewhere else."

"We're just kidding. No reason to get so pissed off," he said and left with his friend.

"Sorry," she said to Doris.

"It's not your fault they're assclowns," Doris said, and Evie laughed.

"Unfortunately they weren't present the day brains were handed out," Evie said, and Doris chuckled while slurping on her straw. "Can I get you more Coke?"

Doris slid the cup in her direction and waggled her eyebrows up and down, and Evie filled it up. Normally there'd be a charge, but Evie let that rule slide.

Doris asked Evie, "What's your name, hon?"

"Evie Barnes."

"I'm Doris O'Neil." She extended her hand, and Evie shook it. "You're the owner's daughter, ain't ya?"

Evie nodded.

"I've seen you around over the years. Looks like you done grown up." She laughed again, a joyful, powerful chortle. "Nice land you got here." She scanned the area and then brought her gaze back to Evie.

"Thanks," Evie said.

"This here is Friedrich," Doris said, and Friedrich tipped his head. His handlebar mustache curved up as he grinned. "And Mouse." She pointed down, and Evie leaned over the counter and smiled at him. "And Finch."

"We've already met," Evie snapped.

He didn't respond and plastered that stupid, arrogant smirk on his face, the one that he knew annoyed her so much. If she was going to be a pistol, he would too.

She rolled her eyes at him, and he sighed in annoyance. "I'm getting me a pair of skates. You guys coming?" he said to them.

"In a minute. I can't let this good popcorn go to waste," Doris answered while chewing. "Your daddy is smart to have this rink and our carnival on his farm." She licked each of her buttery fingers.

"Yeah," Evie said, trying not to sigh. "I guess so."

"Ain't any other farms doing something like this and trust me, I know. I've been all over the country," Doris said.

"You travel a lot, don't you?" Evie said. She propped her hand under her chin and and leaned forward.

"We're on the circuit seven months. This here farm is my favorite. Makes me think of where I grew up, only it wasn't as pretty as it is up here." Doris noticed someone standing behind her, keeping their distance. "Guess we should try our hand at skating. It was real nice meeting you."

"You too," Evie said and smiled at Mouse, Friedrich, and Doris. Finch didn't make eye contact with her and sauntered off, his hands stuck deep in his jeans pockets.

Doris pulled Finch to the side and asked, "What'd you say to set her off?"

He shrugged. "Nothing."

"Didn't seem like nothing to me. Y'all sure spent a lot of time burning holes into each other," she said. "Remember what Kip said. Her daddy doesn't want us bothering her."

"*That* won't be a problem," he said.

Doris laughed loudly. People turned their hands and stared. "You've got it bad," she teased, ignoring the onlookers. "Real bad," she added.

She sat down on a narrow wooden bench and twitched her painted toes – all a shade of pink—and looked up at him, waiting. "Can't reach these skates. You gonna help, or are you too busy gawking at that pretty girl?"

He knelt on the ground and pulled the laces out of the pair of white roller skates. He stuck his hand in each skate, trying to stretch them out as best he could. He grabbed Doris' right foot and squeezed it into the skate. She grunted as she struggled to make her wide foot fit in the confined space. Once she got her right foot in, Finch pulled the laces through, keeping them as loose as possible. She followed with her left foot, and by the time it was all said and done, she was out of breath.

"These too tight?" He tapped on the skates.

"No," she lied, but he could see her toes pressing against the corners.

"Have you ever skated?"

"A few times. When I was a kid. It ain't something you forget, Honey Lamb. Y'all help me up," she said to Friedrich and Finch.

She wobbled and steadied herself. "Whoa. Thought I was gonna tip over." She laughed from a strong case of nerves.

Finch and Friedrich tried to keep her standing straight. "You sure this is a good idea?" Finch asked with concern, breathing heavily.

She placed her thumb under his chin and smiled. "You're sweet to worry, but don't."

She slowly skated onto the concrete slab, with Friedrich,

Mouse and Finch skating right beside her. Passersby muttered rude comments, and Finch scowled at them, mumbling a few curse words.

Friedrich held onto Doris' hand as she attempted to twirl in a semi-circle. She let out a whopper of a laugh, oblivious to the heckling.

Mouse tugged on Finch's t-shirt. "Gimme your hand. I'm gonna fall otherwise," he said, swaying from side to side, his tiny feet balancing precariously on four wheels.

"No way," Finch said.

Mouse gave him a serious look. "I got a bad hip. You wanna be the cause of it breaking?" He almost fell, and Finch jerked him upright.

He begrudgingly offered him his hand, and the two slowly skated around the rink.

"So, not only are you freaks, but you're fags, too?" Todd pointed to them, snickering with his friend.

"Ah..piss off!" Finch said and rolled in the opposite direction.

"Fags and freaks! Fags and freaks!" Todd shouted after them.

Finch spun on his wheels, dragging Mouse with him. Mouse nearly fell over and tried steadying himself by clenching firmer onto Finch's hand.

"What are you, twelve?" Finch replied in a sharp tone to Todd.

"I call it like I see it," Todd said.

"Just ignore him, Finch," Mouse said, pleading with his eyes.

Finch's grip tightened, and his jaw clenched.

"That's my hand you're gonna break if you keep squeezing it the way you are." Mouse pulled on Finch's shirt with his free hand. "Don't let him get to you. You think I care what he's saying?"

Finch looked down at his friend and then back up at Todd and his goons. He let out a heavy sigh. "No."

"Then you shouldn't either. Take me around this rink. I wanna get my money's worth," he said.

Finch snarled his lips and inhaled. He held his breath for a moment, glaring at Todd, then exhaled and peered down at his friend. "All right," he said and started skating.

They made their way to Doris and Friedrich. Doris had stopped twirling, and Friedrich's hands were touching her waist. She wiped at her brow. "Lord, I'm pooped. Ole' Friedrich sure knows how to show a girl a good time." She winked at him and flashed a wide grin.

"I was in good company," he said with a glint in his eyes.

"Always the gentleman," she replied. "What's that all about?" she asked, motioning her head in Todd's direction.

"Just some assclown thinking he's clever," Mouse said.

"He's about to find out what my fist feels like against his preppy face," Finch said.

Doris lay her hands on Finch. "Don't get your undies in a wad over some idiot. We can't go fighting with the townies. You know that could affect business, and Kip won't like that. We're already on his poo poo list," she said, pointing to Mouse and Friedrich. "He ripped us a new one this morning."

"She's right," Friedrich added, and Mouse nodded.

"That's what I tried to tell him." He pointed to Finch. "But he don't listen to me," Mouse said, twisting his lips to the side and narrowing his eyes to Finch.

Finch held up his hands surrendering. "All right. All right. I won't give that doofus what he deserves," he said.

She placed her palm on Finch's shoulder. "Just let it go. That temper of yours is your own worst enemy."

Finch glimpsed in Todd's direction and saw Evie standing in front of him, shouting. Her arms were flailed, waving up and down. He couldn't tell what she was saying, but from her gestures and expression, he and his friends were being tossed out of the place.

She stretched her arm out toward the exit and impatiently tapped her platform shoe against the concrete. When Finch looked closer, he saw what looked like the words, "Get out! And "I'm waiting" coming from her mouth. He smiled to himself, watching her as she followed Todd and his friends out of the rink. Her eyes briefly met Finch's, and he quickly spun in the other direction, skating to the far end of the rink.

CHAPTER 7

Evie started up her dad's truck and the engine chugged, making a sputtering sound as she shot out of the gravel driveway. It needed repairs, major repairs, but fixing it was not high on the priority list. Evie knew it was only a matter of time until the thing died and they'd have to buy a new one. She tried not to worry and pushed that dreary thought to the back of her mind.

She drove toward downtown Haines. It was only a few miles from her house, and she had spent her fair share of weekend nights on Main Street. Downtown Haines had the only movie theatre within miles and a diner with the best milkshakes and hamburgers in the entire upstate. Sure, she didn't have much to compare it to, but most people agreed, that even if Haines was a tiny podunk town out in the sticks, the food sure was good.

Downtown Haines was the quintessential American small town. Picturesque two-story brick buildings that were almost a century old lined Main Street. Park benches and potted plants filled the brick sidewalks. The town hall was the center of Haines, and a large bell hung from the central arch. The bell was for decoration only and hadn't been rung in years.

She pulled the truck into an empty parking space, slammed the creaky door shut and then made her way into Henson's Pharmacy. Old man Henson, as she and most of the town called him when he wasn't around, had been a pharmacist for fifty years. Henson's was the only pharmacy in town, but it offered more than prescription drugs. Groceries and other household items were sold there. And if time permitted, you could sit down on one of the worn red vinyl bar stools and order a rootbeer float. Henson had a soda fountain and offered Coke floats and ice cream sundaes, as well as other sweet treats.

Evie looked around and picked up a few needed items. She made her way to the counter. "Hi, Mr. Henson," she said.

"Hi, Evie," he said and smiled. His magnified reading glasses sat down on the bridge of his nose, and his thick white mustache covered his top lip.

"I'm here to pick up Dad's prescription," she said.

"I was wondering when someone would come pick it up. Thought I was going to have to drive down yonder to your house," he said and turned to grab the bottle of pills and placed them in a small white bag.

"The carnival's in town." She made a face when she said it.

"I figured that much. They're shutting everything down in town for their parade."

"The parade." Evie sighed. "I forgot about the parade."

Each year, to commence the opening of the carnival, the carnies paraded through downtown Haines on Main Street.

"It's supposed to start soon. Figured I'd go out and watch it, too," he said. "That'll be thirty dollars."

"Thirty dollars," she said in disbelief.

"That prescription is most of the cost. Your daddy's on some potent medication," he said.

She searched through her purse and emptied out her change and wadded bills. She unfolded them and counted. "I'm still short ten cents." She frowned.

"Don't worry about ten cents," he said, waving his hand up in the air.

"I couldn't."

"It's a dime, Evie, not twenty dollars. " He let out a low chuckle. "Now go on before you get stuck in that parade traffic." He peered over her shoulder and looked out the window. "Looks like they're blocking off the road right now. Might want to get out of here real quick."

"Thank you," she said and rushed toward the front door.

She wasn't fast enough. Main Street was blocked in, and her truck was parallel parked right down the middle of the parade route. She cursed herself for her stupidity. How could she be so forgetful? They had the parade every year the day the carnival opened. She knew this.

She clutched the brown paper bag, wrinkling it from her tight grip. Crowds of people flocked to the edge of the sidewalk ready to see what Evie thought was going to be one of the most boring and uneventful parades ever. After witnessing the carnival's parades a few times in the years before, she knew this to be the truth, or at least her truth.

Kip could have chipped in more money to buy a fancy float, or purchased flashy costumes for his employees to wear. He could have paid the local high school marching band to play some lively tunes – the kind that everyone knew, sang along to, and danced to. But no, he was too frugal to spend an inkling of his hard earned cash and figured the parade was fine just as it was—boring and without any fanfare.

Even Haines' annual Christmas parades were better than the carnival's. At least there were floats, firetrucks, Shriners (wearing their strange boxed felted hats with long tassels dangling in their faces), and the local town celebrity, Susan "Susie" Eaton, Miss South Carolina. She was Haines' one claim to fame, and unfortunately for her, got duped into any opening ceremony or town affair to show her pretty, but aged face, smile, and wave at the audience.

The sound of a lone beating drum started the parade, and a short single file line of carnies traveled down Main Street, waving at the onlookers. Two carnies, wearing t-shirts and jeans, held onto a large white banner with the words "Kip Kierkin's Carnival of Wonder" painted in red script. Kip personally added the "of wonder" part thinking it'd lure the townies into his carnival. A cigarette dangled from one of the carnie's lips; the smoke funneled up, tickling his pruned face while he held onto the homemade banner.

Just behind the carnies who held the banner was Kip. He waved and gave a tight smile to the crowd, his thin slicked back hair even more greased down with Vitalis for the occasion. He chose to wear a plaid button-down shirt, and a pack of Menthol's poked out from his shirt pocket. The older carnies trekked closely behind him. Some of them waved and even forced a smile, while others talked amongst themselves, ignoring the on-lookers who had stopped what they were doing to see the spectacle. It was like a bad traffic accident; you knew you shouldn't stop to gawk but you just couldn't help yourself.

The thumping of the drum filled the air. An older woman in a dull red satin unitard twirled a baton as she half-skipped to the sound of the beating drum. Her nylon stockings were two shades too dark. A tall, thin man named Dmitri wore blue striped pants and a long mauve valor jacket. He juggled bowling pins as he walked in small steps, amazing the younger audience with his ability to catch the pins while in constant motion. Doris fanned herself with a hand painted Japanese fan, her talcum powder applied even more liberally to her cherub face. She chose a brighter red lipstick to apply to her full lips.

Dressed in a sleeveless black unitard and exposing all of the rainbow of colors on his body, Friedrich flexed his muscles and smiled at the crowd, his long handlebar mustache curled up as he grinned. He loved the attention he received from the shocked faces who couldn't stop staring at his vibrant array of tattoos. The crowd oohed and aahed, pointing at the various designs that covered his entire body. Mouse threw a colorful bouquet of confetti up in the air, and Finch tossed candy to children who watched with gaping mouths and twitching palms, hoping to get their tiny hands on a piece of the sweet stuff.

Finch hated throwing candy at people. He said it was like tossing fish to seals. And he couldn't believe how excited everyone got over a few stupid Tootsie Rolls and Bazooka gum. "You can buy Tootsie Rolls anywhere, and they look like pieces of dog shit," he'd complain. He was more of a Sugar Daddy guy.

He strutted down Main Street, wearing jeans that were ripped at the knees, pieces of thread dangled carelessly and a Kiss t-shirt that he had obviously cut the sleeves off of (his doing on a hot summer's day). Everyone in the carnival poked fun of him for his love of the band. The older carnies couldn't get past the costumes and make-up, which was ironic in his opinion, since they were all putting on "a show" for people.

The parade came and went, and the crowds started to disperse. Show time would start in a matter of hours. Finch caught up to Doris, Mouse, and Friedrich, who waited in front of The Diner. Haines wasn't known for having businesses with imaginative names.

If anyone scanned Main Street, they'd notice that that the beauty salon was aptly named, "The Salon," and that other businesses, like the hardware store and grocery store, were named Bob's Hardware and Lindy's Grocery.

"Hey, Honey Lamb," Doris said to Finch.

He shook the sweat out of his long dark hair and brushed the longer bangs away from his eyes.

"I can't find Stoney," he said, still scouring the area. He squinted his round dark eyes, as the sun beamed down on him.

"You know him. He probably forgot he was supposed to give us a lift back," Doris said, laughing. "He'll figure it out soon enough."

Mouse checked his pocket watch and then peered up at them. "We got a couple of hours till we have to get back anyhow."

"'Sides, we're hungry, and this place sure does smell good." She inhaled. "You smell that bacon and maple syrup?"

Before Finch could answer, Evie passed by them as she came from inside of The Diner. She chose to spend her time there drinking an ice cold Coke instead of standing out in the stifling heat watching a dull parade. She carried her crumpled brown paper bag in her hand. Her brown leather purse strap kept falling off of her bony shoulder. She jerked her shoulder upright as her opposite hand pushed the strap back on it. She smiled at them, well, everyone except Finch, and said a quick "hello"—the kind that told them she was in a hurry and didn't have time to stop and chat.

"Hey, hon," Doris said as she passed by, and then smiled at Finch, who rolled his eyes at Doris and looked in the opposite direction.

Evie opened the truck door and set the bag down next to her. She put the key in the ignition and turned. The engine choked. She turned it again, but the truck wouldn't start. She pounded her fists against the cracked dashboard, rattling the oscillating fan that Gray had installed the previous summer. She knew the truck sounded different when she started it up earlier that morning and reproached herself for driving it anyway.

She opened her door and jumped out of the truck, heading toward the hood. She lifted it and took a look underneath, not knowing exactly what she was even looking for. It was a maze of hose and wires.

"Your truck not cooperating?" Doris shouted, and Evie glanced in her direction.

She shook her head and yelled, "Damn thing died on me again!"

Doris ambled over to her, with Boris and Mouse in tow.

"We can give you a lift if you'd like," Doris said. "Might be a while though. Our ride has gone off and forgotten about us."

Evie's lips curled up into an appreciative smile. "That's real nice of you, but I'm sure if I wait around a little while it'll work again." She fumbled with some nuts and bolts, unaware of what she was touching.

"Your truck must be female," Friedrich joked. "On her own time."

Doris elbowed him playfully and then looked in Finch's direction. "Finch!" she hollered.

He sighed.

She motioned with her hands. "Come on over here and help!"

"That's okay," Evie said. "I can manage."

"Nonsense." Doris waved her off. "If it's broke, he can fix it," she said. "Trust me."

Finch strutted to Evie. Without saying a word, he moved to the hood and stood side-by-side with her. He looked at her, and Evie stared into his deep dark eyes, thinking that they were almost like black holes. The pupils disappeared into them.

He gestured with his hands for her to move, and she stood off to the side, watching him as he fiddled with the objects that were so foreign to her. She noticed a pinkish scar on his muscular upper arm. "Can you get inside and start her up?" he asked, breaking Evie from her stare. *Did he notice me gawking*, she wondered? He had, and he looked annoyed. With her.

He drummed his fingers against the grill of the truck impatiently.

She moved to her front seat and started up the truck. The engine clicked again but there was no reaction inside the compartment.

"You can stop now!" he shouted.

She got out of the car and waited for him to tell her what was the matter.

"You need a new battery, that's all," he said it with exasperation, like it should have been obvious to her, and she was the dumbest person on the planet.

"So I just need to find someone with some jumper cables?" she asked him, ignoring his petulance.

"It won't do you any good. That thing is shot." He pointed to the battery. "And how will you start it once you're home? It'll just die on you again."

Evie scrunched her face, and bit on her lip, thinking. "Okay," she said.

"What are you gonna do, Honey Lamb?" Doris asked.

"I'm guess I'm going to Mike's Garage. He'll have a battery," she said. She didn't know how she was supposed to pay for a brand new battery. Her wallet was empty, and hopefully Mike would have the time to put the battery in her truck. "Thanks," she finally said to Finch.

He shrugged indifference and shut the hood. He headed toward the front door of The Diner.

"Thank you," Evie said to Doris.

"Didn't do anything, Honey Lamb, but you're welcome." She flickered a wide grin. "We'll walk with you to the garage and make sure you're taken care of."

"That's okay. I'll be fine," Evie said.

"Nonsense." Doris brushed her off and turned to face Finch. "You coming?"

"I'm hungry. Like she said, she'll be fine," he answered in a clipped tone.

She muttered something under her breath, giving him a dirty look.

Doris moved closer to him. "You should come."

He shrugged again. "She's a grown girl. She can take care of herself," he said. "Besides, I'm hungry."

Doris slapped him on the arm.

"Ow," he grimaced. "What the hell was that for?"

"You know what it's for. A gentleman doesn't leave a girl stranded."

"I'm not a gentleman, and she's not stranded. Look." He pointed to Main Street. "She's in the middle of town, a town she's lived in her entire life, and I'd be willing to bet half these townies would give her a lift if she needed it. No need for you all to walk with her. I'm sure she can figure this out on her own." He opened the door and stepped inside.

She shook her head in disgust and walked toward Evie, Friedrich and Mouse. "Let's go see about this battery," she said with a plastered grin.

"Really, I'm fine," Evie said. "You can go eat with him," she said, enunciating "him" with a undertone of anger.

"He's fine by himself," Doris said. "'Sides, if he doesn't change his ways he's going to spend the rest of his life that way so he might as well get used to it."

They made their way down Main Street. Evie couldn't help but notice anyone nearby would stop to gawk, point, and whisper as they passed. "I'm sorry," she said to Doris.

"Ain't nothing we hadn't dealt with before." Doris brushed it off. "That's how we make our money, Honey Lamb – by being different."

Mike's Garage was the only auto shop in Haines. Mike, who was the owner, was a good friend of Gray's. Mike's father started the business many years before, and Mike inherited it when he retired. He didn't suffer for business. Being the only auto mechanic within miles helped matters, but most people trusted him and wouldn't dare go anywhere else.

They entered the garage. Mike lay underneath a raised yellow 1975 Pacer. Evie could see some of his faded gray striped uniform pants and his black work shoes peeking out.

"Mike," Evie shouted over the 1950s doo-wop music that played on the radio. The volume was set high, and Mike sang along ineptly.

He rolled out from underneath the car and looked up at her. "Hey, Evie." He smiled at her and then made a strange face at Doris, Mouse, and Friedrich. He slowly hoisted himself up, moaning as he did so. "Hey there," he said to them with uncertainty.

"Mike, this is Doris, Mouse, and Friedrich. They work for the carnival," she explained.

His head tilted to the side, studying the ink colored designs covering Friedrich's body.

"I need a new battery for Daddy's truck," she said.

He brought his gaze back to her. "I won't be able to put it in for a few hours. Gotta finish up on this here Pacer. I'm on a deadline," he said. "Told your daddy he'd need a new one last time I jumped it for him."

"How much is the battery going to cost?" she asked.

"Fifteen dollars."

She inhaled a sharp breath. "I can't pay you today. Is that okay?"

"Yes, of course, Evie," he said, and she felt relieved. "It's not like I don't know where you live." He chuckled. "Your daddy can pay me sometime this week or next week, or the week after." He laughed again.

Evie gave him an appreciative smile. "Y'all can go on. I'll wait here until he can put the battery in," she said to Doris, Mouse, and Friedrich.

"I used to help my papa tinker with his car. I can put the battery in," Mouse spoke up.

"Are you sure?" Evie asked him.

"Positive." He smiled assuredly.

She looked at Mike, who was still staring at Mouse, Doris and Friedrich in wonder. "Ain't never seen so many tattoos," he said almost apologetically.

Friedrich smiled proudly. "You can look at them." He moved closer to him, allowing Mike to inspect them more closely.

Mike ogled at the plethora of colors covering Friedrich. "I get so busy in this shop, I never get to go up to your daddy's farm when the carnival's in town. It's a shame too. Did it hurt?"

"Some more than others," Friedrich said. "Doris says that beauty is a pain sometimes."

Mike glanced one last time and then made his way to a metal shelf, pulling a battery off of it and carrying it with him to the cash register. "This'll do it," he said to Evie.

She reached to grab the battery from him, but Friedrich took it from her hands before she could pull it off of the counter.

"I insist," he said to her.

"I can carry it," she said.

"Allow me," he said.

"Oh just let him, Honey Lamb," Doris said and then whispered loudly. "He's from the old country."

Evie didn't argue and allowed Friedrich to continue holding it. "Thanks again, Mike. I'll tell Daddy to pay you as soon as possible."

"Ain't no problem at all," he said. "Bye, y'all." He waved and headed back to the Pacer.

***

Mouse stood on top of Evie's truck bumper, peering into the engine. His forehead was crinkled, and he wiped sweat off of his brow. His long sleeves were rolled up to his elbows. He took off his fedora; his thinning hair was wet against his freckled scalp.

He used a crescent wrench from the toolbox in Evie's truck to disconnect the battery terminal, turning slightly. Suddenly he yelped, and flew backwards, falling to the ground.

CHAPTER 8

"Ow!" He touched his hand, rubbing it with his other. Pain filled his face. Evie bent down to inspect his sore hand, and helped him up off of the ground.

"You okay?" she asked.

"Just a little shock that's all." He tried to smile, but Evie could see him tugging on his hand, grimacing as he did so.

"Don't worry about putting the battery in," she said and stood back up. "I'll get Mike to do it."

Finch pushed the door open from the inside of The Diner and without saying anything, he passed by them and opened the truck door. He turned the ignition off, and tossed the keys to Evie, who caught them.

"You have to turn the ignition to off before you change a battery," he said in a condescending tone. He closed the door and mumbled something to himself. Evie swore she heard the words "novice" and "duh." He peered over the engine, disconnected the negative battery terminal and then found the positive terminal. "Wrench," he barked, making no eye contact with any of them.

"You could say please, you know," she said and slapped it on his hand.

"I could, but I won't," he said. Evie was speechless.

He pulled the old battery out and placed it down on the ground. He picked up the new battery, and attached it as quickly as he had disconnected the other one. He turned to face Evie, a look of annoyance filled both of their faces but for different reasons.

"Start her up," he ordered.

She was fuming. Her face was distorted, and if it were physically possible, she'd breathe fire at that very moment. She stomped to the driver's side and yanked the door open, plopping down onto the seat. She turned the ignition and the truck started.

Finch slammed the hood down and wiped his hands against his jeans. He bent over to pick up the old battery and moved to the passenger door. He opened it, placed the battery down on the floor, and then closed the door.

"Next time you want to play mechanic, read a manual first. Rule number one: make sure the keys are out of the ignition," he said to Mouse.

"I was just trying to help," Mouse said.

"I know," he softened. "Stick to what you know and you won't get hurt."

"You get more with honey than you do by being a piss-ant, Finch," Doris said to him.

He ignored her quip and scanned the area, and then said, "Don't think Stoney's coming to get us."

Mouse checked his watch and nodded in agreement. "We better be getting back."

"Stoney would forget to put his underwear on the right way if he didn't write the words front and back on them," Doris said with a laugh. "Hey, Honey Lamb, you think you could give us a lift?" she asked Evie.

"Sure. No problem," Evie said.

"We can catch a ride with someone else," Finch argued.

"You're being a fool," Doris said to him.

Doris, Mouse, and Friedrich headed to the back of the truck and pulled the truck bed door down.

"What are you doing?" Finch said.

"You can ride in the front with Evie," Doris said with a mischievous grin. "You spend so much time staring at her, you might as well sit up-close so you can get a better look."

"Forget it," he replied emphatically.

She waved her finger at him like a pendulum. "You're just being silly," she said.

"I'll sit back here, and one of you can ride up front with her," he said. Even he could hear the childishness in his statement. Last time he thought a girl had the "cooties" he was seven years old. She was Julie Howell, and she'd chase him all over the carnival. When she'd finally catch up to him, she'd kiss him and tell him he was beautiful. Finch would wipe his lips and moan how gross it was that she kissed him, but within a year, Julie and her family made another carnival their home, and he missed her attention. He missed her giggle as she ran to catch him. He would slow down for her this time, just so he could hear her tell him he was beautiful. In her eyes, he was something more, something even better.

"There's no room," Friedrich said and straightened his legs out. Doris stretched out her arms, taking up even more room. "See," he said. "No more room."

Finch threw his hands up in the air and stormed off to the passenger door. He stood there for a minute, watching Evie chew on her fingernails and staring into space. He opened the door and sat down. His legs straddled the battery.

She looked at him and rolled her eyes. "You couldn't ride in the back?" She started up the truck and began driving down Main Street.

"Nope," he said. He scanned the inside of the truck. The green dashboard was cracked, and the seats were stained with dirt, grease, and years of farming.

"You don't believe in rear view mirrors up here?" he said, noticing the empty space where a mirror should have been.

"It fell off, and anyways, I've managed to drive without it this long."

"Doesn't mean it's safe. Last time I checked, you actually need to see what's in back of you when you drive," he said.

"I'm a good driver."

"I'm sure you are," he said, mocking her. He touched the oscillating fan. "I've never seen a fan in a truck before." He turned on the switch, and the fan rotated from one side of the truck to the other, moving air in whichever direction it was pointed. "Kind of a waste, don't you think?"

"How's that?" she asked in a miffed tone.

"It's just blowing hot air. Is this what you farmers call air conditioning?"

"No, it's not what we call air conditioning," she corrected him. "My dad installed it to help cool off the truck during the summer."

"Still kind of a waste," he said. He placed his hand in front of it. "It's hot air."

"You would know since that seems to be the only thing coming from your mouth."

He smiled and chuckled.

She didn't understand why she couldn't make him angry. He'd just look at her, and she wanted to kick him. She knew the perfect place for her foot to land, too.

She let out a long-winded sigh and focused everything she had in her on the road ahead. Finch rolled his window down and let the wind run through his hair. A hint of Pert Shampoo filled the car, and Evie had to acknowledge that for a guy who spent his nights in tents and lived in the elements, Finch had a pleasant scent about him.

He leaned forward and fiddled with the volume to the radio. Music filled the truck.

"Don't mess with that," she snapped and shooed his hand away.

"Sorry. I thought some tunes would lighten up this tomb." He moved his hand away from the knob and set it in his lap.

They rode in silence for several minutes as she drove toward her home, and the music from the radio was the only sound heard. Evie looked out of the corner of her eye and caught Finch studying her.

She felt self-conscious, feeling the weight of his gaze on her. "What are you looking at?" she asked. Irritation filled her to the core.

"You shouldn't do that." He gestured with his head to the tip of the fingernail she had in her mouth.

She quit chewing on it. Her nails were down to the quick, blood crept underneath most of them.

"Why do you care?" she hissed, hating herself for asking him that question but she was dying to know.

"I don't. It's just..." he said, searching for the right word, "gross."

That wasn't what she was expecting him to say. "Well, so is smoking," she replied, feeling triumphant for being quick with her cut down.

"It is," he agreed. "Good thing I don't do it," he said with a smirk.

Evie's confidence quickly faltered.

"You gnaw on your nails like that on a date, and no guy will ever kiss that mouth of yours." He sat back against the seat and folded his arms behind his head.

She gasped and then gritted her teeth. Her hands gripped onto the steering wheel. "You're just, just..." she couldn't find the right words. She was too incensed. "Rude! You're rude," she said with more certainty. "The rudest person I've ever met!"

He laughed, which made her even angrier. "I've been called worse. Much worse. I'll take being called rude by you as a compliment," he said, making sure that he exaggerated his smirk, knowing how much it irked her.

She slammed on her brakes. Doris, Friedrich and Mouse crashed against the back of the cab and hollered, and Finch flew forward, his palms were pressed on the dash board.

"What the?" he said, pushing himself back against the truck seat.

"You alright, hon?" Doris shouted from outside.

"I'm perfectly fine," Evie said in a cool tone. She turned to face Finch, glaring at him, and said, "Out!"

"You're kidding, right?" he scoffed.

She motioned to the door. "You can walk back to the farm."

He mumbled under his breath. "Just like I thought. A real princess."

"What's going on in there?" Doris shouted.

"Nothing. Your friend has decided he wants to walk the rest of the way," she said and stared at him, waiting for him to open the door.

He shook his head in disbelief and opened the door, closing it gently behind him. He stood in front of the rolled down window and said with a sardonic grin, "Try not to gnaw those nails off."

Finch gripped onto the rail of the truck bed and swung himself up and over and into the back. Evie pressed her foot against the gas and sped off thinking she had the satisfaction of leaving Finch standing on the side of the road sucking on her exhaust. He squeezed himself in between Doris, Mouse and Friedrich.

"What'd you say to her?" Doris said in an accusing tone.

He shrugged. "She's overly sensitive," he said.

"I'm sure you were a real prince charming," Doris said. "If your mama was here..."

"She's not, so drop it," he snapped, and Doris read him loud and clear.

"She seems like a nice girl," Friedrich added, failing to notice or care about Finch's temperament. "You are spending a lot of energy being cruel to her."

Finch pointed to himself in disbelief. "I'm being mean?"

They all three nodded, and Finch tilted his head up toward the clear blue sky. The clouds even looked different in this part of the country than they did in Gibsonton. He took a whiff, smelling the cow manure and fresh cut grass, and knew he was almost to the farm. He could get there blindfolded just by the scent alone.

"You go on ignoring us, but you know we're right," Doris said.

Evie reached the split in the drive leading to her house and left the truck running, waiting for them all to get out.

"Thanks, hon," Doris shouted as she, Friedrich, and Mouse exited the truck. Finch jumped out and walked over to Evie.

He leaned into her window, and his elbows rested on the top of the truck door. "Thanks for the ride." He smiled, and Evie's mouth was agape.

"You are a butt hole!" she yelled and pressed her foot onto the accelerator.

Finch let out a boisterous laugh. He watched as her tires spun in the loose gravel, kicking up a cloud of dust as the truck sped away.

CHAPTER 9

She wanted to turn the truck around and run him over and over again until she flattened him like a pancake and got rid of that annoying smirk of his. She had no idea where her urge of violence stemmed from, but he could make her madder than a wet hen. She was still fuming when she pulled up to the front of her house. She grabbed her crumpled paper bag and got out, looking up at their house and seeing all of the things that needed to be repaired. It needed to be painted, and the columns on the front porch were rotting from the bottom up. The list was getting longer and longer. She could feel the weight of it all laying on her shoulders.

She pushed the front door open and heard her dad clanking around in the kitchen. He was as loud as a raccoon sifting through garbage cans, and when she entered the kitchen, his eyes widened and a look of guilt filled his round face.

There, in front of him, was the apple pie Evie had made the night before. He was eating from the pan with his hands, liquid apple oozed from the corners of his mouth.

"Daddy," she moaned. "You're supposed to have one slice."

"You can't just have one," he said, food still in his mouth. Chunks of apple fell onto his faded maroon t-shirt, and he scooped those off with his fingers and stuck them into his mouth.

She took the pie away from him.

"Where'r you going with that?" he asked.

"I'll make you a sandwich. You can't eat pie for lunch," she said with frustration. Sometimes she felt like she was the parent, and he was her child. She took ham out of the refrigerator and placed it between two slices of bread.

"It's what I wanted," he said, almost sounding like a whining child. He got up and took the pie out of the refrigerator and sat it in front of him, scooping a heap of a piece with his fork and placing it into his mouth.

She sighed and finished making the sandwich.

"Where've you been?" he asked with a full mouth, but Evie learned long ago how to read him.

"At Henson's. I got stuck in the parade, and then the battery died." She sat across from him and bit into the sandwich that she had made for him. He gave her a smug look when she did so, but she wasn't biting. Dealing with Finch had worn her out. She wasn't in the mood to argue with anyone else. She didn't even know if that's what she was doing with him – arguing. It felt like more than that – exciting and frustrating at the same time. A part of her wanted it. She shook that thought away, wondering where the absurdity of wanting someone to drive her crazy came from.

"Did someone jump it for you?"

"No. I had to buy a new one," she said.

"How much is that gonna cost us?"

"You owe Mike fifteen dollars," she said.

"Lawd have mercy, if ain't one thing, it's another."

She opened up the brown paper bag and took out the small bag that had the bottle of pills in it. She unstapled the bag and took out the bottle. "I picked up your prescription." She pushed the bottle his way and watched as he ignored her and continued eating. "Henson said he's been trying to get in touch with you to pick it up."

He took a swig of his sweet tea, washing down the pie.

"He said it's pretty potent medication," she continued.

"You think it'll make me act like Sally Stratton?" he teased. Sally Stratton was one of Haines' notorious drunks. She spent many nights in the tank for drunken and disorderly behavior, and her husband, Tom, never drank an ounce of alcohol in his life. Most people said that she drank enough for the two of them and that's why he avoided it.

Her brow wrinkled. "It's for your blood pressure."

"My blood pressure's fine till I have to go see the doc. What does he know anyhow?"

"Maybe those ten years of college make him qualified," she said sarcastically.

"I would've gotten around to getting these," he said, picking up the bottle and squinting his eyes to read the label.

"When? At the end of summer?"

"Hardy, har, har," he said. "When I had time. Bet they cost as much as the battery."

"It doesn't matter. If your doctor says you have to take them, you should."

He grinned and said, "You're a bossy butt."

"Just make sure you take them," she pressed.

***

Opening day for the carnival was a success. Kip liked the stacks of bills his bookkeeper counted at night's end. Gray's farm was the perfect location – near the interstate and close enough to the North Carolina border. He knew it'd only be a matter of days until the townies from other areas flocked to the carnival.

Finch's job was simple. Fix anything that appeared to be broken. He had repaired his fair share of rides over the years. Some too many times. He told Kip to replace a few, that their years were

coming to an end, but Kip would just say, "You can fix it, kid."
He could put a Bandaid on it, but eventually, it'd peel off and then what?

He walked the property, hearing people scream in joy from the thrill of being flung side-to-side and up and down at unimaginable speeds. All of the motions the rides produced would make anyone giddy like a kid. He knew, because he was like that once. He'd shriek and throw his hands up in the air, feeling like he was having the time of his life. But then something happened, like when a kid discovers Santa Claus isn't real, and then Christmas is never the same. The excitement of staying up late, waiting for Santa to arrive disappears and Christmas just becomes another day. It was a day with pomp and circumstance, but for most people it was all just a facade that hid their true feelings about the strife it created for them. The carnival became like that for him. It became monotony – the mysticism was gone, and in the end, it was just a job.

A group of people were in line waiting to see Doris, Friedrich and Mouse. A lump caught in Finch's throat, and he swallowed hard. He knew it was their job, that they didn't mind the stares and comments, but something about it bothered him. He couldn't stand the sight of it – people waiting in line to ooh and aah over his friends, to gawk at them, and then whisper insults and other rude comments under their breaths.

"Bunch of dumb rubes," he muttered as he passed them by, almost running into Dmitri, the carnival's juggler, and his wife Olga.

"Sorry," Finch said.

"It is fine," Dmitri said, his arms were wrapped tight around Olga's petite waist. He offered Finch a faint smile.

"How was the show?" he asked.

"A success. These townies like our act," he said with a strong accent and without much of an expression.

"That's good," Finch said, feeling happy for him. Dmitri and Olga were well-liked for their quiet and kind demeanors, although no one in the carnival really knew them. They mostly kept to themselves and often spoke in Russian, which no one else in the carnival understood or even wanted to try to comprehend.

Anyone that didn't cause drama and stayed out of trouble in the carnival was liked. So much senseless drama ensued – too many drunken brawls and fights over who was sleeping with whom. It was welcome when a normal married couple was amongst the crew. Dmitri wowed the crowds with his ability to juggle several items at once. He could juggle up to ten bowling pins, often silencing any crowd who wondered how in the world could he do it. People asked, and he'd just act like it was no big deal. Like it was a talent any hack off the street could pick up and master. Olga didn't have any talents. She worked the concession, selling funnel cakes and cotton candy to hungry townies, who were thankful to be waited on by such an angelic face. Olga's features were soft around the edges. It was rumored that she was a model in her home country, but this was never confirmed or denied. She was definitely eye candy for all of the men on the circuit, leaving Dmitri with an even tighter rein on his wife.

"Goodbye," Dmitri said, and Finch nodded his head once.

Finch went on with his day, counting the minutes, and wondering if this was it. If this was his lot in life—fixing what needed to be repaired. If only he could find someone to "fix" him. A non-stop job indeed. It would be as constant a battle as fixing

Kip's antique rides.

***

He walked alone, enjoying the gentle breeze the night air offered him. All of the rides' bright lights were off, and the carnival was closed for the night. A warm glow from the moon filled the dark, starry sky. Crickets chirped incessantly, and the fireflies flickering lights danced in the shadows as he made his way through the maze of tents – the place that the carnies would call home for the next five weeks.

He heard shouting from the inside of Doris' tent. He ran inside and held his hand up to his nose, a powerful stench of manure permeated the air. Doris and Friedrich stood behind Evie's pet ox, Miles, pushing against him with all of their might, while Mouse sat on top of it, tapping it against the neck, yelling, "Move! Move!"

"*Bewegung! Bewegung!*" shouted Friedrich in his native German language. Finch had managed to learn basic German phrases over the years—a skill he didn't see any use for—but that seemed to impress girls.

"Sie wollen, dass mit Ketchup?" he'd whisper, and they'd giggle at the sound of his voice saying something so foreign to them. They were oblivious to what he said, thinking he was whispering sweet nothings in their ears, but translated into English, Finch was telling them "Do you want ketchup with that?"

He begged Friedrich to teach him phrases like these. Things he thought were fun to say, because learning how to say important things like "how much" or "I need medical attention" just didn't have the same snazzy ring to them. He had mastered the accent, and any clueless girl who heard him speak in German was unnecessarily dazzled.

Miles wouldn't move an inch. He was obviously too enthralled with the candy bar that currently occupied his mouth. Half-eaten wrappers of other sweets and candy laid on the ground around him, and the place looked like it had been ransacked.

"He won't budge," Doris said between heavy breaths. "I didn't even think they ate candy."

"Every living thing eats sugar," Finch said.

"We've been trying to get him to leave, but he's intent on eating everything in sight." She shoved Miles again, and nothing happened. "I'm pooped." Sweat trickled down her face.

Friedrich leaned forward and pushed as hard as he could. Finch could see veins protruding from below the surface of his thick neck. He gritted his crooked teeth, moaned, and let out a wail of frustration. "*Dumm Kopf!*" he shouted, nearly spitting the words out.

"This places smells like the whole damn town took a shit in here," Doris said, plugging her nose and waving her hands back and forth.

"Help me off," Mouse said, and Finch lifted him and placed his feet firmly on the ground.

Finch looked Miles in the eye. The two were having a stare off, and neither of them moved. Finch whispered under his breath, "Time to go on."

Miles took a small step forward and nuzzled up close to Finch, his mouth grabbing hold of Finch's Led Zeppelin t-shirt – one that was frayed and had seen its last days. Finch gently pushed Miles' head away from his shirt. "Not the shirt," he said, but Miles refused to listen.

He grabbed hold of it again, and let out a soft "Moo."

"He likes you," Doris said. "You finally found a fan." She laughed.

Finch scowled at her. "He won't let go." He shooed Miles again, but the stubborn ox only held on tighter. "What'll I do?" he asked them, feeling helpless. The ox had attached itself to Finch, and it wasn't going to let go.

"Take him to Evie. He's hers, ain't he?" she said. "And while you're out, better grab a shovel." She looked down at the pile of cow manure and grimaced.

"You take him," he argued.

She cocked an eyebrow. "You saw how well that was working out."

"Fine," he relented and took a step forward; Miles went with him.

"Just don't be a piss-ant. She ain't ever gonna go on a date with you if you keep killing her with your charm, Mister Charming Pants," Doris said.

Finch was able to get the ox to quit chewing on his tethered shirt. "Can't wear this again," he complained, seeing the big chunk of fabric missing. He passed by tents with glimmers of light emitting from kerosene lamps. The chattering of voices and laughter could be heard, echoing through the camp. Even though it was late, most carnies didn't get to sleep until well into the night. Finch knew from personal experience, five hours was a good night's rest, and if he got more, then it was a miracle.

Miles trailed behind Finch following him as he trudged through the dark. He mooed every now and again, and Finch caught himself talking to him, shuddering at the thought. "I can't believe I'm talking to a dumb cow," he muttered.

Their porch light shined in the distance, and he could see a figure sitting on the front porch swing, swaying back and forth as gently as the soft billowing breeze that swept through the cool night air. He moved closer and saw the light shining onto her blond locks of hair, and her face looked absolutely relaxed, serene almost. He couldn't help but spy.

His feet wandered through the long blades of grass, and he made his way to the steps leading to Evie's front porch. He cleared his throat. He never cleared his throat and couldn't understand the strong case of nerves he suddenly had. On his territory, he was much more confident, but being at her house in the dark of night was a different matter. He cleared his throat again, and then shouted, "Hey!"

She jumped in surprise, and then got a hold of herself when she saw it was him. Tripod stood up and let out one pathetic bark, then settled himself back down onto the porch.

"What do you want?" she shouted back at him in an unfriendly tone.

"Your cow was eating all of Doris' junk food," he said, pointing to Miles who was busy chewing on the grass surrounding Finch's shoes.

"Miles!" She hopped off the swing and ran down the steps. Tripod trailed behind her, rumbling down the steps as only a three-legged dog could do. She stood a few feet away from Finch and the smitten ox. "You know better than to wander off," she scolded, and Finch tried hard not to laugh, but to him it was comical that she was talking to the ox like he was her kid. She peered up at Finch and said, "Tell Doris I'm sorry."

Tripod inched closer to Finch and sniffed him. Finch peered

down at him with a strange look and then patted him on the head. "Hey there, what's your name?"

"His name is Tripod," her tone was haughty. "And you don't get to talk to him." She snapped her fingers at Tripod, trying to get his attention away from Finch.

Finch let out a soft chuckle. "He'd fit right in on the midway." He tapped him a few more times on his furry head and bent down to cup his face. "Better go on, boy." Tripod licked Finch's fingers before he slowly made his way to the front porch. Finch wiped his wet fingers against his jeans. "Not much for watch dogging, though, is he? I could have been Jack the Ripper."

"His senses must be off," Evie mumbled. She raised her hand to her lips and started to chew on a nail, and then abruptly stopped, suddenly aware of what she was doing.

Finch cocked an eyebrow but said nothing else. He looked down at her ensemble – a thin, poor excuse for fabric barely covered her. The light coming from the porch shone through the piece of clothing that adorned her and created a perfect silhouette. He could see the outline of her body and the curve of her breasts. She was dressed in a night shirt and an old pair of cowboy boots. Wind crept underneath her gown. She pushed it down with her hands, noticing that her palms were clammy and her heart was fluttering. She felt a shiver, and crossed her arms over her chest, seeing that Finch's gaze lingered longer than it should have.

"How'd you get him here?" she asked, one arm was draped across her chest, while the other tugged on her night shirt.

He shrugged. "Don't know. " He scratched at his head. "He seems to like me, or maybe it's my shirt." Finch pointed to the big patch of bare stomach, and Evie quickly averted her eyes, trying not to ogle. Finch noticed, and his lips curled upward.

"I'm sure it's the shirt," she said quickly, trying to rattle Finch's confidence. "He likes Zeppelin."

"He has good taste then," Finch said. He wasn't in the mood to tease her or give her a hard time. It was getting late, and he had quite the hike back to his tent. Plus, he didn't want to stand within ten feet of her when she was wearing that stupid frock – the one that was sheer and lime green and possibly made out of satin or rayon, he couldn't tell, and had a strip of lace at the top of her chest. It kept tickling her legs, blowing from the hush of the wind, and showed the perfect shape of her hips and her legs that were long and smooth looking. He wanted to shout up at the air and tell it to stop moving so swiftly so he could gather his thoughts and quit gawking at her.

Things suddenly felt awkward, and a wind chime clattered. "I gotta go. Try to keep that cow of yours away from Doris' tent," he barked before he walked away.

"He's an ox, not a cow!" she snapped.

He turned to face her. "What?" He didn't know why he even bothered to ask. A cow, an ox, who cared?

"Cows are female, oxen are male. He's male. If you knew anything, you would've noticed." She felt a surge of triumph, content that she had finally brought his ego down a notch or two. She could outsmart him when it came to agriculture.

"Maybe you spend your free time checking out animal's private parts, but I got better things to do with my time," he shot back. "Try not to chew those nails off."

He began to walk away, and Miles charged toward him, following behind him.

"Miles!" Evie called, desperation surfaced in her voice. "Get back here," she said angrily.

"Even he knows when something's better," Finch said. "Go on back, buddy," he whispered to Miles and gently pushed him. "Go on," he cooed, feeling a tinge of guilt after seeing Evie's hurt expression. Sometimes he wanted to sock himself in the face.

She pulled on Miles and gestured for him to go her way, and all Finch could see was that dumb swath of fabric of hers flying up. He never loved and hated a night gown so much.

CHAPTER 10

Evie chewed Miles out, and then apologized profusely for being so mean to him. She was just so – mad. Finch made her angry. She wanted to punch him on both sides of his face and then run her fingers across his stomach, touching the smooth firm surface. She groaned aloud and balled her fist. To any outsider, she looked like a two year old having a tantrum.

She darted up the steps and sat herself back down on the swing. Tripod moved her way. "Oh, now you want to be near me," she said. "Benedict Arnold." Tripod cowered and decided a spot further away would be a prudent choice at that time.

She could hear her dad clomping around in the house, probably sneaking something from the pantry. She sighed and tried to think about anything but Finch. She swung back and forth with her knees up to her chest. The tips of her boot heels were covered in specs of dirt and touched the edge of the swing.

***

Birthdays were always a big deal in the Barnes household – Gray made them that way. For weeks he'd sing, "I know a secret, and I ain't gonna tell. And it's really swell." He'd smile and wink at Evie, as if she were supposed to be on her knees begging him to tell her what that secret was. "You can't pry it out of me no matter how hard you try," he always said.

Evie wasn't into surprises. Just let her birthdays come and go without any fanfare and forget the whole thing happened. That's what she preferred, but her pleas for a quiet affair fell on deaf ears where Gray was concerned.

On her sixteenth birthday, Evie would have been perfectly

content letting the night pass without so much as a congratulatory message from friends and family. Gray had other thoughts and threw her a small party. Small being the operative word. Evie didn't have a long list of friends, real friends, the kind that Evie knew she could count on if her life depended on it. Katie was it, and Evie was just fine with that. Having more than one was too complicated, at least for her.

Cooper, Gray, and Katie watched as Evie opened each present. Gray bent over and picked up the large box, which had obviously been wrapped by a professional with its curled ribbon and shiny red bow.

He rubbed his hands together. "You're gonna love your gift."

She tore the paper open and opened the brown box, pulling out the brown cowboy boots with accents of turquoise running up and down the textured cow hide. "These are the ones I saw in the window," she said with a wide smile.

"Ole Katie told me you've been eyeing 'em for a while. Put 'em on," he said.

She slipped her feet into them, feeling the perfection. It was as if her feet were made for them, or the other way around. She got up and walked around the living room, beaming from the comfort of them. They were cushiony and soft. "They're perfect," she said.

Gray looked pleased with himself. "I had to play P.I. to find out what size you wear," he said. "Katie helped me out some," he added and winked at her. Katie giggled.

"Lawd have mercy, I had to special order them from Berk's. Took a whole month. I was worried you weren't gonna get them in time," he said.

"I love them," Evie said and rushed to hug him, squeezing him as hard as she could.

He patted her on the back, letting her go and smiled down at her. "There's a first," he said. "If I had known all it'd take was a pair of boots, I would've gotten you a pair every year just to have a hug like that."

She hugged him again and traipsed around the house in her new pair of boots. They rarely came off her feet from that time on, unless she had to shower or sleep, or had to work in the barn. They were a part of her, a gift from her dad, and she'd never toss them out in the trash or donate them to Goodwill. They'd be with her for life.

***

Another day passed, and Evie kept herself busy working the farm. It was time to deworm the cattle, a task that'd take an entire day, and one that Evie dreaded. No farmer was ever up for the task, but it was one that Evie hated more than anything about the job.

Wrangling them into the barn was enough of a feat, but getting them lined up and standing still long enough for Gray to shove the thick, gooey liquid up their nose was even harder. They were smart enough animals to catch on. Once a few went through the head gate— a contraption that trapped their big heads inside a round metal circle—they hesitated to move forward, only frustrating Gray even more.

"Get in there!" he hollered.

Evie tapped on the cow's behind with the poker stick, but it was wasn't hard enough. She just didn't have the stomach for it. She wouldn't want to get struck with one, so she knew they wouldn't either.

"Come on!" he cried desperately. His cheeks had turned three shades of red, and his voice was crackling, like he was on the verge of tears.

He grabbed the stick from Evie and hit the heifer in the rump. She instantly moved, and Evie pulled the lever on the head gate. This went on for hours, and the putrid scent of cow manure and urine bristled in their weathered, run-down barn. The air was stifling hot and thick with humidity. Several beams of wood had rotted and were being smothered by mud dauber nests. Cylinder tubes resembling organ pipes constructed of dirt reached the barn ceiling.

Evie took a step backward into a pile of cow shit, thankful she was wearing her old rubber boots – the pair she didn't care much for. "Dammit!" she said, seeing that some of it had gotten onto the bottom of her jeans. She'd have to rinse them off before she got back in the house.

"Watch your mouth!" Gray warned, but he was being a hypocrite because Evie heard him swear more than once that day. He always apologized when he did. Gray hated to curse and loathed it when he said a bad word in front of a woman. "A gentleman never curses around a lady," he'd often say. "You make sure no man ever curses around you. Ain't no reason to unless his life is at stake."

"Did you...?" she began, but thought the better of it.

"What?" he asked, eyes widened and hopeful that she was seeking more guidance from him about the dos and don'ts of dating.

"Did you curse around *her*?"

He knew who the "her" was without a mention of her name. "Once. The day before she left," he said, and Evie was sorry she asked. He changed the topic and added a few more snippets of wisdom, hoping his daughter would end up with the perfect man, or at least his impression of what the embodiment of perfection looked like for his one and only child.

Gray had a long set of guidelines that a man must meet to be worthy of his daughter. "He should pick you up for your date. None of this meeting somewhere." He frowned. "I see so many girls meeting a guy some place. Seems somewhat tawdry if you ask me."

Evie rarely had a response. She'd let him ramble, dishing out advice that had somehow stuck with her. "And I know all you women's libbers like to open your own door, but let the poor fellow do it. Let him wait on you hand and foot treating you like the princess you are," he'd say.

It was like this the entire day. Her pulling the lever while Gray's hands were covered in the nasty, snotty looking consistency. She had to keep track of every heifer, writing down their number, making sure that each of them was dewormed. Each heifer had a yellow tag attached to one ear with bold black numbers. Evie never named them anymore. She learned a long time ago not to because they weren't ever coming back.

"This one's a beauty," he said, smiling at the heifer. He talked low and sweet to them, and patted them on the head. Some said he had a natural knack with them. That they'd do anything for him, but he'd always shrug off those compliments and say, "It's how Daddy was. I learned from him."

Evie scrawled the heifer's number down on a sheet of paper. "That's ninety-three," she said. They were almost finished.

Her legs were achy, and her lower back hurt. She knew that at eighteen years of age, she shouldn't be in that much pain, but a day's work was just that – work.

Heifers, she equated, were like her mother, but heifers were more forgiving. Her mother wasn't, and for that, she could never bring herself to stop hating her.

Her mother couldn't deal. She didn't want to wait out Gray's next business decision or fanciful venture, one that was sure to make them some serious money. She wanted real cash, the kind that they could roll around in and spend frivolously on trinkets and trips and things that no one needs. The type of things rich people had just because they could. She hated that she wore the same old frocks and shoes that dated back to the Kennedy administration, and that her daughter was content running around in grimy denim – worn and torn from a day's hard work. Her hands weren't the beautiful buttermilk complexion they once were, but tanned with new found wrinkles and age spots to match. She loathed that she saw a reflection of a haggard woman in her mid-thirties whose life, she supposed, was over.

It didn't take long for her to muster the strength or lack of consideration, depending on how one viewed it, to leave her family. On a beautiful autumn day, while Gray and Evie sat at a cattle auction, she packed up a few of her treasured belongings and left. A note sat on the kitchen table. Just a few words – none of remorse, none of promises. She said she couldn't deal with it anymore, and wanted to start her life over without them. Gray blamed himself – like any father and spouse would. A small part of Evie wanted to blame the carnies for her mother's escape – that maybe she wouldn't be able to deal with seeing strange folk on her land every summer without reaping copious benefits in exchange. But mostly, Evie learned to hate, because her own mother, the one who had given birth to her, had chosen to live her life without her.

Rumors skyrocketed through the roof. Where had Rebecca Barnes gone? Why did she leave? Was it for another man? When Evie was asked, she'd bark and say, "Who cares," because she didn't. Why should they? She told herself that anyway. She refused to grieve over her mother. She had made her choice, and Evie had made hers.

She received a letter from her once, a few months after she left. Evie never opened it, and tore it to shreds right in front of her stupefied father. "We don't need her," she said to him. The tattered rose color paper was spread across the linoleum kitchen floor. Evie watched her father stoop to the ground, trying to put the pieces back together one at a time.

She bent down and picked up all of the fragments of paper in one swoop and tossed them in the garbage. "Don't," she pleaded to him. "It'll only make things worse. She's gone now, Daddy," she had said. At the young age of eight, Evie had moved on with her life without her mother in it.

"That anger will kill the good in you," her dad told her on more than one occasion, but she let it go in one ear and out the other. She could focus all of her energy hating her mother for what she did to them, especially for what she did to her father. Leaving him took a piece of his soul, and even at a young age, Evie was aware that a glimmer of light had died from Gray's big blue eyes. For that, she could hate her and have no remorse for harboring that feeling. It was real and true, and she would never apologize for feeling that way.

CHAPTER 11

Evie lay on her couch, trying to watch a show on the television, but the reception was poor, and the screen rolled continuously. She got up to move the ears of the antenna and let out a frustrated sigh. The television was worthless, showing nothing but black and white images in scrambled fashion and blurred images of actresses and actors on shows Evie would have liked to have watched but rarely got the chance to see. At best, they were able to get three stations, but most of the time, two of the three weren't even viewable.

Gray was out with Cooper, hanging out at the bar and playing pool – things that she thought sounded dull and like a waste of time. But he needed his guy time, and if bonding over a few watered down beers and shooting at some colored balls made him feel manly, then she could understand. Besides, she liked having the house to herself. She so rarely got the chance to hang out in her PJs and eat a bowl of ice cream for dinner. When he was home, she had to make sure that they ate right, and a little bit of her was always on edge – like a mama bear with its cub.

Someone pounded against her front door, and Evie screeched, heading toward the front window. She checked the time on her clock, seeing it was too late for Katie to be coming over. Katie wouldn't have knocked so hard anyway. She wouldn't have even bothered to knock for that matter. Katie would let herself in and make herself at home. She hadn't talked to Katie since she told her she was pregnant, and she worried about her best friend. If they didn't talk the next day, Evie was going to head over to her house and check in on her. That alone should tell Katie how much she cared, because going over to Nate McDaniels' house was not something Evie did that often. He frightened her, and everyone in the house walked around him like they were walking on egg shells, afraid to stir the pot. Evie knew that was the reason Katie chose to stay at her house all the time—to get away from that sterile environment. She often wondered how a person as full of life as Katie could be related to a toad like Nate.

Evie pulled the curtains out of the way and saw Finch standing outside on her front porch. *What's he doing here?*

She looked down at her flimsy night shirt, grabbed a sweater off of the coat rack and put it on. She slipped into her cowboy boots and opened the door.

Finch's white t-shirt was wrinkled and tight—showing clear definition in his arms and chest. His cheeks showed hints of rose, and he was perspiring. He stuffed his hands into his jean pockets. "Your gate is open, and a few cows got out," he said. Evie could see his chest rising and then falling flat.

"Where?" she asked.

"Down that way." He pointed behind Evie's head. She knew which gate it was – the one that was on the far end of the property near their fishing pond and a dirt road that only led to a few neighbors farms and nowhere else.

"Okay," she breathed. "Thanks." She closed the door behind her and began walking toward the barn.

"Where are you going?" he asked, running to catch up to her.

"I can't leave them out there," she explained. "I'm gotta get the ATV and wrangle them in."

"Do you need help?" He continued to follow her as she pushed the barn door open.

She stopped to face him. "I don't think you can do this," she said, appraising him.

He folded his arms against his chest. "Try me," he said in a challenging tone.

She shrugged and said with doubt, "Okay." She tossed him the keys to one of the ATV's. "Follow my lead."

She sat down and turned the ignition, the rumbling chug, chug, chug of the engine's motor silenced every other sound. They each turned on their headlights. Finch's ATV's light shined onto Evie's back. He was thankful she wore that gosh awful sweater over that frilly frock he had dreamt about more than once the last couple of days.

She gestured with her hands, and off they sped, driving up and down the hills. Finch loved the feel of the wind blowing through his hair—the breeze against his back—as he coasted on the foothills.

They finally reached the gate, and Evie drove out onto the dirt road, leaving Finch straddling the ATV, watching her in amazement. Recent flooding rains made it difficult to navigate on the muddy terrain. She jerked hard on the steering wheel, and stood up as she pressed her foot hard against the accelerator—looking more like a horse jockey riding a horse than a farmer riding a machine.

"Sug! Sug!" she shouted at the six-hundred-pound heifers.

The obstinate cattle remained planted, unaltered by her sudden movement and barking orders.

"Yaw! Yaw!" she yelled. She turned her ATV around and headed toward them, and Finch thought she was going to run them over. She called to Finch as she moved in haste, "Get on this side!" She gestured with her hand.

He drove forward and was opposite to Evie – the cattle in

between them like a game of Monkey in the Middle. His bright lights shined into the heifers' big brown eyes. The light startled them, and they suddenly moved away from him and to the other side, with Evie right beside them. They had nowhere else to go but forward and onto the property.

"Sug! Sug!" she shouted as she forced the scared heifers onto the property. "Come on!" she yelled over her shoulder to Finch, waving her hand in the air. He drove through the open gate and reached Evie.

She let the ATV idle and jumped off, running to shut the gate behind her. Finch watched as she closed the gate and jerked on the latch, ensuring that it was shut.

She hopped back on her ATV, still standing on it as she rode up the hill. The light from Finch's ATV shined on her golden locks of hair as it blew haphazardly, jostled by the rushes of air coming at her. She was going so fast that he was finding it hard to keep up. He pressed his foot onto the accelerator and focused on the honeyed vision in front of him.

He should have paid attention to where he was going. He felt the left side of his ATV raise a few feet off of the ground, and before he knew it, the ATV was tipping over, with him still on it.

He landed in what he thought was the softest spot he could. He felt a sense of relief, thinking it was mud, but when he looked down and saw that it was not mud, but in fact, cow manure, he moaned in disgust and shifted to the right. More manure covered his rear end. He gagged from the stench and felt the mushiness against his butt and lower back. The ATV laid on it's side, the bright light shining off into the distance, showing a glimpse of the cattle they had rescued now making their way back home over the rambling hills.

Evie heard all of the commotion and quickly turned the ATV around, heading to where Finch lay. She let it idle, with the beam of light honing down on him, as she jumped off and bent over to check on him.

"Are you all right?" she asked.

He could see she was concerned. The crinkle between her brows was especially prevalent. "Yeah," he said, knowing that his ego was the only thing he had wounded.

"I told you that you weren't cut out for this," she admonished. She took a whiff and then looked down at him more closely. "You landed on a pile of shit!" She laughed. Hard. A strong bellowing noise came from the depths of her and surfaced – the cackle echoed into the quiet night.

"Yeah. Yeah. It's a riot," Finch said with sarcasm.

Evie continued to laugh. "You just formed a crater on that moon pie!" she teased. She was getting carried away, saying things like "meadow muffin" and "cow pie." She was rambling one cow joke after another. Like she had them stored for such an occasion and she couldn't wait to use them.

He let her have her fun and finally said, "Help me up, please." He offered his hand to her.

She grabbed a hold of it, and he pulled her down next to him, her bottom pressed into the pile of cow dung.

"This moon just got another crater," he joked.

"You are such a butt hole!" she screamed. He couldn't tell if she wanted to laugh or cry. She wanted to do both. If her dirty looks could light a fire, the whole farm would be a hazy blaze, him included.

"That old frock of yours needs to be tossed anyway, Granny," he kidded, lying through his teeth. He wanted to kiss the seamstress for making such a beautiful piece of fashion.

She looked down at her night gown and pulled her sweater closer around her chest, feeling his eyes burning onto her. "I'm not a Granny," she retorted. "And your fashion sense isn't so spectacular, either, Mister 'I wear rock band t-shirts all the time because I think it makes me look far out,'" she said.

"Humph," he mumbled. He pushed himself off of the ground and offered her his hand.

"No way," she said, shaking her head.

He raised an eyebrow. "I won't do it again. Promise."

"I can get up on my own." She placed her palms against the dirt and heaved herself up, standing a few feet away from Finch. "We gotta get this thing back up," she said, tilting her head down in the direction of the ATV.

Finch bent over and struggled to lift it.

"It'll take two of us," she said and got on one end while he stood on the other. Together they tipped it over upright.

"Think it's broke?" he asked, breathing heavy.

"Nah," she breathed. "Try her out."

He turned the ignition and the engine purred.

"See," she said. "Turn it off," she ordered as she moved to her ATV and turned off the ignition. Silence surrounded them, and restless crickets created an impromptu concert.

Evie walked in the direction of the fishing pond.

Finch increased his step to meet her pace. "What are you doing?" he asked.

"Swimming," she answered, like it should have been obvious to him.

"Now?"

"Unless you want cow shit on your clothes, I'd suggest you do the same thing." She took a whiff. "You stink!"

He cocked an eyebrow and tilted his head. "You're one to talk."

Her eyes cast down bashfully, and she sniffed, realizing some of that wretched stench was coming from her.

She stomped off, failing to have a comeback. After she kicked off her boots, she took off her sweater and laid it on the ground. She trudged through the murky ground and allowed the tepid water to overcome her. Tips of her blond tresses were drenched and clung to her soppy skin. The air outside was nippier than the water. "There aren't creepy crawlies in here if that's what you're afraid of!" she called to Finch.

"I'm not chicken," he said and tore off his shirt and unbuckled his belt. He headed her way and ran into the pond, water splashed everywhere.

"Good Lord. You're gonna wake the snakes with all the racket," she said with frustration.

"I thought you said there weren't critters in here," he said, and Evie could hear a hint of fear in his statement.

"You're scared," she teased and grinned wide.

"A snake's bite is worse than yours," he said with a smirk.

"I don't bite," she said with a serious expression.

He swam closer to her, thankful that it was dark out and he couldn't see much of anything. He knew that lime green night shirt was soaked, and he shoved that thought to the back of his mind, storing it for another time, maybe when he slept.

"Sure you do," he said. "The first time I met you, you barked at me for a pile of cigarettes that I hadn't even created."

She couldn't argue with him and flashed back to their first encounter, thinking how rude she was. "You're no saint, either," she snapped, and her tone grew softer, "I mean, you're always trying to rile me up."

"Rile you up?" he mocked. "You mean, get a rise out of you? Yeah, I guess I do." He laughed to himself, and Evie noticed he made no effort to apologize.

"Well... it's rude," she started.

"We've already established that you think I'm the rudest person you've ever met," he teased.

"You are," she said it like it was a fact. "But..."

He gave an expression of curiosity and for the first time, Evie noticed a change in him. He seemed insecure, desperate to meet her approval, but maybe she read him all wrong.

"It was nice of you to help me tonight... with the cattle," she said.

He lay back on the water and floated, staring up at the starry sky. "It's no big deal. No need to get mushy about it."

She splashed water at him. He wiped his eyes and swam upright. "What'd you do that for?"

"You deserved it," she said and scowled at him.

"For what?" He wiped the remnants of water out of his eyes.

"I said thank you, and you had to be arrogant about it."

He thought for a moment, and finally said, "You're welcome. But there's no need to say thanks. I did what anyone should have done." He said it like it was plain as day or as obvious as the sky being blue. "If someone is in trouble, you help and don't think about getting something in return."

"Oh," she said, blowing against the surface of the water, creating a ripple.

"Did someone else leave the gate open?" he asked.

"Why do you say that?" Her gaze met his.

He shrugged his head to the side. "Seems like something you and your dad wouldn't do since you've been doing this forever, and that's a beginners mistake," he pointed out. "You got someone working for you that could've done this?"

She shook her head. "My dad thinks it's some dumb teenaged kids playing pranks on us, but I don't know."

"Pranks? Like cow tipping?"

"Cow tipping is a myth. No one cow tips," she said, rolling her eyes at him.

"Really?" he asked with surprise.

"Do all carnies smoke and drink?"

"Most, but not all," he joked.

"See my point," she said. "Not all farmers wear overalls and smoke corncob pipes. And we sure as hell don't spend our time tipping over cows."

"What do you do?" he asked with interest.

"What do you mean?"

"For fun?" he asked. "What do you do?"

"I don't know." She swam further away from him, hoping the distance would build a nice little sound wall, strong and sturdy enough to keep him from asking anymore questions like this one.

He swam her way, and Evie wondered where he learned how to swim so well. His arms moved like an Olympic swimmer, and his head and mouth knew where to turn, breaths taken at the most opportune time.

"Sure you do," he pressed.

"I guess I don't do anything worth mentioning," she said with a tinge of sadness, looking up at Finch with her mouth cast down.

"If I lived here, I'd spend my days outside enjoying this view. I'd have a garden and would rebuild that barn – the kind of barn you see in pictures – red with white trim. And I'd have a donkey and goats," he said, and Evie let out a laugh. "What's so funny?"

"A donkey and goats?" she said in disbelief.

"Sure," he said. "Why not?"

"Goats are more trouble than they're worth. And donkeys are jack asses," she said, laughing at her pun.

"The point is, you got something wonderful here. A nice little place to call home. That's worth a lot," he said, and her smile faded, realizing the weight of his words. Life on the circuit didn't equate to permanence.

She didn't offer a comeback and allowed his words to linger. She swam away from him again and got out of the pond, trembling from the difference in temperature. Her body felt the shock instantly.

With her sweater wrapped tight around her, she peered over her shoulder. "You coming?" she asked him.

He was trying really hard not to stare. It took everything in him to turn his head, eyeballing some tree branch that swayed flimsily in the wind. He studied that tree branch like he was going to be tested on it. Those darn underwear of hers. He could see that they were hip huggers. He wanted to offer a big bear hug to whoever made them. He'd even give a quick kiss to the maker of that hideous sweater. Was there anything that didn't look good on the girl?

She looked down at her soaked night shirt and saw the outline of her underwear. Dear God in heaven, even her nearly blind great-uncle Joseph, who had cataracts, could see that she had on floral undies.

Finch jerked his head in her direction and called out, "Coming!" He gazed at the ground, refusing to take one look at her. So help him, he was not going to gawk at her like some dopey love-struck high school boy who just discovered girls.

He swam to the shore and sloshed his way out, pushing the large plant life out of his way. His jeans hung low, showing the grooves on his stomach, and Evie noticed a tanned pinkish spot under his rib cage. He placed his palms on his hips and hoisted them up. Sprinkles of water sporadically landed on his shoulder blades and upper arms as he shook his hair. He was unaware that Evie was ogling at him like a little girl in a room full of dolls.

He bent over and pulled his shirt over his head. Evie made her way to the ATV and sat on it, ready to go and get away from him. He hopped on his and followed her back to the barn.

They turned their engines off and dismounted the ATV's. Finch's wet jeans sucked to his skin like a vacuum cleaner. His shoes squished with each step he took, and Evie chuckled.

"What's so funny?"

"You wore your shoes in the pond." She let out a laugh again.

"Yeah. So," he said defensively.

"That's why you're squishing around. I can't believe you wore your shoes," she said, shaking her head.

"It's a pond. Gross things live on the bottom, and I'm not getting a foot fungus," he said.

"Who knew you were so prissy?" She laughed again.

"Prissy," he scoffed. "I'm just being smart. Bet you'll wake up tomorrow with some nasty crap in your toes."

She looked down at her boots and wiggled her toes. "Nah. They're not citified like yours."

"Citified?"

Finch held the barn door open for Evie, allowing her to walk ahead of him. It took her by surprise and she muttered a quiet, "thanks" as he did so.

"I've got a stronger immune system," she explained as they stepped outside.

He let out a laugh. "That is ridiculous. Because you grew up on a farm, your feet aren't susceptible to a foot fungus?"

"Yep." She nodded her head.

He scratched at his wet head and tilted his head down. "That's just crazy talk."

Evie saw a hint of a smile on Finch's face, a genuine one and not that irritating smirk he always had plastered on his face. This was real, and she liked it.

"How'd you know the gate was open?" she asked him.

He shrugged. "I'm a night owl and like to walk around at night." He read her expression, seeing a flicker of worry. He twisted his lips to the side and gave a smile. "Don't worry. I'm not peeping in your window or anything. It's just nice here, that's all."

"Well, I guess I'm glad you're lurking around the farm then. Otherwise, we would have been in a world of trouble," she said and her brow furrowed. "Daddy's got a lot of money riding on those stupid heifers." She caught herself, realizing she had said more than she wanted.

He could read the discomfort on her face. Like she had just confessed a deep dark secret. Money was money, and most of the time, discussing finances was a big no-no. He got that.

"I better get going. It's late, and it looks like your dad is home." He motioned to Gray's green truck parked in their driveway. The lights were all on, and she could see the shadow of him moving around inside. "I don't want him to worry about you," he added. "Bye." He crossed through the grass and moved toward the twinkling lights coming from the carnival's temporary homestead.

"Hey, Finch!" she called, and he turned to face her. "Thanks."

He nodded and started to walk again.

"Try not to be so rude next time you see me," she added with a smile.

He came to abrupt halt and spun on his heels, facing her. "You too." He smiled and trudged on.

Evie ambled up the steps and pushed the front door open. She could hear Gray's thunderous steps and moved to where the source of noise came from. He leaned against their kitchen counter sucking on a Popsicle stick. His lips were red all over.

"Where you been?" he asked with a full mouth.

"The gate was open," Evie said.

His eyes widened, and he stood up straight, taking a few steps forward. She held her hand up.

"It's okay. I closed it," she said. "All heifers are accounted for."

He looked down at her with an appreciative, crooked grin. The buttons on his shirt barely closed, and she could see his undershirt peeking beneath his plaid button-up. "Good girl," he said. "You go swimming?" He noticed her gown was wet and her hair was still damp.

"Yes sir," she said and didn't give any further explanation. She knew he wouldn't think it was strange for her to swim in the pond at night or in her gown for that matter.

"Think it's those same dumb kids from earlier this week?"

"I don't know," she said with a deep breath. "Whoever they are, it's getting old real quick."

"How'd you know the gate was open?" he asked.

"I couldn't sleep and was wandering around."

"Well, it's a good thing you were out roaming around," he said, failing to notice the shifting of her eyes and the fact that she was staring at her feet and not at him.

She didn't know why she felt the need to lie to her dad. But the reaction was instant, and confessing what Finch had done would ruin the moment, no matter how small, and she just didn't want to do that. She wanted to keep Finch to herself.

***

Finch strolled through the grass, seeing that most of the lights had flickered out from the inside of the tents. His shoes squished as he moved, and he snickered. She was right: it was ridiculous that he wore his shoes in the pond. They were his only good pair too, and now they'd be water logged for days.

He worried that she thought he was a peeping Tom, walking around on her property in the dead of night giving the lame excuse that he was a night owl. So lame, he thought. But something about those rolling hills made him feel peaceful and at home. He never had that "at home" feeling. The farm gave him a subtle hint of what it felt like to have that much comfort that he could kick his shoes off and lay on the grass while looking up at the stars. He'd take it, even if it was temporary. Four more weeks. That's all he had left, and he was going to milk it for all that it was worth.

He knew he should keep his distance from her, but the more he fought it, the more he had the urge to get near her, just to see her glare at him, or say something snappy to him. She had some decent comebacks, he could admit that, and watching her on the ATV was pretty impressive because he obviously lacked skill when it came to riding on that machine. Still, her dad said to keep his distance, and he had to honor that. If he had a daughter, he wouldn't want some twenty-two year old carny hanging out with the likes of someone like him, either.

CHAPTER 12

Things were quiet at the skating rink. Most of the locals were enjoying themselves at the carnival, and the few who decided to skate, called it an early night. Gray was out of town helping Cooper deliver cattle to the slaughter house. Cooper raised beef cattle, and their lives were often cut short. Evie never went on those trips. It was just too much – sending the cattle to their deaths. She didn't want any part of it, and Gray couldn't understand it. "You gotta toughen up when it comes to them. How else are you gonna be a farmer?"

She didn't know the answer to that question. But being aware of something and actually seeing it happen were two different things in Evie's eyes. She just didn't want to be the one to pull the trigger. It broke her heart when she had to separate the heifers from their calves. The helpless calves' cries stayed with her, and a tinge of guilt lingered within her each time she saw them.

Evie put her favorite album on the record player, Fleetwood Mac's *Rumors*, and placed the needle on the song she loved the most. Stevie Nicks' deep sensual voice blared from the speakers around the rink as she cleaned things up for the night. She could never tire of that song and figured she'd play it at least three more times before she was finished.

She hummed to herself while she re-stacked the shelves with pairs of white roller skates, lining them up by size. Most of them were scuffed with patches of brown, and the wheels were almost worn down to the bearings and needed to be replaced. Gray had purchased them from a roller rink in North Carolina that was closing and boasted to Evie, "I got them for cheap," he had said, rubbing his hands together. Evie never asked how much he paid, but she suspected, no matter how inexpensive they were, it may not have been worth it. She went inside the concession stand and turned off the popcorn maker and emptied the popcorn kernels into a large garbage bag. She wanted to hurl from the buttery fragrance.

Most of her tasks were completed quickly, and she resolved to put on a pair of skates and skate to a song or two under the beautiful twinkling stars in the South Carolina sky. Why not, she figured. She had the place to herself and could do as she pleased. She sat herself down on the bench, pushed her feet into a pair skates and pulled on the laces, tying them into a nice, neat bow.

"Evie."

She shrieked, and her hand flew up to her chest. "Todd! You scared the snot out of me," she said, still trying to catch her breath. "What are you doing here?"

"You're easy to scare," he teased, but Evie didn't think he was very funny. In fact, she didn't think anything he said was funny.

"Why are you here?" she asked. She checked her watch. It was late, way too late for him to be there.

He sat down next to her, and she got up, balancing on four wheels. "What? I can't sit next to you?" He pinched his face, snarling his thin upper lip.

She pointed to her skates. "I was about to skate," she said.

He got off the bench. "Katie told me," he said, and Evie knew exactly what she had told him but she decided to play dumb.

"Told you what?" She could hear the lilt in her voice and knew any buffoon could figure out she was lying.

Todd cocked an eyebrow and looked at her incredulously. Evie figured he wasn't as dumb as she originally thought. "You know what," he spat. She got a whiff of his breath—a stench of booze.

"You should go on home," she said. She knew he liked to drink. Katie told her stories of nights when he drank so much he'd pass out and wake up hours later, forgetting what happened. Evie never got the full story, but she suspected he wasn't the kindest drunk either. Some drunks were funny, some were sad, and then there were the mean drunks. Evie figured Todd fit in that last category.

"You need to help me," he ordered. He wasn't asking; he was telling.

She folded her arms against her chest. "I don't need to help you." She started toward the rink, and he yanked her by the arm.

"Ow. Let go," she hollered, jerking her arm free from his grip.

"I'm too young to have a kid," he said with desperation.

"Well that's too bad, Todd," Evie snapped. "You made your bed. Now you have to lie in it."

"I told her I wasn't ready to be a dad and that she should get rid of *it*." He said "it" with disdain as if "it" was a raccoon that was sifting through his garbage.

Evie's mouth gaped wide open and anger filled her blue eyes. "Get rid of it! What the hell is wrong with you?" She wanted to punch him in his preppy face.

He pulled a sterling silver flask out of his front jeans pocket, took a swig, and then safely put the flask back from where it came.

"You," he pointed, jabbing his finger into Evie's shoulder, "need to talk some sense into her."

She glared at him. "I," she grabbed his finger and pushed it away from her, "don't need to do anything." Her heart was racing.

"She'll listen to you. If you tell her to get rid of the thing, she'll do it," he pressed as his words slurred together.

"The thing," Evie repeated in horror. "He or she is a baby, and he or she is yours, one that you helped create."

"I told her I'd pay for the abortion, but she won't take my money." He pulled out a stack of bills. "Give this to her and make her use it."

Evie placed her hand on her mouth and slowly shook her head. "Todd, I can't..." She backed away from him. He was standing so close—she could count every single hair on his unshaved face, and that was too close for her comfort.

"Take the money!" He threw several dollar bills at her. Evie stared at him with an open mouth.

"I'm not taking your money, and I'm not telling her to do anything. It's her choice."

"Just take it!" he screamed. "And quit being such a judgmental bitch!"

"I'm not taking your money, and you need to go home. Now," she said with a firm voice.

He moved even closer to her, and for the first time, Evie noticed how much taller he was than her. He flared his nostrils and breathed hard and heavy. Evie could feel his body inching closer to hers with every breath. Before she had time to flee, he shoved her against the wooden shed. A nail caught against her back, piercing into her skin. She groaned in pain and tried moving away from the shed. He shoved her again. This time, a little harder.

Todd's long arms hovered around Evie. She felt constricted, smelling his breath on her, and feeling his sweaty palms pinning her arms. "I always thought you were a bitch. You thought you were too good for me."

Evie's mind raced, searching for a way to get out of there. His grip tightened, and she tried to jerk herself free.

He held on tighter. The vein that ran up the side of his neck throbbed. "Stop fighting me!"

As Evie raised her knee to his groin, wisps of her hair blew. The tip of a bowie knife plunged into the shed directly adjacent to her head and barely missed the tips of Todd's fingers.

"What the hell!" Todd shouted. He spun on his heels and released Evie from his grip.

Evie's eyes darted to her right, seeing the blade. She scooted out of his reach. Finch stood a few feet away from them.

"You better go on home," Finch said in a cool, commanding tone and with an "I mean business" expression.

Todd's mouth was agape, and as Finch passed him by and pulled the knife out of the wood, Todd backed up against the shed.

Finch moved himself between Todd and Evie, standing defensively, with his legs wide apart and the muscles in his arms flexed. His jaw twitched. "You need to get going. That was just a warning shot. Next time I'll aim for your head," he said it evenly and smoothly, with command. "And I don't miss."

"Yeah, right," Todd scoffed.

Finch let out a deep sigh. "Man, you really are stupid, aren't you?" He lifted his arm back and held the knife like he was holding a hammer. He gripped onto the handle and stiffened his wrist, and he flung the knife forward, aiming at Todd. It landed within a centimeter of Todd's head.

Todd's face turned scarlet and sweat trickled down from his forehead. His eyes peered up, and he reached his hands up to the knife, touching it to really see if it was there. Once he felt the pearl handle, he turned to dash away but stumbled to the ground. He got up and looked back over his shoulder.

"My aim is perfect. I only miss when I want to. You better start hauling ass," Finch said.

Todd flew out of there, and Finch turned to Evie. "Are you okay?" he asked, his tone gentle and soft.

She nodded slowly, still unsure of what she had just witnessed. She looked at the knife, then at him, and then back at the knife again.

"You sure?" he asked, tilting his head to the side and biting his bottom lip.

Her mouth was wide open, and confusion filled her. She touched the sore spot in her back, and he moved around her. "Mind if I take a look?" he asked.

"No," she whispered, still trying to collect her thoughts and understand what had just happened.

He lifted up her shirt and inspected the mark on her back. "It's red, but not bleeding." He pulled her shirt back down and moved back in front of her. Her eyes were still wide, and her mouth was still partially open. "Are you sure you're okay?"

"Yes," she said and gave him a slight smile. She bent down and unlaced her skates and took them off. She held onto a skate and started running in Todd's direction.

Finch raced to catch up with her. "Where are you going?"

"To throw this skate at his stupid head!" She held the skate up in the air as she sprinted up the hill.

Finch grabbed her by the waist, slowing her down. He didn't have time to think about the fact that his hands were touching her, that her hips were just the right size, and that she had a natural pleasing sway when she ran. "That skate can kill him."

She came to a stop. "And a knife can't?"

"My aim is perfect. I chose not to hit him. You, on the other hand, may not be so kind," he said.

"I just want to hurt him a little," she said, pinching her fingers together. "Just enough to scare him."

"Did you see the wet spot on his pants? I think I put enough fear in him for one night," he said.

Evie paced back and forth and swallowed several times, her blue eyes blinking constantly. "Fine!" She tossed the skate to the ground and threw her arms up in the air. She looked at it, and then at Finch, who had a smug expression.

"I'm not saying anything," he said, laughing quietly to himself. He picked up the skate and gestured for Evie to follow him back to the rink.

"How'd you know?" she asked as they made their way down hill.

He gazed at her curiously.

"How'd you know I was here?" she clarified.

"I was on one of my walks, and I heard people shouting," he said.

The crackle of the needle amplified, and Evie turned off the record player. She picked up the other skate off of the ground. Finch took it from her hands and placed the pair back on a shelf.

"How were you able to throw a knife like that?"

"I grew up in the carnival," he answered. He pulled his knife out of the wood siding of the shed and placed it back in his leather sheath.

"And?" she said.

"And...," he sighed, raking his fingers through his hair. "My mom was a knife thrower, and she taught me how to throw knives."

"Wow," Evie said with an amazed expression, like he just told her that his mother tamed lions. "Your mom was a knife thrower?"

"Yeah," he said with indifference, failing to understand how exotic it made her seem to Evie.

"That is far out," she said with a wide grin.

He snickered and shook his head.

"What?" she asked.

"You're funny," he said. "And it's a little strange that you're not spazzing out right now."

"Believe me, my heart was beating like a kick drum earlier. I'm fine now," she said reassuringly. "You think I'm funny?" she asked. No one ever told Evie she was funny except for Gray and Katie, and Katie thought everything and anything was funny.

"Yep." He smiled.

"When did your mom teach you to throw knives?" she asked, straddling a nearby bench and gesturing for him to join her. He plopped down on it and faced her.

"Well...," he said, his eyes peered up in deep thought. "It took several years. She had me start throwing them when I was five."

"Five?" Evie said in disbelief. "Were you hands even big enough to hold anything?"

He placed his hand under his chin, marveling at her inquisitiveness. She asked a lot of questions and seemed to be interested in anything he had to say. "Yes," he said with a smile. "They were big enough."

"Is your mom in the carnival?"

"No." He frowned. "She passed away when I was fifteen."

"I'm sorry," she said.

"It's not your fault. And, anyways, it was a long time ago."

She looked down.

"It's okay," he said.

She peered up at him, seeing his reassuring expression. "Really," he said with a smile.

"Were you born in the carnival?" she asked.

He chuckled. "Actually, I was," he said. "In Iowa. I was named after the state bird as a matter of fact."

"That's why you've got a bird name." She held her laugh.

"I don't have a refined name like Evelyn, but Finch isn't so bad. I know there isn't another Finch Mills out there. At least I've never met one," he said.

"Let's hope not," she kidded. "How'd you know my real name?"

He narrowed his eyes at hers. "Any idiot could figure that one out. Evie is short for Evelyn, right?"

"Yeah, but..."

He interrupted her and said, "Just 'cause I work in the carnival doesn't mean I'm two beers short of a twelve pack."

"Do you want to skate?" she blurted.

He scrunched his face. "Okay," he answered in a questioning tone.

"What?" Evie said, reading him.

"That was abrupt and totally off topic."

She sighed. "We could've been going at it all night, and I thought it'd shut you up." She got up and walked to the shed. She pointed to the shelf lined up with skates. "What size?"

"Eleven," he answered.

She handed him his pair and pulled out the pair that Finch had put up minutes earlier. She put the needle back on the record, and music filled the air. They laced up their skates and headed to the rink.

Evie skated backward, turning in a perfect circle, while Finch watched her in awe. "You're good." He was impressed.

"I'm all right," she said, turning around again.

He skated slowly, and she noticed he had a slight skip to his step. "You don't skate much, do you?"

"You're awfully observant, aren't you?" he retorted. "I can manage." She moved his way and skated around him in a circle. "Show off," he said with a sigh.

"It's my turn now," she snickered as she said it.

"I didn't know we were in a competition," he said.

"I'm ahead by one point."

"How's that?" He folded his arms across his chest and formed a slight smile.

She counted on her hands as she skated near him. "I'm not afraid of a little pond scum, I can drive an ATV, and I can skate circles around you. Literally," she teased, a quiet chortle came from her.

"I'd think knife throwing would carry a little more weight."

"Hmm," she tapped her fingers against her chin, "okay, maybe we'll just call it even."

"You better watch out. I got a bag of tricks up my sleeve," he said.

"Can you swallow fire too?" She twirled in a circle again.

"Maybe," he teased. "How about you skate to my pace so I don't keep getting dizzy watching you go in circles?"

She slowed her pace and moved along side him. "Were you a knife thrower in the carnival?"

"For a while," he answered.

"How long?"

"About five years."

"What made you stop?"

"You're really nosey," he said, feigning annoyance, but deep down he struggled to be irked with her. She was like a nice little space heater on a cold winter's day. He wanted to hover close to her and let her warmth envelope him.

"And you're evasive," she said with a glint of humor in her eyes. She was teasing him, mercifully, and he knew he'd stand there and take it.

"I've been called worse, even by you." His mouth felt dry, like it was stuffed with cotton balls, and he sounded hoarse when he spoke. He cleared his throat and regained his confidence. "How about you fix me a glass of that famous sweet tea you Southerner's talk about all the time and I'll tell you what you want to know?" He tried to say it in a suave way, but Evie didn't seem to notice or care that his voice cracked as he said it. Or maybe she just wasn't impressed, he thought.

CHAPTER 13

Her nerves were shot, and her hand had a nice little twitch to it that she couldn't seem to stop. Finch made her nervous – but not in the psycho "Son of Sam" way. Her heart fluttered, and she couldn't think straight. She lost her train of thought when she was around him. When he asked her about having tea, and he licked his lips while doing so, all she could think about was kissing those lips with the tip of her tongue and running her fingers through his shiny hair. It looked like satin, and she wondered if he used hair spray or if it had a natural sheen to it.

He was fidgeting with his hands, rubbing index fingers and thumbs together, as she poured two large glasses of sweet iced tea. It was late in the night. If Gray knew a man was in her house without him there, he'd spit fire and grab his rifle, aiming it directly at Finch's shiny head.

"Here you go," Evie said, handing him his glass.

"Thanks." He smiled and took a sip. "It's so sweet."

"How else would you drink it?"

"Without a cup of sugar," he teased. "They serve sweet tea in Florida, but I never order it."

"You live in Florida?" She sat down and leaned forward, engrossed in any tale he'd have to tell her about the sunshine state.

"About five months out of the year," he answered. "I rent a garage apartment from this retired carny named Rolf. He's a cranky old coot and has an obsession with collecting James Bond stuff. He has a fit if you touch any of it though." Finch laughed thoughtfully. "It's an okay place I guess. Not like here," he said. He glanced at everything in the kitchen: the painted white maple cabinets;

butcher block counter tops; white porcelain sink; the oak floors; and the planted begonias that filled the window sill. He brought his gaze back to her. "This kitchen is nice."

"It's old as dirt but thanks," she said. "Florida." She sighed and rested her palms under her chin. "I've always wanted to go there."

"What's stopping you?"

"Oh, just about two hundred cattle," she said.

He fiddled with the cow shaped salt and pepper shakers. "Are these part of that two hundred?"

"Those were my Grandma's. Half the stuff in here belonged to her," she said.

"It's got to be tough working with cattle," he said.

"Probably just as hard as what you do. At least I can stay put. You're always traveling from place to place."

"Yeah. Tell me about it," he grumbled.

"Do you get tired of it?"

He thought for a moment and then stared her in the eyes. "Yeah. I do. I really do"

"What would you do if you weren't working in the carnival?"

"I don't know. It's all I've known all twenty-two years of my entire life, and that's a difficult thing to walk away from. I wouldn't mind owning a farm like this," he said.

"Trust me, the life of the farmer is not at all romantic. You smell shit all day, and if you're lucky, you get a few hours to relax."

"But it's yours. You own it. There's a difference," he said and leaned forward, placing his arms on the table. "When you own something, all the kinks and bad things don't matter as much because you've got some say in it. You've got an investment in it." He took a sip of his tea and swallowed. "You think I have any investment in the carnival? I couldn't care less about it. It's just a job. I fix what's broken and go to work like a drone hoping something will wake me up, but nothing ever does." His lips cast down.

"But you have a choice," she said. "This is my lot in life."

"How many people do you know would hire a carny like me?" She thought for a moment.

Finch answered before she could come up with a number. "Zero. That's how many. If I told anyone I'd been working on the circuit since I could walk, they'd associate me with crooks and weirdos and tell me to scram. It's a double-edged sword."

"Certainly someone would hire you," she said.

"Probably not, but I'm not going to sit here and drown my sorrows in this sugary drink."

"It's tea," she defended with a whine.

"It's sweet," he said.

"There's two kinds of tea: unsweet and sweet."

"There's no such thing as unsweet tea. It's just iced tea," he said, and his lip curled up to one side. "You can't unsweeten something."

"Yankee," she said and stifled a yawn. She took another sip, hoping the caffeine would perk her up.

"I probably should get going," he said. "I'm putting you to sleep, and it's late. I don't think your dad would like me being here."

"He's gone, and I'm not tired."

"So I am boring you then, aren't I?" He playfully nudged her.

Evie felt warm inside, enjoying the feeling of his hand on her arm. She wondered if her face was as flushed as her insides were. "Very much." She smirked at him.

He moved his head forward and peered around. "Where's your

dad?"

"Taking some cows to their death," she said with a frown.

"You don't go with him when he does this?"

"No. I have to stay here and take care of things. Besides, if you've been once, you don't want to go again. Slaughterhouses aren't pleasant places to revisit," she said.

"We've been to some depressing towns on the circuit. They're not killing cows, but they stink really bad and the people are strange."

"If you're calling them strange, then I bet they're *really* weird."

He laughed and finished off the contents of his tea. He stood up and brought the pitcher to the table and poured more tea in their glasses.

"Thanks." Her elbows rested on the table, and she folded her hands together under her chin. "You've been all over the country, huh?" she asked.

He thought for a moment. "Not everywhere. I've been all over the south and the mid west, though."

"That's more places than I've ever been."

"I don't really get to see the towns. I'm so busy working, and on the few nights I'm off, I'm too tired to sightsee."

"Is your dad in the carnival?" she asked.

He laughed out loud and shook his head. "Your questions are all over the place."

She tapped on her head. "I have a whole bunch stored up here waiting to come out."

"The prospect of that scares me a little." He flickered a grin. "My dad is in the carnival, but not this one. He works for another unit."

"What does he do?"

He scratched his eyebrow and squinted. "Last I heard he was a ride operator."

"You don't talk?" she said.

"No, not really. He's never been around, so I don't have a relationship with him," he stated without emotion.

"I'm sorry," she said.

He took a sip of his tea and said with indifference, "No reason to be sorry. I'm not."

"But doesn't it bother you?" she asked and then added with an embarrassed expression, "Sorry. I'm prying."

"You are nosy," he said and laughed. "But I guess I promised you I'd answer your questions if you fixed me some tea, and no, Evie, it doesn't bother me. I got over that a long, long time ago."

"Did he leave you?"

"When Mom found out she was pregnant, he high-tailed it out of the carnival faster than you can spit. Mom was always dumb when it came to men. She'd pick the worst guys and swear she was going to change them. Even when I was a kid, I knew you can't change people," he said in a sharp tone. "David, my father, is definitely not the type that should be a dad. Mom fell in love with his looks and charm, and that's about it, because he doesn't have much else to offer the world. Then he left her at the ripe ole age of eighteen fending for herself and an unborn baby. I run into him about once a year, but there isn't much to talk about. He lives in his own world. "

Evie's eyebrows pulled down in concentration. "My mother left," she confessed. "She left when I was eight years old, and I haven't seen her since."

He gave her a sympathetic look and slightly shook his head. "It seems we have something in common."

"Yeah, I guess we do," she said with a breath.

She yawned again, and Finch made a face. "There I go boring you again." He stood up, taking their glasses to the sink. Evie got up and followed him to the door.

"Thanks for the drink," he said.

"You mean the tea," she corrected.

"The sweet tea." He smirked. "It was good, and the company wasn't half bad, either."

"When you don't have that dumb smirk on your face, it's not that bad." She stretched to look up at him.

He peered down at her and grinned. "When you're not glaring at me, I don't mind your face so much, either." He pushed the screen door and walked outside. The outside porch light shone down on him.

"Hey, Finch," she called.

He turned around and looked at her.

"Thanks for helping me tonight. Maybe you'll teach me how to throw a knife like that?"

"I would, but I'm afraid you'd try and use those skills on me when you're mad at me," he said.

"Only if you smirk," she shot back.

"Sometimes when I see your face, I can't help but smirk," he retorted.

"Well, sometimes when I see yours, I want to hurl," she said, grinning.

"Night, Evie," he said.

"Goodnight, Finch."

***

Sniffling and moaning woke Evie up. She shot up out of bed and jerked her head to the right; Katie stood in front of her carrying a suitcase and sobbing hysterically.

"Katie," she said with uncertainty. It was dark in the room, but the shadowy figure looked like her best friend.

She set the suitcase down on the floor. "Oh Evie," she cried and sat down on the bed, sobbing into her chest.

Evie patted her gently on the arms and said in a soft voice, "Shh, it's okay."

"No it's not," she said while crying, making it difficult for Evie to understand the words coming out of her mouth. She was talking so fast.

"It's going to be all right."

"I ran away, Evie," she said.

"You what?" Evie widened her eyes.

"I had to." She pulled away from Evie's chest and sat upright. Evie reached over and turned on her bedside table lamp. Katie's face was ruby red, and her eyes were bloodshot and puffy.

"What happened?" she asked and leaned forward, placing her hand on top of Katie's.

They sat with their legs crossed, facing each other. Katie took an uneven breath and wiped her eyes. "I told my parents I was pregnant."

"It didn't go well," Evie said more as a statement than a question. Knowing Nate, it didn't go well at all. He had a short fuse, and Evie knew he'd be more concerned about how it looked – his one and only daughter pregnant before marriage. The town was sure to talk, and an uptight, stodgy man like Nate would care more about *that* than his own daughter.

"My dad was really mad. I've never seen him so angry, Evie," she said. "He told me I had to go stay with my aunt in Georgia until I had the baby. He said," and she whimpered, sucking in a deep breath, "he said I'd have to give it up for adoption. I told him I wasn't giving the baby up. I'm having the baby, and I'm gonna raise him, even if it's without Todd."

Evie found her eyes welling up with tears, and she fumbled for the right words to say. "I'm so sorry, Katie," she said. It was the only consoling thing she could offer.

"He said the most horrible things to me. He's never been this mean to me before." She sniffled and pain filled her small brown eyes.

Evie had heard Nate call his daughter plump and fat on more than one occasion. One of the few times Evie went over there for dinner, Nate grabbed Katie's plate and dumped half the food in the trash. "You keep on eating this way, you'll be so fat we'll have to get a crane to carry you out of here. Look at Evie. Her plate doesn't have that much food." Katie just lowered her head in shame and toyed with the rest of dinner.

"He called me a slut and said that's what I get for spreading my legs. He even defended Todd and said that I was messing up *his* life." Katie shivered and shook her head slightly, looking down at her stomach and rubbed it gently. "He said he wasn't going to let me have a bastard."

Evie was at a loss for words. Hearing that Katie's father would say such things was beyond her understanding. She knew Gray would never do that. He'd be mad if she got pregnant, but he'd never make her feel lower than dirt. Nate McDaniels was a bad man, and Evie knew why so many people in town avoided him—

only a man with a blackened soul would utter such hate to his own flesh and blood without any remorse.

Evie was shaking on the inside, her hands were clenched into tight fists, and she was so damn angry. She wanted to get in her truck and throw pair after pair of skates at that awful man. She was tempted to find Finch and ask him to throw knives at the asshole, but she knew she had to contain herself. Criticizing Katie's dad wasn't going to make the situation better, and going over there to tell him off would only make matters worse.

"He locked me in my room and told me I was going to my aunt's tomorrow morning," she said. "But I snuck out. I'm not going to my aunt's, and I'm not giving this baby up. He's mine." She brought a pillow to her chest and squeezed it. "You can't tell him I'm here," she said with a quivering voice. "If he knows I'm here, he'll make me go." She looked into Evie's eyes with a pained stare. "Promise me you won't tell him."

"I won't, Katie. I won't," she said. "What are you going to do?"

"I don't know, but I'm not going back there, and I can't count on Todd. He told me to get an abortion. As if I'd even consider that." She peered down at her stomach, and touched it with both hands.

Evie decided not to tell Katie about her run-in with Todd. She knew it wouldn't help matters.

"I hate them all," Katie said, looking off distantly with fire in her eyes. "How can you love someone and hate them at the same time?"

"People disappoint you," she said matter of fact. "Love takes time, but it's sure as hell easy to hate. You can't stop loving someone overnight," she said and thought about her mom when she spoke. "But you sure as hell can hate them in a split second."

"I can't believe I thought Todd loved me."

"Maybe he does, but he's just too young to understand the kind of love you need," Evie said, knowing that Todd was incapable of loving anyone but himself.

"No. He doesn't love me. If he did, he wouldn't have reacted the way he did."

"He's such a jerk," Evie muttered and then realized she said it aloud. "I'm sorry."

"Don't be. I know you never liked him," Katie said.

"Katie..."

"Don't try to deny it. You make your emotions really obvious," she said. "I know you too well, Evie."

"I guess I do." She let out a sigh.

"My dad's going to come here tomorrow. It'll be the first place he looks."

"I know," Evie said.

"I can't stay here, but I don't have anywhere else to go. I hate to get you caught up in this mess."

Evie held her hand up. "I'm not leaving you to the wolves. We'll figure this out." Evie's mind raced. She scratched at her scalp and bit on her lip. She snapped her fingers and smiled. "I got it!"

"What?"

"My mom and dad's house," she said. "Their old house on the other side of the farm."

"The one you lived in when we were kids?" Katie asked.

Evie shook her head vigorously. "That's the one," she said. "No one will think to look there. No one's lived there since Granddaddy died and we moved in here, and that was years ago. I can't promise it'll be nice inside, and there isn't much furniture in it."

"No. It sounds perfect, and I'm not in a position to be picky anyway."

"At least this way Daddy won't have to know."

"You can't tell him, Evie."

"I know, and that's going to be tough. I don't like lying to him."

"It'll just be for a little while until I get things figured out," Katie said.

"We're going to have to get you situated early in the morning. Daddy will be here first thing, and you know your dad is bound to show up soon after."

"I know. I just hope this works."

"Me too," Evie said. "Me too."

CHAPTER 14

It was a cozy, ranch style house that was painted an egg yolk yellow embellished with emerald green shutters. A large white oak tree stood tall and proud adjacent to the house, creating a canopy of shade welcome during the hot summer months. Most of the plant life had died long ago, but what remained had taken over, spreading like wildfire. Some plants had trailed up the brick facade of the house, creeping their way to the roof. Weeds and dandelions were prominent, and a rusted rocking horse sat in the front of the house. The once apple-red paint had chipped, and the horse was missing an eye. A solitary patio chair sat off in the grass, and it too had rusted, the white paint barely visible.

Evie touched the horse for a split second. It rocked back and forth. The spring vibrated, and the horse squeaked as it moved. "I remember this," she said, reminiscing about her early childhood memories when she, Gray and her mother lived in the small house. Her mother would sit on a lawn chair, wearing nothing but a pair of shorts and a bikini top, and watch Evie rock back and forth on the horse. She'd smoke her cigarette and lay her head back basking in the sun, while Evie shouted "Whee" each time she felt the shift of the novel amusement.

One time, when she was four or five, she couldn't remember her exact age, Evie fell off that horse. The fall had hurt, and she had skinned her knees enough for them to bleed. Her mother wasn't outside with her. She cried her way through the house and found her mother talking on the phone, laughing at what the person on the other end had said. Her voice was hushed, and when Evie entered, her tone changed completely.

"What do you want, Evelyn?" she asked. "I'm on the phone."

"I need a Band Aid," she choked on her sobs while saying it.

"You're always getting hurt, and Mommy is on the phone," she snapped.

Evie cried even more, and her mother said a quick, clipped goodbye, slamming the phone against the receiver.

"Mommy had to get off of the phone with a very good friend because of you. I hope you're happy." She yanked Evie by the hand and stormed into the bathroom.

"I remember playing out here," Katie said. "We would make mud pies, remember?"

Evie nodded. "I liked this house, but Daddy didn't see any reason in living in it once the big house was empty."

"Why didn't he ever rent this house out? He could've made some money."

"Sentiment, I guess." She shrugged. "It's the only thing left of his marriage to my mother. Well, besides me."

Evie unlocked the front door and pushed it open. They were immediately overcome by dust, a musty scent, and a wave of stifling heat. "Geez Louise, this place needs a maid." Evie fanned her hand in front of her nose and scrunched her face. "It's hotter than a hen house in here."

"It's not so bad," Katie said and coughed. Beads of sweat formed on her olive-complected skin.

Evie frowned. "This probably isn't good for the baby."

Katie touched her on the arm. "It's better than home," she said.

"I guess we better open some windows and do some spring cleaning so you can make this place bearable for the time being," Evie said, heading outside to the truck. Katie followed her, and they grabbed a broom, dustpan, mop and bucket from the back of the truck bed. They made a second trip to get a set of sheets, towels, and a bag of food Evie had packed earlier that morning.

"You go on. I have this," Katie said.

"You sure?"

She nodded. "You've got work to do, and I can manage."

"I'll be back later on tonight to check on you, and I'll bring a fan too."

Katie leaned in to hug her, and Evie patted her lightly. "You and your cruddy hugs," Katie said and gave a dry laugh.

"It's the best you're going to get," Evie said.

"I know. Thanks for helping me out."

"We're best friends. Of course I'll help you."

"I'm just learning who I can count on, and anyway, thanks."

"I'll see you later." Evie left and drove home.

***

Shortly after noon, Nate McDaniels pulled up on Gray's property in his brand new 1977 Dodge pickup. Nate liked new things: new cars, new mistresses, new toys and gadgets. While most farmers were content driving a truck until it reached its death, Nate bought a new one every few years, tiring of the old and replacing it with a newer, bigger, flashier model.

This one was painted beige with brown trim, and a rail was attached to the bed. A heavy duty brush guard covered the front, making it appear more rugged than it really was. Nate professed to be an expert hunter and outdoorsman, but most people knew he trapped his animals before the big kill.

He wore a cowboy hat, a button-down short-sleeved shirt, and a brand new pair of Wranglers. A sterling silver belt buckle glistened in the shining sun. Gray always said that Nate dressed too nice to be a farmer, and some of the townspeople swore he manicured his nails. He walked slow and kept his hat low on his head, and his five o'clock shadow was always present.

He knocked on the front door, and Evie got up from eating lunch and answered it.

"Hello, Evelyn," he said. He never called her by her preferred name, and it really annoyed her.

"Hello," she said.

"Can I come in?" His hand was already on the screen door. She nodded.

He walked inside and took a look around. "Still looks the same," he said with a twisted lip. A toothpick hung from the inside of his mouth.

She knew that wasn't a compliment. "What can I help you with?" she said.

Gray entered the room with a frown. "What do you want McDaniels?" his tone was curt.

"I'm looking for my Katie," he said. Evie thought it was pompous that he referred to everything as "my." My truck, my wife, my Katie. Everything was his.

"She's at home, ain't she?" Gray said with some confusion, looking at Evie.

Nate all but rolled his eyes and said with an exasperated tone, "If she were I wouldn't be here, now would I? She left last night, and I figured this would be the first place she'd go." He narrowed his eyes on Evie's.

"We haven't seen her," Gray said.

"You sure?" Nate asked him but looked at Evie as he did so.

"Yeah I'm sure. Go check somewhere else 'cause she ain't here," Gray said with annoyance.

"Has she called you?" he asked Evie, flippantly ignoring Gray.

"No," Evie said, relieved she could answer that question honestly.

"And she's not here?" he questioned.

"No," Evie said. Katie was indeed not there.

"Hmm," he mumbled and scratched at his chin slowly. It sounded like sandpaper rubbing against wood. "If you see her, you call me. She needs to come home. Her mother and I are worried."

"Okay," Evie said. Her heart beat rapidly, and her palms were already damp. The man made her nervous.

"We'll let you know. You best be going now, McDaniels. We need to finish our lunch," Gray said, gesturing for him to the front door. "And we have work to do. I'm sure you can relate to that," he added in an underhanded tone. Gray had said more than once that Nate didn't work: his cronies did.

He tipped his hat and walked outside, peering over his shoulder at Evie before he left.

"What in tarnation was that all about?" Gray asked Evie.

"I don't know," she said.

"I reckon you do, and it must be for good reason you aren't telling me," he said, tilting his head to the side and looking at her skeptically.

Evie gulped. "Really, I don't know what he's talking about."

"Well, if she's run away, I sure hope she's safe. I'm surprised it took her this long. If that man was my father, I would've run like the wind the moment I could walk. He's a snake," Gray said, shaking his head in disgust as he went back to the kitchen.

Evie peered out the window, watching Nate's truck speed off. She knew he'd come again, and she hoped she could keep her wits about her and fib convincingly when that time came.

CHAPTER 15

She hadn't been to Kip's carnival since she was in her early teens, and that was because Katie had forced her. Some guy who Katie had a crush on told her he'd meet her there and would bring a friend for Evie too. Not that Evie was too thrilled. Katie heard a lot of grumbling, and Evie, after much persuasion and begging from Katie, reluctantly went with her best friend.

His friend wasn't at all Evie's type: pimply faced, thick bottle cap glasses, and a slicked- down bowl haircut. He breathed heavy and always seemed to be sniffing. Katie's date was a dream compared to Evie's, and after an hour of watching them having the time of their lives on those rides while she was subjected to countless Dungeons and Dragons stories and annoying factoids, Evie said a quick good night and walked home alone, thanking the stars above that the disaster of a date was finally over.

When Katie learned Evie had gone, she left her date and showed up at Evie's house, profusely apologizing. "I'm sorry. If I had known, I wouldn't have set y'all up."

"You didn't have to end your date on my account," Evie had said.

"Silly goose, we're best friends. I'll always choose you over some dopey guy," Katie had said. Evie swore to Katie she'd never go on another blind date again, and Katie never asked her to double date after that.

She knew Gray would suspect something was up if she went somewhere that night, saying she was going to town. Evie was a homebody and rarely went anywhere unless it was with Katie. She figured the most believable thing she could say was to tell him that she was going to the carnival to see how things were going. She needed to check on Katie, and realized she'd have to tell a thousand more lies to him by the time Katie had decided what she was going to do.

"You're always checking on things over there. Let me go for the night," she said to him. She decided the only way to partially tell the truth was to actually visit the carnival. It would at least make it believable when he asked her how things were coming along.

"Sounds good, Punkin. I'm right tired anyway," he said, and she could see the strain on his face and the newly formed circles under his eyes. He laid back on the couch, his bare feet dangled over the edge. "You hear anything from Katie?" he asked.

"Nothing yet," she answered and shot out the door before he could ask her more questions. It was only a matter of time until she'd cave-in and tell him the truth.

She strolled through the midway, hearing the clack, clack, clack from the carnival games – the ones where people paid too much so they could possibly win a stuffed animal. Kids ran past her, hurrying to ride yet another ride, and the smell of cotton candy, popcorn and funnel cakes permeated the air. She gagged a little and continued on, hoping she'd spot Finch soon. Flashes of colored lights filled the night sky. Rides were decorated in them – blue, red, white, and yellow. Edison bulbs lit the midway. Food and games filled tents.

A man wearing a black Bowler hat, a red vest and black shirt hollered to the crowds passing him by. "Play the game; everyone is a winner!"

Evie put a little more effort into her fashion choice for the night – lip gloss was applied, and she chose to wear a pair of white shorts to show off her farmer's tan and a white and blue ringer shirt that was a snug fit against her breasts. She'd deny it if she was asked. She'd swear that she had no interest in Finch Mills, and she was just curious about how things were going at the carnival, that's all. And a part of her would believe what she was saying because her attraction for Finch was buried deep in her subconscious.

"Heya, hon," shouted Doris.

Evie turned and saw Doris standing outside an orange striped tent, fanning herself. She moved her way. "Hi," she said.

"Don't think I've seen you here before," Doris said. Her make-up was more extreme than usual, and cornflower blue eyeshadow covered her eyelids.

"It's been a long time," Evie said and peered at the sign hanging above their heads, boasting "Kip Kierkin's Freaks and Curiosities Presents: The World's Strangest People." It bothered her, and she wondered how Doris could be so unaffected by being called a "freak."

"That sign ain't doing us no good anymore," Doris said. "Used to have a lot more of us freaks. I think the townies don't feel like they got their money's worth when they realize they're just looking at an old fat lady, a shortie, and a man with a bunch of tattoos," she said with a half shrug. "Our lines get shorter and shorter each year. They want to see the juggling acts and the knife throwing. I hear one carnival has a guy that rides his motor cycle through a ring of fire. Look at the line waiting to see Dmitri." As she pointed at the line wrapped around the tent, a flicker of sadness showed in her almond-shaped eyes. "They'd rather see him juggle, I guess." She sighed, and her lips cast down.

"Does it bother you?" Evie asked.

"Makes me worry that I won't be able to make a living much longer," Doris confessed with a sense of sadness, failing to understand what Evie was really asking. "Kip ain't going to keep us on much longer, I figure." She let out a long sigh.

"I'm sorry," Evie said. "Does it bother you that he calls you a freak?"

She shook her head. "No. I've been made fun of my whole life. At least this way, I can profit from it."

"Oh," Evie whispered, not sure what else to say.

"So what brings you to our neck of the woods? Finch said he helped you wrangle in some cattle the other night."

Evie's cheeks turned red, and her face felt hot. She quickly recovered and said, "Yeah. He saw the gate was open. It's a good thing too. My dad's banking on those cattle."

"Came sauntering in here like a wet mop," Doris continued. "I used to do a little moonlight swimming myself." She winked and gave an impish grin.

"Oh no, it wasn't anything like that," Evie said.

"Sure, whatever you say, Honey Lamb."

"No, really. We were washing the manure off of us," she said. The rise of color once again appeared on her cheeks.

"Is that what they call it now?" She let out a hardy laugh. Mouse and Friedrich came toward them, smiling.

"Hi, Evie," Mouse said and tipped his burgundy fedora. He was dressed in gray trousers, a white shirt, and a gray plaid vest.

"Hi." She waved and smiled at him. She thought he looked smart and realized she had never seen him in anything but nice clothes.

"Hello, Evie," Friedrich said. He wasn't in his typical garb and wore a blue t-shirt and jeans with pointed boots. Evie noticed that they were alligator skin and wondered if he had wrestled one in Florida to get them.

"You seeking Finch?" he asked her.

"No," Evie said, trying to refrain from groaning.

"She says she's checking on things for her daddy," Doris said in a tone that evoked, "she's full of shit but I'll go along with it anyway."

"I am," Evie defended.

Doris winked and her lips curled up. "How about you come inside for a Coke?" She pointed to the empty tent.

"You sure?" Evie said.

"Ain't no one gonna come in here. Our last show was an hour ago, and I highly doubt we're gonna have an influx of townies trying to peep at us."

Doris gestured for Evie to follow her. The inside of the orange striped tent was lined with wooden benches – narrow and long. A raised wooden platform faced them. Friedrich sifted through a styrofoam cooler and pulled out two bottles of Coke. He popped the caps off and offered them to Doris and Evie. Evie grabbed the bottle and took a sip.

"We always keep Coke handy," Doris said. "So, it's a good night for a swim," she continued. "Or a good night to wash manure off of you." She raised her perfectly trimmed eyebrows, and upon further inspection, Evie determined that they were painted in.

Evie didn't respond.

"Well, I can see I'm not funny," Doris said. "How's that bull of yours? Took us a few days to get that stink out of my tent."

"I'm sorry about that," Evie said with a frown.

Doris waved her hand at her. "Don't be. It was a sight to see, us trying to get him to move. Seems like Finch was the only one with the touch."

The mention of Finch's name made her feel warm inside, and she fought a blush from forming.

Doris opened her package of Twinkies and offered Evie one.

Evie hated Twinkies and tried not to crinkle her nose in disgust. "No, thanks."

"How is your truck working?" Mouse asked her.

"Fine," she said. "It's just old and needs new parts."

"Like us." Doris pointed to herself, Mouse and Friedrich.

"Speak for yourself woman. I am fit as a twenty-year-old man," Friedrich said, and Doris guffawed.

"Well, you do have a nice bod, but don't let it get to that big old head of yours," she said to him.

"They're like this all the time," Mouse whispered to Evie.

"Oh," she said. "Are they married?"

"Might as well be," he answered and placed his hand under his chin, letting out a soft sigh.

"So, tell us about yourself. We only get snippets from Finch. He ain't the sharing type," Doris said.

She felt their eyes burning into hers, and the situation felt awkward, like she was on trial. "Well, I don't know what you want to know," she said with uncertainty.

"Don't matter. We're just trying to know you is all," she said. "Tell you what, you can ask us something and then we'll do the same. Go on," she encouraged, and Evie felt the pressure to come up with something quick.

"Why is your name Mouse?" she asked.

They all three laughed, and Mouse took off his hat and rubbed the top of his head. "I came from a big family. There were nine of us, and I was the smallest. Mama used to get on to me because I was so quiet. She'd say, 'Hugo, you move around like a mouse. I almost stepped on you!' The name just stuck, and everyone has called me by it since," he said.

"We all got names for each other," Doris said. "I call him Sexy," she said, pointing to Friedrich and waggling her brows. "And sometimes I call Finch 'Piss-ant' but he doesn't respond when I do. He's fixing one of the rides if you're wondering where he is," she said.

"I don't care..." Evie began.

"Sure you don't. If I were an eighteen-year-old girl, my hormones would be going crazy for 'Mr. Tall, Dark, and Handsome,'" she said, and Friedrich frowned. "Don't you worry, Honey Lamb, he ain't gonna steal me away from you," she said to him and turned her gaze back to Evie. "As it is, I'm old enough to be his mama, and the more I get to know him, the more I can see what a little piss-ant he can be."

"That's for damn sure," Evie agreed with Doris about the "piss-ant" part, well, and the "tall, dark, and handsome" part too. Any fool would agree that Finch was easy on the eyes.

"Still, even piss-ants have their finer points, and he has the heart of a lion just like his mama did." Mouse and Friedrich nodded in agreement. "I'd bet if you opened him up, you'd find half of his inside was his heart," she said it with resounding confidence. "You wait around long enough, Honey Lamb, he's bound to come in here."

The last thing she was going to do was hang around like a swoony idiot hoping for a few minutes of Finch's time. "It was nice seeing you again," she said, getting up.

"That was fast. Guess we scared you off, didn't we?" Doris said.

"No," Evie lied. "I should be going."

"Bye, Honey Lamb. I'll be sure to tell Finch we saw you," Doris taunted.

Evie wandered through the carnival, hearing screams of excitement as people were twisted and jolted on the rides. She was tempted to try her hand at the ring toss but figured it'd be a waste of money, and what was she going to do with a stuffed bear anyway. She'd never really made time to stop and look around, to see all that the carnival offered. And from what she could see, it offered enough to keep people coming.

Time passed, and throngs of people passed her by. It was a mass exodus. Every single person was leaving at the same exact time, and Evie was stuck right in the thick of it. Trying to walk against traffic was pointless. She decided to wait it out until the crowds disappeared, and then she'd make her journey to Katie. The music had stopped, and the noise from the rides had silenced. Now the sounds of nature were more prevalent. Carnies talked amongst themselves uttering phrases Evie knew her dad would definitely charge a dollar for. She tried to commit a few to memory thinking that some of them would be useful in the future.

The crowds were finally gone, and Evie started to her childhood home. She felt silly for even trying to see some guy she barely knew, who, when she thought about it, wasn't much of a charmer anyway. Well, neither was she for that matter. They were two of a kind, and that scared the bejesus out of her.

***

The place was spotless. Katie had been cleaning all day, and when Evie arrived, she was fast asleep on the sheet covered sofa. It, along with a table and two chairs, were all that was left in the home.

Katie yawned and fought to keep her eyes open. "Did my dad come by?" She was drenched in sweat.

"Yeah," Evie answered. "I think he believed me."

"Good." She breathed a sigh of relief. "He'll come back."

"I know, but don't worry," Evie said. She held the fan up and said, "I brought you a fan." She plugged it in, and it hummed as it circulated air.

"Thanks, Evie." She yawned as she said it, and then her eyes started to close.

"Go on to sleep. I'll check on you tomorrow," Evie whispered.

Katie lay back down and fell fast asleep.

***

She made her way back to Gray's truck. Gray had insisted that she drive to the carnival even though she told him she was perfectly fine walking. "You don't need to be walking around in the dark by yourself," he said. She was glad he persuaded her to drive. Trekking from one end of the property to the other made her feet sore, and wearing platform shoes wasn't the most prudent choice for the evening.

Gray's truck was one of the few vehicles left in the make-shift parking space. It was a quiet night, and all she could hear were the voices of carnies.

"I heard you were looking for me," he called at her.

It was dark out, and she was surprised he could see her. He moved out of the shadows, and she was able to get a better look at him.

"No," she said, the keys jingled in her hands.

"That's not what Doris said."

He stood a little closer to her and smiled.

"I was just checking on things at the carnival," she said.

"And what'd you find out?" He was teasing her, and Evie was getting more flustered by the minute.

"That I still hate the smell of funnel cakes."

He laughed. "I'll let you in on a little secret." He moved closer to her. "I do, too."

She bit on her lip and fidgeted.

"Where were you coming from?"

"What do you mean?"

"Well... I would've seen you at the carnival, and I saw you walking up to your truck from there." He pointed north.

"I was checking on the property, and anyway, why are you watching me?" she griped.

"You're hard to miss," he kidded. "Why are you checking the property in the dark?"

"I was just making sure the gates were locked."

"Have you had more problems?" he asked with concern.

"No. But it's better to be safe than sorry."

"True," he agreed and paused for a moment. "Did you ride the Super Slide again?"

"No," she said with annoyance.

"Too much fun for you?" He laughed.

"Don't you have somewhere to be?"

"You're on my turf, remember?" He widened his arms, pointing at everything.

"But who owns the land?" she said in a haughty tone.

"Your father," he said.

She lowered her head in defeat.

"I saw *Smokey and The Bandit* was playing at the theatre downtown," he said with his hands in his pockets. "I'd like to go see it."

"So go see it."

He shook his head and rubbed the back of his neck. "I'm planning to. I was thinking maybe you'd want to see it with me."

"Oh," she said, feeling like an idiot for missing the painfully obvious. "When?"

"I get off early tomorrow night. I could pick you up at seven."

"Um...I have something to take care of."

"Oh," he said with disappointment.

"No, I mean you can't pick me up, but I can meet you at the theatre" she said.

"Oh, okay," he said, and she could see he looked relieved. "Are you sure you want me meeting you there? It seems wrong somehow." Finch may have had experience with women, but going on dates wasn't something he was skilled at. He only knew what his mother, Friedrich, Doris, and Mouse told him, and what he'd seen in the movies. And one of the things he always saw a guy do was pick a girl up at her house the night of the date.

"Yeah. It's fine," she answered. "I'll see you out front of the theatre tomorrow at seven." She reached for her door handle, and Finch placed his hand on top of hers and opened the door for her. "Thanks."

"See you tomorrow," he said and shut the door.

CHAPTER 16

"Let me curl your hair just like Farrah Fawcet," Katie said. "Pretty please." She clasped her hands together and made an exaggerated begging face.

"It's not a big deal. Really. We're just meeting at the movies," Evie said but even she had put in a little extra effort and washed her hair with the special Short and Sassy Shampoo that Katie always bragged about. Although her hair wasn't short and in the Dorothy Hamill style like Katie's, she swore she noticed some new sass from the effects of the shampoo.

"It's a date, you dope," Katie said. "And from your description, he sounds dreamy."

Evie blushed.

"I knew it!" she squealed. "He is, isn't he?"

"Calm your horses," Evie said.

"Just let me live vicariously through you. I probably won't ever go on another date again, unless there's a man out there who likes an unemployed woman with a fatherless kid," she said with a resounding sigh.

"You'll find someone," Evie said.

"Maybe. Maybe not. I just gotta focus on this little guy from here on." She looked down at her stomach and then back up at Evie. "But that doesn't mean I can't help my best friend look even more gorgeous than she already is. I brought my make-up case. Lord knows why. I won't need it anymore." Katie picked up a compact blue suitcase and unlatched it. Eyeshadow, lipstick, blush, eyeliner, and mascara filled it. She sifted through it and pulled out blue eye shadow and pink lipgloss. She squinted her eyes and placed her palm on Evie's face. "We're gonna do the natural look on you. Sit down," she ordered.

Evie sat down on one of the wooden chairs and remembered the times she sat there as a child, eating meals that her mother had made.

"Are you going stir crazy in here?" Evie asked.

"Not yet. I'm reading those books and magazines you brought. So that's keeping me busy. He likes to kick," she said.

"You keep calling him a he. What if he's a she?"

"Then she'll have a complex when she's born," Katie joked. "I really don't care as long as he's healthy and doesn't act anything like Todd."

"He'll act like you," Evie said with confidence.

"Curling iron's hot," Katie said and grabbed a handful of Evie's fine blond hair. She wrapped her hair around the hot iron and held it in that position for a few seconds. She then repeated the process over and over again until Evie's hair met with her satisfaction.

"Close your eyes," Katie said. She applied blue eyeshadow to Evie's eyelids and handed her the tube of pink lipstick. "You can put this on." Evie applied the lipstick and blotted her lips on a napkin.

Katie opened her compact. "Here, see how beautiful you look."

Evie saw the hair surrounding her face was feather back, and the make-up showed off her blue eyes. She smiled and said, "I like it!"

"Like or love?" Katie questioned.

"Love." Evie said with a smile.

"Good. He should too." She gestured for Evie to stand up. "Let's get a good look at you." Katie appraised her and shook her head, muttering to herself, "Why does red look better on blonds?"

Evie looked down at her red tube top and then back at Katie.

"Think I should wear another shirt?" She yanked on her top, pulling it up.

"You pull that thing up any further, and it'll cover your neck. Don't worry, your boobs aren't flopping in the wind," Katie said.

Evie crossed her arms over her chest.

"Quit being so insecure. You look great!"

"Thanks."

"You have to come here after the date. I want to hear all about Mr. Tall, Dark and Handsome's kissable lips."

Evie widened her eyes. "Katie. I'm not going to kiss him on the first date."

"Why not?"

"Because..."

"It's a kiss. You can't get pregnant from a kiss. Trust me, I know." She pointed to her stomach. "Well, if he kisses good enough, you could end up pregnant." She twitched her brows and grinned.

Evie's face turned red.

"You've kissed a guy before, right?"

"Yeah," Evie said with a lilt in her voice.

"You haven't? How have I not known this? I'm your best friend."

"You never asked, and when would I? I've never had a real boyfriend," Evie said with a pout.

"I just assumed you kissed Nick Tate that one time."

Nick Tate and Evie spent seven minutes in a closet together at Wendy Jenson's house during her sixteenth birthday party. While the other kids heckled them, snickered and shouted encouraging phrases like, "Slip her the tongue, Nate," and "Slide into second base," Evie and Nick spent their time standing awkwardly in the dark cramped space wondering what to do with their hands and their mouths. Nick wasn't a skilled casanova, and Evie was just as much of a novice when it came to the opposite sex. Their seven minutes ended with a quick sloppy peck on Evie's lips from Nate, lasting all of a millisecond, which in Evie's mind didn't count as a real kiss. She wanted a *From Here to Eternity* Kiss, passionate and intoxicating, the kind where you hate to come up from air.

"No, well, kind of, " Evie fumbled her words. "It doesn't matter," Evie brushed her off.

"Oh yes it does," she said and balled her hand into a fist. "Practice on here with your tongue." She demonstrated by licking her clenched index finger and thumb.

"Ooh, Katie, that's gross." Evie grimaced.

She formed a devious smile. "Fine. Practice on him, then."

Evie's face turned rosy. "I gotta go," she said and headed for the door. "You'll be okay, right?"

Katie nodded vigorously. "Definitely. Have fun."

***

Finch waited outside of the theatre, his hands tucked in his jeans pockets, and he paced back and forth, rocking on his heels. He could smell his aftershave and hoped that it wasn't overpowering. The cheap stuff was always too strong. He tugged on his denim jacket and stared down at his ensemble: a Kiss t-shirt and bell bottom jeans. He hoped he looked nice and berated himself for being so self-conscious. He never put much thought in what he wore before, so what was different about this night? Evie, for one. She was what made him want to impress her, and he couldn't figure out how she could have that effect on him so easily. There was no doubt that if she happened to twirl her hair or bite on her lip, he'd be a goner.

He saw her walk up and tried to remember he was supposed to be a decent guy but that darn red tube top of hers squeezed tightly against her, and her breasts bounced with each step she took. He wondered if she was wearing a bra underneath that meager piece of fabric and brushed that thought away as quickly as it had come. Her jeans fit snug and showed the curve of her hips.

"Hi," she said.

"Hey," he said. "You look nice."

"Thanks. You too." She licked her lips, and he noticed they were glossy and pink.

"You ready?" he asked. He had to quit looking at her or so help him, he'd grab her right there and then and kiss her hard.

She nodded.

He placed a bunch of quarters on the counter and slid them toward the movie attendant. She gave him a strange look, and he nodded with encouragement. "Two tickets for *Smokey and The Bandit*."

She gave him the tickets, and Finch walked inside with Evie. "That was a lot of quarters," she said to him as the attendant tore their tickets in half.

"It's how I'm paid most of the time. It gets heavy sometimes," he said, patting to his full front pocket.   "Do you want anything?" He pointed to the concession stand. A bright neon sign flickered above popcorn machines, candy and soda fountains.

"A Coke," she answered.

The line was long and he said, "How about you save me a seat, and I'll take care of this?"

"Okay," she said.

Finch had no idea what Evie liked, so he bought popcorn, two

Cokes, Milk Duds and Dots. He'd buy the whole damn kit and caboodle if it suited her.

He put the boxes of candy in his two pockets and then stacked the Cokes on top of each other, resting them under his chin and holding them in his palm, and carried the tub of popcorn in his other hand. He felt like Dmitri trying to juggle it all at once and wondered if someone was going to offer him a dollar bill if he'd toss it all up in the air and catch it.

Evie had chosen to sit on one of the last rows toward the back of the theatre. She waved her hands up in the air so he'd see her. He precariously shuffled toward her, hoping to God that he wouldn't drop anything. His sense of balance was good, masterful even, but balancing it all and being a nervous wreck wasn't a good mix.

Evie saw Finch's full hands and got up, meeting him halfway. She took the Cokes out of his hand. "Thanks," he said.

"Are you feeding an army?" she whispered as they sat down and he emptied his pockets.

"I didn't know what you liked," he said.

"Dots," she said with a grin and instantly grabbed the box from his hands. She stuck a straw in her Coke and took a sip. "Thanks."

The theatre grew dark, and a preview for *Grease* showed. Evie leaned into Finch and whispered, "I want to see this."

"It's a musical," he said with a sigh.

"Duh."

"How can you sit through a film where they randomly break out into song and dance?"

"Shh," a man in front of them turned around and glared at them.

"We'll finish this debate after the movie," Evie shot back.

"There's no debate. Musicals suck," he teased.

"Humph," Evie mumbled and rolled several Dots together into one big glob. She plopped them into her her mouth and chewed.

Finch glanced at her, and Evie sensed him staring. "What?"

"Nothing," he said with a smile and grabbed a handful of popcorn and put it in his mouth. "Want some?" He handed her the tub.

"No thank you," she said emphatically, pushing the tub away. "I hate the smell of popcorn."

"I guess I'm not getting a kiss goodnight then," he joked and then rolled his eyes at his last comment. He had to take it slow with her and saying crass things like that wasn't going to win her over. They'd only push her away. She was too smart to fall for bullshit lines.

Her cheeks and ears burned, and then her gaze lingered to his lips for a second.

He leaned in and whispered into her ear, "Sorry."

Her stomach did a summersault, and she could feel the warmth of his buttery popcorn breath against her. She could learn to love popcorn. "It's okay," she barely managed to say.

"No, you didn't let me finish," he whispered. "Sorry you don't like popcorn."

The movie started and everyone in the theatre grew silent. As the Bandit sped off, trying to evade Smokey, Finch's eyes wandered down to Evie's hands, wondering if he should make a move for it or not. Her palm faced up and was begging for his to join it. He couldn't understand his strong case of nerves. With any other girl, he'd be on first base and slowly pawing his way into second. He quit dwelling on it and placed his hand on top of hers. If she didn't want it there, she'd move it away, he figured.

Evie felt the warmth of his calloused hand on top of hers. She'd only held hands with one other guy, Mark, and his hand clearly bore no resemblance to Finch's hand—one that had labored daily for the last seven years. Mark's had been soft like a baby's butt and wet and sweaty. She felt repulsed holding it, and never went on a date with him again.

Maybe she was too picky, she wondered. She asked herself that question a lot. Did she seek too much in a guy? She had a running list in her head, and Finch didn't meet all of the criteria, but at that moment, with his hand on hers, she forgot about that list. She wrapped her fingers around his hand, and their hands didn't unlink until the movie was over.

The credits rolled, and they made their way out of the theatre and to the outside, watching as people passed them by. A few recognized Evie, stopped to stare, and gave her a strange look when they saw her talking to Finch.

"Do you want something to eat?" he asked.

"I'm full, but thanks."

"I'll walk you to your truck," he said, taking her by the hand again as they headed to Gray's truck.

Evie leaned against the truck door, and asked, "So what have you got against musicals?"

"Who breaks out into song and dance like that?"

"They do," she said.

"Exactly," he said. "They're actors, not real people."

"Anyway, I still want to see *Grease*. I love Olivia Newton-John."

"She's a little too folksy for me. I like rock and roll," he said. "But I'll take you to see it if you want," he tried to feign indifference.

"Are you sure you could manage it?" She narrowed her eyes at him and raised an eyebrow.

"Yeah. I may just have to cover my ears when they sing," he said with a laugh.

The sound of cars passing by and people talking filled the air, and they stood there staring at each other, wondering what the other was thinking. Finch finally said, "I had a good time tonight."

"Me too," she said and smiled.

"I don't get off work early for a few more days, but I was thinking we could grab some dinner," he offered, noticing that his fingers were fidgeting inside of his jean pockets.

"Okay," she agreed.

"I'm picking you up next time, though," he said.

"No, that's okay. You don't have to."

He sighed and brought his hand against the back of his neck and rubbed it. "I'm not going to keep meeting you somewhere like some back alley trollop. I'll pick you up at your house," he said with a firm voice.

"It's not a big deal," she said with a half shrug. "And did you just use the word 'trollop?'"

"Yeah, so, and anyway, it is a big deal to me," he said seriously.

"Fine," she said with a huff. "Go ahead and pick me up then. Wait till you meet my dad," she said with sarcasm.

"Most girls wouldn't be pissed off the guy wanted to be a gentleman, and what do you mean by your dad? I've met him. He's a nice guy."

"He's not going to be happy I'm going out with *you*," she snapped.

Finch grimaced for a split second and then quickly recovered. "Well, he'll have to get over it," he snapped back.

"You're a real jerk off, you know that?"

"I'm a jerk off because I want to pick you up at your house so you're not driving home alone in the dark? Yeah, I'm a real jerk," he scoffed. "You know what, just forget it!" He threw his hands up in the air.

"Fine," she said and opened her truck door. "I didn't want to go out with you anyway. Mister Smirkity Smirk!"

"Ooh, burn. Okay, Miss Queen of Insults, I'll be sure to cry into my pillow tonight on the account of you not going out with me."

"You..." she struggled for words. "Your face is stupid."

"Oh yeah, well your face won first place for being the dumbest in the world!" he said, and fought hard to keep himself from laughing.

She gasped and said, "You're mocking me!"

"Well, you kind of make it hard not to. 'My face is stupid'? Who taught you how to insult people, because you really suck at it?" he said.

She sighed heavily and tapped her fingers against the truck door. "You suck." She scowled at him and mumbled something.

He laughed and shook his head in amazement. "You've got some temper."

"This is not funny," Evie said, trying hard to not laugh with him, but the more she heard his loud cackle, which for some reason really pleased her, the more her grin grew wide, and she couldn't help but smile along with him.

He stopped laughing and looked at her seriously. "I won't take you out on another date unless I can do it the right way." He leaned into her and placed his arm above her head. If he bent his head down, he could kiss her, and he knew she wouldn't fight him. There was no denying the chemistry. But he was going to save it, for another time, a better time, when the whole world wasn't watching and it was just them. He knew once his lips touched hers, it'd be with so much force, nothing could stop them, and that kind of kissing could get them arrested. He wasn't sure if he wanted to wrestle her to the ground, tickle her, or French kiss the living daylights out of her.

"Okay," she relented with an uneven breath. "Okay."

"I'm following you home. They say you're not supposed to drive when you're angry."

She was flustered, and her body felt warm all over. "I can drive fine. And who are *they?*"

"The same jerk offs you say enjoy breaking out into song and dance." He helped her in the truck and closed the door. "Good night, Evie."

CHAPTER 17

Gray insisted that he and Evie go out for dinner – "a fancy meal" as he aptly referred to a steak dinner. It wasn't a nice dinner unless steak was the main ingredient.

"What's the special occasion?" she asked him. He was dressed to the nines, no baseball cap, an ironed shirt, and a dark, never-worn-before pair of Wrangler jeans.

"Just wanted to take you out," he said and smiled at her. "You look nice." Evie was wearing a spaghetti strap blue floral sundress with white shoelace trim at her chest.

"Thanks. You too," she said, and they left the house, heading toward The Strip Club.

The name alone caused anyone to chuckle, anyone with a twelve year old sense of humor, that is. Gray loved to tease that he was going to The Strip Club, waiting to see if people's faces would turn red from embarrassment. He'd laugh and say, "They have the most succulent..." and he'd wait a few seconds for their reaction, and then would say, "steaks."

The Strip Club was located in Chester, one town over from Haines. Most of Evie's friends from high school went to The Strip Club the night of prom, because it was the only decent, white-table-clothed restaurant within miles. Evie had only ever been there with Gray and didn't see what the hype was all about. They could easily buy steak from Cooper, and it'd cost them half the price.

A flicker of dim light shone from the table-top lamp that sat on their table. Yellow bubbled glass walls divided each dark wooden round booth. Every booth was semi-circled with red tapestry seating and faced a black grand piano. A musician played tunes only Gray recognized, and he hummed along, reminiscing.

"Did Katie ever call?" he asked.

"No," Evie said. "She hasn't called." If an expert detective were at the table he'd pick up on her lie. Anytime Evie told a fib, she went to great lengths and included useless information that just wasn't needed. A simple "no" would have sufficed, but she just had to add the last part making it abundantly clear that Katie, had in fact, not called her.

"Where do you figure she ran off to?"

"I don't know," she said, trying to sound worried.

"Don't fret, she'll show up. I've seen that dumb boyfriend of hers in town. So I know she didn't' run off with him," he said.

"It was nice of you to take me here tonight," she said, changing the Katie subject.

"Thanks. I've been working you so hard. You're doing a great job taking care of all them calves."

Evie was responsible for bottle feeding the calves. Once the calves were delivered, the cows were sent off to a larger dairy farm to produce milk, leaving Evie in the role of mother to the needy calves.

"It's no big deal," she said.

"Still, all the same, you deserve something nice."

They ordered their food and listened to the piano player try his hand at Billy Joel's "Piano Man." Gray sipped on his beer and said, "I love this song."

"Me too," Evie said. It was one of the few songs they could agree to.

"Your mother and I never liked the same music," he said.

Evie had no interest in talking about her mother, but he continued anyway, "She liked The Beatles, Jefferson Airplane, and

The Doors. I could never get her to listen to Motown."

"Humph, doesn't surprise me," Evie said in a snippy tone.

"That wasn't the only thing we didn't have in common." He leaned closer to Evie and scrubbed his hand over his face. "I met her at The Diner. Did I ever tell you that?"

"I think so..." Evie had only half-listened to any story about her mother.

"She worked there during her summer break from college. I always felt like she was smarter than me, going to college and all."

"You're smart," Evie said.

"Thanks, Punkin, but your mother was sharp. She knew things I'd never even heard of, and she was the cutest little iddy biddy thing," he said with a smile. "I was surprised when she went on date with me." He took another swig of his beer and continued, "Her and Nate were high school sweethearts, but that summer they broke things off. I think she caught him cheating on her."

"I didn't know they dated," Evie perked up. This was news to her.

He nodded his head. "Up until that summer. When I found out they broke up, I'd go in that restaurant just about every dern day just to see her. I was sweet on her all through high school, and when she finally agreed to go on a date with me, I was in hog heaven," he said.

"She was lucky you asked," Evie said.

He shrugged. "I ain't too sure about that. What I should have done was let her be. We were different as night and day. She wanted the moon and more, and I was just a farmer's kid. Nate McDaniels was a better match for her."

"How can you say that?" Evie said in disbelief. Nate was pond scum in her book.

"'Cause it's true. Sometimes you covet something, and when you finally have it, you figure out you don't need it, and it ain't yours to want anyhow."

"Do you regret her?" Evie asked, leaning forward.

"I regret what happened between us. Punkin, she wasn't in love with me, and I thought I was head over heels in love with her, but the older I get the more I realize I was in love with the idea of her. She was something beyond my reach, and once I finally had her, I still felt empty because no matter how much you love something, if it don't love you back, you ain't ever going to be content." He frowned and ran his fingers across his mouth. "I'll never regret you. You're the best thing that came out of that marriage."

"She chose to leave." Evie's jaw tensed. She felt her heart beating against her chest. Anytime her mother was brought up, she always had this type of reaction; even ten years later, it felt like it only happened yesterday.

"I could've stopped dating her. I knew we were worlds apart, and then I got her pregnant. I was just as selfish as she was," he said remorsefully. "She was trapped, and I knew it." He shook his head and looked down at the table, peering into his half-empty beer.

"It takes two to tango," Evie said.

"It does, Punkin, but I should have let her go. If I had really loved her, I wouldn't have gone on more than one date with her."

"She knew she didn't love you. She had a choice, and she blew it," Evie said with anger.

"She wasn't happy. I wasn't real surprised when she left. I knew it was coming. Every day I came home, I kept expecting her closet to be empty and for her to be gone. I just knew. Lord knows why it took her as long as it did? I guess she finally gave up," he said. "The point is, I want you to quit being so angry towards her. You can't keep blaming her, because I've forgiven her. I've forgiven myself. I learned the hard way, and I hate that you have so much anger festered up inside you. You keep at it, you'll end up bitter and alone. That kind of anger will make you brittle and hard, and you don't want that, Punkin. Believe me, you don't want that."

"But how can you forgive her for leaving us?"

"I had to make my peace. She was wrong to leave, and I was wrong to covet her. She's got enough regrets to live with. We don't need to hate her."

"Ha," Evie scoffed. "What regrets is she living with?" Evie never knew what happened to her mother, but she imagined that she was living with a wealthy man, spending his money on things Evie thought were superficial. She didn't know if she had a half-sister or brother, but if she did, she felt sorry for them.

"She left you, and I figure that deep down that is burning her up inside. That's the kind of mistake you never recover from. You don't need to hate her, Punkin. She's hating herself plenty for the three of us," he said and finished off his beer.

The waitress delivered their plates, and they let the topic wither away as they ate their steak dinner. Evie tried to let what he said sink in, hoping that maybe one day soon, she'd learn to stop hating her mother.

***

Evie knew Gray would be asleep in no time. Steak dinners did that to him, and coupled with beer and a butter and sour cream filled baked potato, by the time she tiptoed to the door and closed it, he was snoring. Anyone within ear shot could hear him.

She made her way toward the other side of the property and prudently chose to wear her boots for the trek. She was still wearing her dress from her dinner with Gray, and she carried a bag filled with food, drinks, and magazines she had picked up for Katie.

The moon was full and cast a gleam of light as she padded her way through the property. She thought about the things her father had told her that night and wondered if she could stop hating her mother. It was all she'd ever known for so long, and letting go of that feeling was going to be hard. Really hard. Because she had set her mind on despising her when she left, and now, she thought, how would she feel about her? Nothing? Was she supposed to feel nothing about her? At least if she felt nothing, she could finally say with all certainty that she didn't care.

She saw him coming her way, and her heart raced just a little faster.

"Hey," he said with a quick head nod.

"Hi," she said.

"You're out late," he said.

"I can say the same for you."

"Whatcha got in the bag?" He pointed to it.

"Nothing," she answered.

"Looks heavy," he said. As he took it off of her shoulder, his fingers brushed against her bare skin, and goosebumps formed up and down her arm. He put the strap on his shoulder and patted the bag. "It's pretty heavy. You trying out for the weightlifting team?"

"No," she said, trying to figure out a lie, any lie would do at that moment. She was grasping at straws.

He folded his arms against his chest and stared directly into her eyes. "What's going on, Evie?"

She bit on her lip and tucked her hair behind her ears. She brought a finger to her mouth and started to chew. "I can't tell you," she said, shaking her head.

"Are you a Soviet spy?" he teased and narrowed his eyes to her finger. She pulled it out of her mouth and gave him a dirty look.

"I wish," she sighed. "If only it were that simple."

He scrunched his face. "You'd make an awful spy, by the way."

"Why's that?"

"You don't hide your feelings very well," he said as he followed her. "And I bet spies have better comebacks."

She looked at him as she ambled her way through the grass. "You're going to follow me even if I don't tell you, aren't you?"

He shook his head up and down. "You've got me curious. Plus, you gotta stop walking around by yourself at night. Some of the guys I work with are real creeps," he said, and his tone had an edge to it.

"How do you know I walk around by myself at night?" she asked, trying to sound appalled.

"The other night... when I saw you at the carnival."

"Oh," she said. "You're observant. Maybe you're the Soviet spy?"

He looked around before he whispered, "East German, but don't tell anyone." He appraised her and said, "You're all dressed up."

"My dad and I went out to dinner."

"When your face isn't getting in the way, you can really clean up," he said.

"Thanks," she said with sarcasm. "Your face is always getting in the way."

He let out a loud, hardy laugh and walked beside her. Evie knew she shouldn't let him in on her secret, but she had to tell someone, and her instincts told her that Finch could be trusted. That beneath his piss-ant exterior, he was trustworthy and earnest and may be able to help Katie.

They reached her old house, and Evie stopped outside the front door. "You can't tell anyone," she said.

Finch looked around and his eyebrows squished together. "What am I going to tell? Are you hoarding a Soviet spy in there?" He moved his head side to side and cupped his hand over his head.

"I mean it, Finch. You can't tell." Evie begged.

"Okay," he said. "But if I go in there and find out you've got your high school rival's mascot, I'm leaving."

"Yeah. I saw that Brady Bunch episode too." She let out a sigh. "You're making this into a joke."

"It's kind of hard not to. You're being all Barnaby Jones about it," he said.

"You watch that show?" she asked with surprise.

"I'm a carny, not a recluse."

Evie unlocked the door and pushed it open with Finch right behind her. Katie lay asleep on the couch with a magazine draped over her chest.

She whispered to Finch, "This is my best friend, Katie."

He cocked an eyebrow and tilted his head to the side, giving her a silent look.

"It's a long story," Evie said. She sat the bag down on the table and tiptoed over to Katie. "Katie," she whispered. She poked her on the arm.

Katie opened her eyes and widened them, moving her head and looking around in surprise. She let her eyes focus and looked at Evie and then at Finch. She frowned and said, "You brought him here?

Evie," she whined. She sat upright and messed with her hair.

"He won't say anything," she said and plopped down next to her, facing her. "And I really didn't have a choice anyway." Evie glared at Finch and then peered back at Katie.

They continued to argue as Finch quietly grabbed one of the chairs and carried it with him to where they were, sitting just a few feet away from the couch. He rubbed his hand along his jaw and over his mouth and didn't say anything.

Katie noticed him looking at them. "Does he talk?" she whispered.

"Usually too much," Evie said.

"Well, why is he just sitting there staring at us then?" Katie asked.

Evie shrugged.

"Finch Mills," he said and stood up and shook hands with her.

Katie grimaced. "You've got quite the firm grip on you," she said with admiration. She turned to Evie and said, "You were right; he is dreamy."

Finch looked directly into Evie's eyes with a superior expression. "So, I'm dreamy, am I?" he said, pleased with himself.

She flared her nostrils. "No. Not in the slightest."

Katie giggled. "Y'all got it bad," she said. She extended her hand and he shook it. "I'm Katie McDaniels."

He sat back down on the chair and crossed his leg over the other. "Nice to meet you, Katie." He flashed a smile, the warm sincere kind that Evie liked so much.

"You too," she said. "Evie's told me all about you."

"She has, has she?" He jutted his chin and raised both of his eyebrows, directly looking into Evie's blue eyes.

"Yeah. I told her what a piss-ant you can be," Evie chimed in.

"You've been talking to Doris too much. Only she calls me that lovely name," he said to Evie. "I can't be that bad. You did agree to go on a date with me, remember?" He gave her a smug look.

Evie struggled for a comeback.

"Don't strain yourself. I've got all night if you need it," Finch said.

Evie pursed her lips.

He leaned forward and cupped his hand over his mouth, pointing at Evie. "I have that effect on her," he said to Katie. "Is she turning red?"

"A little," Katie said and chuckled. "I like you."

"Well one person in this room has taste," he said. "I like you too, Katie." He paused, watching as she brought her hands to her stomach, and it all started to add up. "How far along are you?"

"How did you...?"

"You're holding your stomach like you've got something golden in it, and we've had a lot of pregnancies in the carnival," he said."I can just tell."

"Still?" Katie said impressed. "You're observant."

"Just good at putting two and two together."

"And cocky," Evie added with a moan.

"I think I'm thirteen weeks. I haven't been to a doctor yet, but that's what I've come up with," she said and bit on her bottom lip.

"And your parents had a fit?" Finch said.

Katie nodded. "To say the least." She breathed. "My mom cried herself to sleep, and my dad, well, he said some pretty horrible things." Finch frowned and continued to listen. "He said he was sending me to my aunt's and I'd have to give the baby up," she said with a quivering lip. "But I'm not giving him up. I'm gonna raise him on my own despite the whole world being against me. Is that crazy?"

"No," he shook his head, "it just means you're going to be a great mother."

She wiped at her eyes. "Look at me. I'm a blubbering mess." She sniffled.

"It's the hormones," Finch said. "Wait until you get to your third trimester." He stood up and walked to the table and took a few napkins. "Here." He handed them to Katie.

"Thank you," she said and gave him a warm smile. "Evie, if you don't marry this man, I will."

"Quit stroking his ego," Evie said. "All he gave you were a few crummy napkins."

"Sorry, but most of the men in my life, with the exception of your daddy, don't have half the manners he does. Right now, a napkin is as good as a diamond ring in my book."

Finch sat back and folded his hands behind his head, smiling at Evie. "She likes me."

"She's hormonal and doesn't get out much."

"Hey," Katie whined. "I'm sitting right here, you know?"

Evie turned to her with an apologetic expression. "Sorry. He just gets me so frustrated." She grunted.

"I can leave the room so y'all can make-out and get it over with. Or there's a closet." She gestured to a linen closet down the hallway. "How about y'all go in there for seven minutes and see what happens?" Katie teased.

Evie blushed at the thought. She knew that a trip in a closet with Finch would not have the same result as it did with Nick Tate.

There'd be more than a stupid slobbery peck. She'd kiss that smirk off his face for every one of the beautiful seven minutes she was in there.

Even Finch turned a slight shade of pink, thinking of all the things he and Evie could do in a closet for that length of time. He'd hold her tight and run his hands along her cheeks, combing his fingers through her long blond hair. He'd kiss that tiny freckle on her ear lobe, and then the corner of her mouth, whispering how truly amazing she was.

"She's likely to get a coat hanger and strangle me with it," Finch said.

"Maybe," Katie said and formed a slight smile. "But something tells me y'all would find other things to do to occupy your time."

Evie's ears were boiling hot. The rest of her was a rising inferno. She knew she was as red as a tomato and hated that he had that kind of effect on her. But there it was. And even though he crawled under her skin, she couldn't stop wanting to be around him, wanting to say something to him, anything, if it just meant they were talking.

"It seems that you're in a predicament," Finch said seriously, rubbing his chin. "What are you going to do?"

"I'm not sure yet," Katie answered. "I can't stay here forever, but I don't have anywhere else to go."

Finch gave her a sympathetic nod. "I'll see what I can do to help."

Katie waved her hand up. "That's all right. You don't have to trouble yourself."

"It's no trouble," he said reassuringly. "Let me see what I can figure out. Try not to worry."

"Thank you, Finch. I can see why Evie likes you," she said. She turned to Evie, "So, what'd you bring me tonight?"

Evie took a few seconds to respond, still in awe over Finch's kindness.

Katie waved her hand in Evie's face.

"A deck of cards, some food and more Coke," she finally answered.

Katie pointed to her belly "He's got a hankering for Coca Cola," she said to Finch.

"Mom said I was a Pepsi guy," he said. "It's all she drank when she was pregnant with me."

Katie rubbed her hands together and smiled. "Cards, huh? We should play a game before y'all leave."

"I'm in." Finch got up and sauntered to the table, pulling the deck of cards out of the bag.

He brought the other chair over and placed it in the middle of them, spreading the cards out on it and shuffling them.

"What are we playing?" he asked them.

"I only know how to play Blackjack," Evie said.

"Blackjack it is," he said and dealt them their cards.

***

An owl hooted high up in a tree, and coyotes howled in the distance. Frogs croaked, and crickets chirped incessantly. A slight chill filled the summer night air, and Evie shivered, feeling the coolness against her bare shoulders.

Finch took off his denim jacket and offered it to Evie. "Thanks," she said, putting it on.

She could smell him all over it: cologne that was strong but not too overpowering; a slightly musky scent from the days he wore it to work; and the Earth. Finch was a conglomeration of all three.

He grabbed a hold of her hand and held onto it, just enough of a tug to let her know of his presence, that he was there, right next to her. She didn't fight it and laced her fingers into his, feeling the leathery texture of his tanned skin.

"You were nice to offer to help Katie," Evie said. It had surprised her. He was so kind, so empathetic.

He stopped for a moment and stared down at her. "I feel sorry for her, and it's not right what's happening to her," he said. "The same thing happened to my mom, except she wasn't pregnant. Her lousy parents booted her out of the house when she was seventeen, and as much as Kip frustrates me, he saved my mom. If he hadn't taken her in, she could've ended up with some loser drunk or worse." He raked his fingers through his hair. "I guess I just don't want the same thing happening to Katie. She's a nice girl, and it's a shame she's gonna have to grow up so fast."

Evie didn't know what to say. He was being so open and so honest with his feelings, she wanted to give him a hug and pat him gently on the shoulder. The only words she could muster were, "Sometimes you confound me, Finch."

He gave her a tired smile. "How's that, Evie?"

"You're a piss-ant one moment and a teddy bear the next. I can't figure you out." Her fingers grazed across her chin as she stared at him incredulously.

"And you, Evie, are a good friend. Katie is lucky," he said, and they started their walk back to Evie's.

In the quiet of the night it was easy for them to get lost in their feelings. They stole the short amount of time they had been given to learn more about each other, talking about anything and everything—which movie was their favorite, and why their favorite song meant so much to them.

"I better go inside," Evie said in a hushed voice. Her voice was dry, and she felt like butterflies were fluttering around in her stomach. "Daddy's probably asleep on the couch, but if he wakes up and sees I'm not there, he'll have a fit."

"I still want to take you out for dinner," he said. "If you'll go," his tone soft.

"I'd like that," she answered. "That was a much nicer way to ask."

He kicked his foot back and forth and looked down, feeling ridiculous for mistrusting himself. He was a glob of nerves. "I was thinking since you check on Katie every night, I could walk with you, you know, to make sure you're not traipsing around out here by yourself."

Even Evie could hear the insecurity in his tone, that underneath there was hope, hope that she'd say yes. "Okay." She smiled, happy that he had offered.

"We can continue our talk tomorrow night then," he said. "Your taste in movies needs work." He curved his lips up.

"How can you not like *Willy Wonka and The Chocolate Factory*?"

"They're a bunch of ungrateful kids, and people randomly break out into song and dance," he said and paused for a moment, glancing at her house and then back at her. "Won't your dad suspect something if you're out walking around every night?"

Evie shook her head. "He's so tired lately. After dinner, he falls asleep on the couch, and doesn't wake up until after midnight." A flicker of worry ran across her face and faded as quickly as it had come.

He gave her an understanding nod. "I will see you tomorrow after the carnival closes," he said.

She stood on her tip toes and quickly pecked him on his cheek before saying a hurried "Good night." She refused to make eye contact and wondered if his face was as flushed as hers. His cheek had felt warm, and she could still feel the sting on her lips from his five o'clock shadow. If she turned around to look at him, she'd die from embarrassment. It was just a quick peck, but she knew it was the start of something.

CHAPTER 18

He was punctual. True to his word, he met her outside of her house after the carnival had closed. Without saying a word, he took a small bag out of her hand and carried it, while he held onto her hand with his other. He was going to hold her hand anytime she let him.

He peered down into the crumpled brown paper bag and asked, "What have you got in here?"

"Candy for Katie, and I picked some up for you," she said sheepishly.

"What'd you get me?" He stuck his hand down in the bag, rummaged around, and pulled out some Sugar Daddies. "Aww, my favorite. How'd you know?" He flickered a wide grin.

"You told me," she said.

"Well, thanks," he said with surprise, and she could see that for once, Finch was the flustered one. "I was thinking about Katie," he said as they walked side-by-side. "Couldn't she just live with you? I mean, her father can't force her to live with her aunt and give up the baby. She's eighteen."

"She could stay with me, but he'd find a way to force her to leave. She's so scared of him, and if you knew him, you'd be too. He's the only man I've ever met that makes me say a few Hail Mary's anytime I'm near him." She shivered slightly.

"He sounded bad when she talked about him, but he must be worse than I thought. You're afraid he'll do something if he knows she's here?"

Evie nodded with a sad expression. "I'd bet Miles' life on it."

Finch took a deep breath and pinched on the skin of his throat.

"Give me some more time to think of something. Maybe she could join us on the circuit?" He shook his head slowly. "But I wouldn't stick my worst enemy in this job, let alone a nice girl like her. The carnival is no life for someone like her."

Evie blew air out of her lips. "Hopefully, we'll get something figured out. She doesn't want me to tell my dad, but I can't keep this from him much longer."

"No, you can't," he agreed.

***

Finch thought about Evie as he headed back to his tent. They were spending more time together, and she had kissed him. Okay, so maybe it was just a peck on the cheek, but her lips did touch his face even if it was for a brief moment. He couldn't get her out of his head, and the more he got to know her, the stronger the pull was. He'd see her in his dreams, when he fixed a ride, when he smelled popcorn or tasted a funnel cake. She was everywhere.

"Haven't seen you around lately," Doris said. She was lounging on a lawn chair, fanning herself.

He half-shrugged. "I've been around."

"Around in what sense, Honey Lamb? You've been hanging out with Evie, haven't you?" She giggled. "Stoney said you borrowed his truck the other night."

"Yeah. So," Finch said with annoyance.

"So... did you take her out on a date?" She leaned forward with a groan. "Can't imagine you borrowed his truck to sight see."

"Don't you have something you could be doing?" Finch asked with exasperation.

"Nope. I'm just waiting for Friedrich to come back with my Coke," she said. "It's been a quiet night anyhow, hon. Kip ain't so pleased with us right now." She frowned.

"Business still slow?" Finch asked with a note of concern. He had heard Kip chewing Doris, Friedrich and Mouse out earlier that week, threatening to sack their asses if they didn't conjure up some more business soon. But they weren't magicians, and they couldn't create magic if it wasn't there.

"Slow is an understatement. Dmitri's doing great with his juggling act, though," she said with a pout. "The rumor mill is buzzing, and it ain't anything good."

He looked down and rubbed his forehead.

"I didn't tell you this to get you down in the dumps. Don't you worry about us," she said. "So, are you taking her out again?"

He let out a heavy sigh. "I'm hitting the hay," he said and started off.

"Kip ain't going to be so pleased when he hears you're sweet on the owner's daughter. We're supposed to stay away from her."

He stopped and turned around, facing her. "Well, it's too late for that, isn't? Maybe her dad won't feel that way when we meet?"

She made a tsk-tsk sound. "You're not a real charmer, hon. He's gonna take one look at you and lock his daughter up in that farmhouse of his."

"Thanks. A lot," he huffed. "I'm not an asshole, Doris."

"You know how much I love you. I just don't want you getting your hopes up is all. People like him don't want to know people like us, and they sure as hell don't want someone like you knowing their daughter."

A lump caught in his throat. "She doesn't have a problem with me," he said. "Maybe he won't, either."

"Daddies can make things complicated if they want. All I'm

saying is tread carefully." She lay back down and fanned herself. "She's not some ten cent floozy."

"I'm well aware of that," Finch snapped.

Friedrich approached them carrying two glass bottles of Coke. "One for you my dear and one for me." He handed Doris her drink and sat in the empty chair next to her.

"Thanks, hon. Finch is in serious trouble," she said.

Friedrich stood upright and widened his eyes. "What is the problem?"

"Calm down. He's okay. He's just got the love bug is all, and guess who that bug is?"

"Evie," Friedrich said and smiled, showing his crooked teeth. He sat back down and looked at Finch appraisingly.

"Bingo!" Doris sang.

Finch drew in a deep breath and released it. "I'll see you guys later." He stomped off, hearing Doris singing, "Finch and Evie sittin' in a tree..."

***

She was a basket of nerves and couldn't stop clomping around the house, chewing on her nails and twirling her hair. At least she had the guts to tell her dad Finch was taking her out on a date. His reaction was just as she suspected: pursed lips twisted to the side. He didn't say much, only that he wasn't happy about it and would make mention of it to Kip.

"You can't, Daddy," she begged.

He sighed. "You're an adult. I can't stop you from going on a date with this boy. But of all the people to go out with, a boy from the carnival."

Finch was right; he was judged. People automatically thought of him as a crook, a loser, just because he made his living as a carny. "Give him a chance," she pleaded, and from the look on his face, she knew it'd be a hard sell.

"You're old enough to make your own mistakes," he said.

That was a first. Gray never snapped at her like that, and she couldn't tell if he was mad at her choice of date or just angry she was going on a date in general.

"Sorry," he said softly and rubbed the back of his neck. "I'm just tired and cranky is all."

"It's okay."

"No it ain't." He shook his head solemnly. "If I get a bad feeling about this fella, I ask that you respect me and don't go out with him. Can you do that for me?"

She nodded slowly.

"Thank you." He formed a tight smile.

Finch knocked on the door, and Gray moved to open it. "Mr. Barnes," Finch said with a stammer. "I'm Finch Mills." Gray was big and tall, and the look he was giving Finch was intimidating.

Finch extended his hand and Gray shook it. "Come in," he said. "What kind of name is Finch? Your parents into birds or something?"

Finch cleared his throat and let out a nervous laugh. "No sir. I was named after the state bird of Iowa, where I was born."

"A yankee boy, huh?" Gray muttered.

Finch walked inside their home and did a quick look around. It was exactly how he had remembered: sheer lace curtains hanging from the big picture windows; a green plaid sofa; and a huge rug centering the room.

"Evie tells me you're taking her out to eat," Gray said.

"Yes sir," Finch answered, and Evie was surprised the word "sir" was a part of Finch's vocabulary.

"So, what do you do in the carnival?" Gray asked him.

"I fix all of the equipment," he said.

"Hmm," Gray nodded appraisingly. "That's a useful skill."

"Yes sir, it is," Finch answered politely. "You have a nice farm," he added.

Evie had to stifle a laugh. Finch was trying too hard, and it was painfully obvious.

"Thank you," Gray said. "Why don't you sit down so we can talk for a bit?"

Finch moved to the sofa and sat down. Gray plopped down in his recliner and leaned forward. "How old are you?"

"Twenty-two," Finch said.

Gray smacked his lips. "And where are you from?"

"I can't pinpoint a place. We travel so much, but if I had to say somewhere, I guess Florida. That's where I spend half of my time each year." Finch shrugged.

Gray continued interrogating Finch, and Evie noticed that Finch remained cool and collected, answering each question that Gray asked without a hint of irritation.

"Y'all better get on going. I'm sure you're hungry," Gray said and got up.

Finch stood up and shook Gray's hand again. "It was nice to meet you."

"Make sure you have Evie home by eleven o'clock," he said. "On the dot, and not a minute late." He shot Finch a stern, "I mean business" look.

"Yes sir, I will," Finch said and motioned for Evie to follow him out the door. He rushed to Stoney's truck and opened the door for her.

Evie stepped up inside and sat down. Finch slumped against the seat and let out a deep resounding breath. He leaned over and buckled her lap belt.

"What are you doing?" She looked down at his hands.

"Sorry," he mumbled. "I used to be a ride attendant at the carnival. I guess I'm used to buckling seat belts."

She chuckled and said, "So, you survived the interrogation."

He laughed in response and turned the ignition. "It was my first," he admitted. He'd never had to meet a girl's father before, and he thought he didn't do half-bad for having a lack of experience in that department.

"I didn't know 'sir' was a word you even knew," she teased.

"Ha, ha," he said sarcastically. "I wasn't raised in the wilderness. My mom did make sure I had some manners." He looked in the rear view mirror and reversed the truck before doing a one-eighty.

"Still," she continued. "It was funny to watch."

He shot her a quick glance. "I'm glad I amuse you so much."

"You do." She placed her hand on his and gave it a gentle squeeze.

***

It was a slow night at The Diner. Finch and Evie were immediately seated in a corner booth that faced the front window, giving them a bird's eye view of pedestrian traffic. Everything inside was beige, brown and orange, a product of refurbishing from a few years earlier. Evie missed the aqua green tufted booths and light blue counter tops, but Antonio, the owner, thought a renovation was in order. Music played from the jukebox as a waitress took their order for drinks.

"Pepsi," Finch said.

"We don't serve Pepsi here," the waitress said. She wore a beige uniform with a white apron tied at her plump waist. Her silver hair was tied in a bun, and green pointed glasses fell down the bridge of her nose. She pushed them up. "We only got Coke."

"Tea then," he said.

"Pepsi?" Evie shook her head with disappointment.

"You go north of the Mason Dixon line and you'll see that most people prefer Pepsi."

"Ha," she scoffed. "Then they're all stupid."

"Do they have stupid faces too?" he teased and grabbed a hold of her hand, gently rubbing the surface of it with his thumb.

She struggled for words and let out a soft, "Yes."

The waitress brought them their drinks and took their order. Finch took a sip of his tea and grimaced. "Sweet," he said.

"You ordered tea," Evie said.

"Tea, not sweet tea."

"You have to order unsweetened tea if that's what you want, otherwise, it'll always be sweet. Poor Yankee." She patted him on the arm, feeling the hard muscle underneath his shirt. He had dressed up for the evening, wearing a button-down shirt instead of his usual rock band t-shirts, and his hair had obviously been combed.

"Since when are Floridians yankees?"

"Since they don't know the difference between sweet tea and unsweetened tea," she said. "Does the sun really shine while it rains down there?"

"Sometimes," he said. "I'm only there in the late fall and winter, though."

"I bet it's beautiful," she sighed while she said it.

"Some parts are. But it's nice here too," he said. "You'll have to come down there sometime when I'm there. I could show you around," he offered.

"I'd love that," she said, and she meant it. "I really want to see the Gulf of Mexico. It sounds amazing."

"It is, Evie."

They waitress brought them their food and they began to eat. They continued to talk as they ate, sharing more things about themselves.

"How did you go to school?" she asked.

"I was home schooled, and Rolf was my instructor. He was a teacher in Germany," he explained. "When I turned sixteen I got my GED. I never had the normal high school experience," he said, using quote marks with his fingers. "No proms, no football games, none of the events that will give me nostalgia later on when I'm old."

"You didn't miss much," she said. "Dances are overrated, and football is stupid."

"Because the players have stupid faces?" he kidded.

"Exactly," she said with a smile.

They continued to talk, discussing politics and war, and other adult topics that they had never been broached with anyone else. They discovered their commonalities and their differences, what bothered them, and what brought them to tears.

"You named a calf after James Brown?" he asked with disbelief.

"He's from South Carolina, and he's the godfather of soul. Anyways, James suited the calf," Evie said. Finch laughed aloud, causing the few restaurant patrons to stare at them.

Time passed, but neither of them could tell how late it was. To them it felt slower, frozen almost. So many stories and secrets were unraveled in a short amount of time. And there were so many more stories and tales that they could share if time allowed.

The waitress approached their table and said, pointing to the clock on the wall, "Sorry y'all, but It's closing time."

"Sorry," Finch apologized, seeing they were the only ones left in the restaurant. It was 10:30. He only had half an hour before he had to take Evie home, and he wished at that very moment that he could freeze time. One more hour wasn't enough. He wanted a day, no a week, actually, maybe a month would be good.

They stepped outside, and he placed his arm over her shoulder as they headed to Stoney's truck. It felt natural to both of them, and Evie snuggled closer into him, feeling the warmth of his breath on her hair.

"Evelyn," Nate said, stepping from the shadows and inhibiting them from taking another step.

"Hello," she said, and Finch could sense the change in her mood. She was tense.

"Have you heard from my Katie?" The way Nate McDaniels stared at her made her a big bundle of nerves.

"No," she lied.

"I find that hard to believe," he said. "Y'all are best friends, aren't you?"

"I, I," she stuttered.

"She says she hasn't, so why don't you step aside so I take her home," Finch said.

Nate glared at him. "You've got some nerve. Who the hell are you to tell me what to do? This conversation is between me and her."

He let go of Evie and took a step forward in front of her. "I promised her dad I'd have her home soon, and I aim to keep my word," Finch said.

Nate held up his hand and said, "No snot nosed carny kid is going to talk to me like that! You better watch your mouth boy." His jaw tensed, and his stare hardened. He leaned over him. The way he said "boy" infuriated Finch. He sounded like those prison cops in the movie *Cool Hand Luke*.

Finch wasn't frightened in the slightest. He opened his jacket and tapped on the head of his knife. "Now if you'll excuse us, I'm gonna be getting her home on time like her dad expects me to," he said.

Nate backed off and scowled at him. "You better hope you don't run into me again."

Finch stepped to the side and held onto Evie's hand as he walked to Stoney's truck.

They sat inside, neither one of them said a word for a few minutes. Evie breathed heavily, trying to calm her heart.

Finch punched the steering wheel. "That guy's a real piece of work."

"I thought you were going to knife him," Evie said.

He turned his head in her direction. "A guy like that has his head so far up his ass, I have to paint a picture for him to understand my language," he said. "Sorry." He shook his head, looking down at his balled up fists.

She scrunched her face. "For what?"

He looked up at her. "I'm trying to mind my manners when I'm around you."

"You think cursing offends me?"

"No," he said. "But I'm trying to be a nice guy."

"Don't try, just be, Finch, 'cause I like you as you are," she said and turned away, feeling a blush rise to her cheeks. "Were you really going to cut Mr. McDaniels?"

"No, Evie," he laughed as he said it, still feeling the weight of her last words. She liked him. There, she said it out in the open for him to hear. She liked him. "This isn't *West Side Story*. I just knew that a man like that wouldn't listen otherwise. Trust me, I've met plenty like him in my life."

"I told you he was scary," she said.

"I'm not scared of him," he said seriously. "His type cowers behind others and gets them to do his dirty work." He brought his hand down to hers and stared her in the eye. "Are you okay?"

"Yeah," she said. "I'm just worried about Katie."

"I can see why, Evie. I can see why," his voice trailed off, and he started up the truck and drove her home.

He opened her door and walked with her to the front door. She peered inside her window and saw her dad asleep on the couch. The television blared, and Gray's snoring echoed to the outside.

"I had a nice time," Evie whispered. "Thank you."

"Me too. We should go out again," he said, wanting to add the words, tomorrow, and the next day, and the day after that, but no way was he going to be a bumbling mess.

"Definitely," she agreed. "You're going to have to learn how to order a tea, though."

"Ugh with the tea. Cut me some slack," he kidded. "You're going to have to acquire some taste in movies."

"I told you I liked *Rocky*," she said. After a heated debate about their favorite movies, Finch conceded that Evie had an inkling of taste because she thought Rocky was a good movie. It was one of his favorites, and if she had said she hated it, he knew he'd still want to date her.

"That's true," he said. He looked down at her and tilted his head.

Evie's heart raced, feeling the anticipation.

He placed his hands around her waist and brought her closer to him. His touch was firm but gentle. "I really want to kiss you right now, Evie Barnes, but your dad is on the other side of that door, and I don't want to make him mad." He kissed her forehead and released her from his embrace.

She tried to catch her breath. Her mouth was open, and she could see the yearning in his eyes.

He moved to the top step and stopped, spinning to face her. "Good night, Evie."

"Night, Finch," she managed to say before she pushed the door open.

Gray woke up in an instant. He checked his watch and said, "A few minutes early." He gave a nod of approval.

"I think he knew if he had me home late you would have broken both of his legs."

"Nah," he swiped his hand, "just the one." He smiled. "You have a good time?"

"Yes." She nodded with a wide grin.

"He seems all right, I guess. He laid it on a little heavy with all the 'sirs,' but I figure he wanted to make a good impression, and that tells me he must like you a ton if he's trying to win my approval."

"I don't know about that," Evie said.

"What do I know? I'm just a dumb ole' farmer. Seems to me that he's real sweet on you, though."

Evie stayed silent.

"You seem sweet on him too?" Gray probed.

She turned three shades of red. "Daddy!" she whined. "I just went on a date with him. We're not getting married."

"All marriages began with a first date," he said.

CHAPTER 19

Finch immediately read the look of concern on Evie's face and noticed her stooped shoulders. She wasn't her usual self, and he was desperate to know what was wrong. "What is it?" he asked.

"We lost a calf today," she said with a downturned expression.

"I'm sorry," he said. He wanted to fix it, just like he fixed everything else, but he didn't know the first thing about cattle.

"We think there was mold in the hay," she said. "Daddy had Tom, our vet, come out, and he says the others should be fine, but I still worry we're going to lose more and that could cost us. A lot."

"If the vet says they'll be okay, I'm sure they will," he said. "Try not to worry too much." He moved his hand to her shoulder.

She bit on her lip and sighed. "We're so behind as it is. We need these heifers to birth the calves so they'll lactate. If they don't, we don't get our money, and we can't pay our bills."

"It's going to be okay, Evie. The vet said that they'll be fine. Worrying isn't going to solve the problem," he said.

He pulled her into him and hugged her. Tight. She felt the urge to pull away, after all, hugging wasn't her thing, but he was like a magnet and she couldn't let go. She just let him hold her and gave into it, pressing her face against his chest and wrapping her arms around him. It felt nice being held by him, like a part of a chain link fence, connected together.

She finally let go and looked up at him, hopeful and thankful. *When will he kiss me*, she wondered? *What is he waiting for*, she thought.

"We better go check on Katie," he said, and Evie felt a wave of disappointment cross over her.

She nodded, feeling the tug of his hand on hers, and the more she thought about it, the more frustrated she became. She stopped walking and let go of his hand. "When are you going to kiss me?" she asked with irritation.

"What?" he said, truly surprised by her question. He'd never been asked that question by a woman before. Never in his twenty-two years of life.

"You keep giving me hints that you want to kiss me but you never do, and it's driving me crazy!"

"I," he began, bumfuzzled with his words. She could shock the hell out of him, and he absolutely adored that about her, but man could she irritate him.

She tapped her foot against the grass and folded her arms to her chest, waiting, for something. A response. An action. Something to tell her she wasn't a buffoon for what she just said. Because it was out there in the open now and she couldn't take those words back. She had made it known that she wanted his lips on hers.

He threw his hands up in the air, mumbled under his breath and started walking. She ran to catch up with him.

"Where are you going?" she shouted, and he ignored her. "Hey, I'm talking to you!"

He spun on his heels and gave her a frustrated look. "I heard you, but I don't respond well to demands."

"I didn't demand anything," she said defensively. "I asked a simple question."

"You all but demanded that I kiss you, and I want to Evie, but I want to do it when the time is right. Kissing you right after you told me about your calf dying and you're worried about money isn't very romantic or considerate, is it?" He let out a groan. "You frustrate me so much! You know that I'm aching for you." He gave her a pained expression.

She stared at him with her mouth wide open, at a loss for words.

He pulled her to him, and she didn't fight it. She was ready to surrender into him. He held onto her tight and leaned down, kissing the freckle on her ear lobe, the one he'd been eyeing since the day they had met. She shivered, feeling the touch of his lips and the warmth of his breath against her skin. He pushed her hair to the side and lightly grazed the nape of her neck with his lips, creating a trail of kisses up to her partially open lips. She felt intoxicated and couldn't move. He was taking her breath away with each and every kiss.

She titled her head to the side and pressed her palms against his back, feeling the heat from his skin. She was lost in him. So incredibly lost.

His lips finally met hers, and their tongues joined together, swirling in motion. She tasted him, the warmth and pleasance of him, and he closed his eyes, enjoying the absolute beauty of that moment.

He finally let go of her and stared deep into her eyes, thinking that he could do that again and again. She brought her hand up to his cheek, gently rubbing it with the tip of her thumb. She stood on her tip toes and cupped his face, kissing him on both sides of his cheeks, then his forehead, and finally the dimple in his chin.

She was flushed, and so was he. It was a simple kiss, but the aftershock still lingered. His heart was beating ferociously, and hers was pitter pattering at the same pace. She steadied herself. Her knees wobbled, and he wiped his hands against his denim jeans before he took a hold of her hand.

"That was…" He couldn't say "nice" because that was a trite description. It was more than that. It was the best kiss of his life, and he knew anytime he closed his eyes he'd see her and he'd replay that moment.

"Wonderful," she finished his sentence. But "wonderful" didn't evoke her feelings. It was more than that. Amazing. Breathtaking. So much more. Her lips still burned, and she licked them, tasting the saltiness of him on her.

***

Katie knew. It was written all over their faces. "Y'all have been kissing," she pointed out without reserve.

"Katie, geez," Evie snapped and shot her a dirty look.

Katie laughed. "It's about time," she said.

Even Finch was speechless. Since when did he get so shy, he wondered. He kissed her, big deal. He had kissed many before her. But this wasn't the same. He never wanted to hold Evie so bad after kissing her, and when she kissed him on his cheeks and his chin, he nearly lost it. The frightening prospect that she could persuade him to do anything, that she could ask him for anything and he'd give in with no questions asked, scared the hell out of him.

Katie glanced at Finch and then Evie. "Good Lord! That must have been some kiss. The look on y'all's faces is priceless. I wish I had my Polaroid." She laughed to herself.

Finch turned his chair around and straddled it, facing Katie. "I've been thinking about your situation," he said seriously, and Katie quit laughing. Evie sat beside her, facing her, and urged Finch to continue. "You could stay at my place in Florida. I won't be back until the end of October, and by that time, I'm sure we can find you another place to stay in Gibsonton."

Finch had mentioned the idea to Evie, who figured it was worth a shot. It wasn't long-term, and it wasn't a solution, but it would get Katie out of harm's way – out of Nate McDaniels' reach.

"I can't impose," Katie said.

"It's not imposing. Rolf, my landlord, he won't mind the company," he said and read Katie's expression. "Don't worry, he's not a creep. Just an old carny who talks too much. He'll talk your ears off." Finch laughed, thinking of Rolf's motor mouth. "I'm thinking there are plenty of carnies like Rolf that'll take you in. Worse comes to worst, I could move in with him when I get back and you could stay in my place."

"It's the best way for you to get away from your dad," Evie added.

"I can't keep taking so much from everyone. I'll never be able to pay you back, and what will I do once I have the baby?" she said.

"There's plenty of work down there. Besides, you aren't taking if we're offering. Most carnies understand what it means to be down on your luck. Rolf, he helped my mom out when she was your age. He'd want to help you out," Finch said confidently.

"I don't have any money. I can't take advantage," she said.

"Don't worry about the money, and like I said, you're not taking advantage," Finch interrupted. He and Evie had figured they could come up with enough cash to get her on a bus down to Gibsonton. Todd had thrown his money at her, but Evie couldn't take it, and she knew that Katie never would.

That money was mailed to him with a nasty letter attached, the day after he threw it at her near the rink. The note contained more than a few expletives, and anyone who saw it would be shocked that Evie knew so many foul ways to describe someone.

"I don't feel right about this," Katie said.

"Too bad," Evie said. "We're doing this, whether you like it or not."

"I guess what she's trying to say is we want to do it," Finch added, trying to soften the mood.

"How can I ever repay y'all?" Katie said, tears streamed down her face.

"I'll call Rolf tomorrow," he said. "He'll say yes, so we'll just need to get that bus ticket." He gave her a reassuring smile.

"I can do that," Evie said.

"Eves, you don't have the money," Katie said.

"Sure I do," she lied. She had gotten some graduation money from her great-aunt. It wasn't much but it'd be a contribution to the money Finch was donating.

"And you," Katie said to Finch. "You don't even know me. You don't have to do this."

"You're Evie's best friend," he said and sighed. "I'm just repaying the favor someone did for my mom, and maybe one day you can do the same."

***

They stood far enough away from the house in case Gray woke up. Evie was going to miss these late night walks. Would they continue once Katie moved to Florida, she wondered, and then a feeling of sadness filled her. Her best friend was moving, and Finch would be gone at another carnival soon. Change was a part of life, but this wasn't what she had in mind. Pining for a guy and losing her best friend at the same time?

"You're a good man, Finch Mills," she said.

"I wouldn't say that," he said with an air of humility. "You're the one with the big heart, Evie."

"Once you talk to Rolf, I'll go buy the bus ticket. I'll have to go to Chester to get it," she said.

"I can go with you," he said. "Kip won't notice if I'm gone for a couple of hours."

"No. I don't want you risking your job," she said.

"Evie, I'm the only one who can fix the rides. You think he's going to fire me? He knows he can't," Finch said. "Besides, I wanna take care of the ticket, and I know if you go alone, you'll pitch-in your money."

"You can't buy the whole ticket," she argued. "I won't let you."

"It won't cost much, and I've got enough saved up anyhow," he said. He tilted his head down and brought her closer to him. His lips almost touched hers. "Quit fighting me," he said, and kissed her before she had time for a comeback.

CHAPTER 20

Evie and Gray sat at the breakfast table. Gray sipped on a cup of black coffee while Evie thought about everything but the farm. Normally it all but consumed her, but it was the furthest thing from her mind at that moment. Gray noted the distant look on her face, the lack of conversation. They weren't the types to sit around and chit chat. Gray wasn't known for being a conversationalist, but normally Evie would try and make an effort, or vice versa.

"You okay, Punkin?" he asked.

"Sure," she answered with a lilt.

"Tom says the heifers are going to be fine," he said.

Sadly, she wasn't even thinking about the heifers. She should have been. She knew that. After all, they would be her bank or bust. "That's good." She looked up at him and gave him a half-smile.

"I was thinking once these calves are born maybe you and I can go on a trip together."

"Who will take care of the calves?"

"Cooper. He sold all but a few of his beef cows, and he owes me a couple of favors anyhow," he said. "You've always wanted to go to Florida. We could go to the beach." A glint of hope shone in his sky blue eyes. "Ain't that far from here, you know?"

The mention of Florida reminded her of Katie, of Finch, of everything that had happened so far that summer. "We should save the money."

"Don't you worry about the cost," he said. "We've never gone on a real trip together. I've done made up my mind about this so there's no use in arguing with me."

Evie and Gray had never been on a real family vacation—the

kind with snapshots filling a photo album.

She twirled her hair in deep thought. "It sounds nice," she finally said. A trip did sound nice, but the idea of it seemed unreachable.

"It's just what we both need," he said with certainty.

**

Finch called Rolf, who said yes once Finch explained the situation. At one time, Rolf was a knife thrower for Kips' carnival, and one of the best in the nation. He took Finch's mom under his wing and taught her everything he knew. He was the only true father-figure she ever had, and Finch thought of the old man as his replacement grandfather. Finch rarely asked him for anything, and anytime he did, Rolf gave in without question.

The closest bus station was in Chester. Evie picked up Finch once all the calves were bottle fed and the heifers were taken care of. She didn't bother to shower, and the grime and grit of a day of farming out in the sun still lingered on her.

Her wet hair was pulled up into a pony tail, and the soles of her work boots were encased in mud. The two of them were a pair, Finch thought. His hands were covered in grease, and she was a hot mess of mother nature.

She met him outside the gate that they locked up together that one night. The truck was idling, and he hopped the fence to join her.

"Show off," she said when he plopped down beside her.

He wiggled his brows. "You know you're impressed," he said and leaned over to kiss her on the cheek. He inhaled and said, "You smell pleasant."

She shot him a dirty look and then smiled. "Same goes for you."

Chester's population was twice the size of Haines, and the bus station was busy despite it's obscure location on the map. Given that it was the only bus station within fifty miles, it managed to keep a steady flow of traffic.

Finch and Evie walked to the counter to purchase a ticket. The closest city to Gibsonton was Tampa, and a bus was headed in that direction in one week. Finch pulled a wad of bills out of his pocket and handed them unfolded to the clerk.

Evie argued with him, but Finch just shook his head. "We already settled this."

"Look. I've got money." She opened her purse, pointing to the small stash of bills inside of it.

He closed her purse and muttered under his breath.

"Y'all are too young to sound like an old married couple," the clerk said.

"Oh, we're not married," Evie corrected.

"You sure act like it," the clerk said.

Finch took the ticket and handed it to Evie. She placed it in her purse and then grabbed the crumbled up bills. She stuffed them in his front jeans pocket and gave a satisfactory grin.

He clutched her around the waist and leaned into her, and Evie thought he was going to kiss her right there in front of everyone. Instead, he took the bills out of his front pocket and stuffed them in her back jeans pocket. He cocked an eyebrow and said, "tsk-tsk."

Evie huffed and glared at him.

"Just like Nancy and me," the clerk said and laughed.

Evie stomped off with a grunt and opened the truck door. Finch sat beside her and stared at her incredulously. "Let me get this straight. You're mad at me because I paid for the ticket?"

"Yep," she snapped.

"And that makes sense how?"

She didn't like his tone. "I told you I'd help pay."

"And I told you I'd take care of it. Why do you fight me, Evie?" He rubbed the back of his neck and closed his eyes for a moment.

"I'm not fighting you." But even she knew that was a lie.

He looked up at her, and for a split second Evie saw his dark chocolate eyes were more like a puppy's. "You are, Evie," he said with a breath. "Just let me do this, okay." He reached for her hand and held onto it.

After a few heavy grunts, Evie finally conceded and started up the truck. Few words were said on their journey back home. Evie wanted to ask him why he was doing it. Why would he make the sacrifice? But the words wouldn't come out because she suspected the reason, that this thing, whatever it was between them, was more than a summer fling. She'd ache for him when he left, and it just couldn't be one-sided, she thought.

***

A funnel of smoke filled the air, and a firetruck raced to the entrance of the property, cutting Evie off before she could take the left turn. Evie pressed her foot against the accelerator and followed the red truck in haste.

"What the hell?" Finch said. He stuck his head out of the truck window and tried to get a better look.

Evie screeched the truck to a halt. Finch jumped out before she could turn the engine off. He ran toward the smoke; a fire was ablaze, burning its way through one of the tents. Flocks of townies fled past them, rushing to get into their cars. Carnies tossed buckets of water onto the tent, but the fire continued to spread.

Friedrich ran with Mouse in his arms. Doris followed behind him. Finch took one look at Mouse. His face was gray and covered in remnants of ash. "Mouse!" he shouted in distress, heading their way.

"Go put out that fire!" Friedrich hollered.

Finch dashed toward the direction of the smoke and grabbed a bucket full of water. He tossed it on the tent. Evie joined him, in hopes that the flames would die out soon.

A trail of embers dusted the ground. Finch stomped on them with all his might. "Step on them, Evie," he said with a stressed expression.

The air was thick with smoke, and Evie choked as she stomped around, squishing the embers into the clay.

Every member of the Haines Volunteer Fire Department was there. Most were retired from their previous jobs at the Post Office and moved as quickly as one would expect sixty-five-year-old men to move. They linked their hose to one of Gray's spigots, struggling to hold onto the high-pressured contraption. A few carnies joined alongside them and sprayed the tent with full force.

Finch and other carnies continued to toss water onto the tent as the firefighters doused the lingering flames. The ground was soaked. Nothing remained of the tent, just a few scorched benches, too burned to be of any use. Kip appraised the area, shaking his head in defeat.

Mouse sat nearby. He hacked a dry, painful sounding cough. Doris handed him a cup of water. He chugged it down and handed her the empty cup, indicating he wanted another. A few townies coughed as they wandered the property in a daze. They were offered water, but they rejected the offer, and fled the carnival.

"This is a disaster," Kip said to any carny that would listen to him. Most were too stunned to hear him.

"Luckily, no one was hurt," Finch said to Evie. He ambled to Mouse and patted his friend on the back. "You okay?"

Mouse looked up at him with glazed eyes and coughed. "Just swallowed some smoke," he croaked. Doris dabbed his face with a wet handkerchief.

Evie latched onto Finch's hand. She'd never seen anything burn to the ground before, and the sight of it was horrifying.

Children of carnies cried, still shaken from the fire. Olga pulled them close to her and consoled them, singing a Russian lullaby to sooth their nerves. Dmitri frowned and placed his hand on her shoulder. He wiped her tears and looked at Finch with a mournful expression.

"What happened?" Finch asked Doris.

"Don't know," Doris answered. "We were in the middle of our show, and the next thing we know the whole damn tent was on fire." Her ample chest rattled as she let out a cough. "Poor ole Mouse got the brunt of it, and some of the townies that were sitting in the front row."

"I don't understand how the fire started," Finch said.

"Me neither, Honey Lamb. Thank God no one was hurt. 'Course Kip is sore we lost some business. I don't think those townies will ever come back," she said. "People could've died here today."

Firefighters rolled their hose and scanned the area for any last remaining embers. The chief, or at least that was what everyone called him, spoke to Kip. He took off his cap and ran his fingers through his thin, sweaty hair. "Ain't got any idea how this started, but it was a doozy," he told Kip.

"They said it started in the middle of their show," Kip said, pointing over to Doris, Friedrich and Mouse.

"Most fires just start. Ain't no slow goin' with 'em," he said.

Finch covered his mouth with his hand and glanced back at the empty spot in the ground. He brought his gaze back to them.

"What is it?" Evie asked him.

"It just doesn't add up. There's no reason for a fire to start," he said.

"Think it was the electrical?" Doris asked.

"No," he said. "I checked those wires myself, and Harry never does a crappy job installing them." He scrunched his eyebrows together. "This doesn't feel right."

"I agree with you," Friedrich said to him. He wrapped his arm around Doris's shoulder.

Dmitri and Olga passed by them, the children still latched onto her. Dmitri turned to Finch and said, "When I was preparing for my show, I saw a man behind the tent. I did not think anything of it at the time, but now I wonder if he had something to do with the fire."

"What did he look like?" Finch asked.

Dmitri thought for a moment. His eyes darted back and forth. "He had brown hair and was wearing a blue shirt, but I didn't get really get a good look at his face," he said. "I'm sorry."

"It's not your fault," Finch said as Dmitri gave a half-shrug and continued moving.

Kip approached them, a scathing scowl covered his gaunt face. "You." He pointed at Finch. "Where were you?"

"You can't lay this one on me," Finch said.

"I saw you jumping out of her truck after the fire started. You wanna hanky panky with her, don't do it on my time," he spat.

"Don't talk about her like that," Finch snapped, taking a step forward. He clenched his jaw and breathed hard and heavy. "Don't blame this on me, because I had nothing to do with it!"

"You should have been here." Kip pursed his lips and stormed off, cursing.

"He's just worried is all," Doris said, trying to calm the situation.

"Doesn't mean he has to talk about Evie like that," Finch said through clenched teeth.

"I'm fine," Evie said, squeezing his hand. "Let it go."

"You're better than that, and I don't want him saying those things about you like you're nothing," he said.

"It doesn't matter what he says, Finch."

"She's right, Honey Lamb. All that matters is what you two think about each other. Ain't no one else's opinion gonna matter unless you let it matter, and if you do, then y'all are in a world full of hurt."

CHAPTER 21

The days passed, and everyone seemed to be on edge. The fire impacted the carnival's business, and Kip saw a decrease in ticket sales. Townies talked. And once word got out that there was a fire, the faint of heart steered clear. There were those that continued to come, generating some business, but not enough for Kip. He snapped at anyone and everyone in the carnival. Doris, Mouse, and Friedrich bared the brunt of his wrath. Finch wasn't in his good graces, either, and was smart enough to run the other way when he saw him coming.

Gray's dark circles shadowed his blue eyes, and worry filled him. He expected a huge lump sum, a good sized profit from the carnival. If business continued to slow for the next two and a half weeks, that trip to Florida he had planned for Evie and himself was going to be a bust.

"Don't forget to take your medicine," Evie said to him while they ate dinner. The bottle had more pills in it than it should.

"I won't, Mother," he said sarcastically.

"He's been a grump lately," Cooper said to Evie.

It was their night to work at the skating rink, and Cooper decided to join them for dinner. "Tell me about it," Evie agreed.

Gray stood up in a huff and walked outside, slamming the door.

"He's been like that all week," Cooper said to her.

"Why?"

"I ain't sure. Men don't talk to each other like you women do. Maybe you can draw it out of him," he said.

"I'll try, Cooper. I guess we better get to work," she said.

***

Evie sat patiently while Katie painted her fingernails ruby red. "You know that this will just chip off, right?" Evie said.

Katie squinted at Evie's pinky finger and applied a coat in one even stroke. "Shh, you're breaking my concentration."

"Probably by tomorrow, too," she continued.

"Sshh," Katie said. She held Evie's hands and appraised them. "Looks good." She smiled and placed the brush back in its bottle.

"I'm going to miss you," Evie said, and a lump caught in her throat.

"Eves, since when did you get all touchy feely?" Katie said.

"I'm not. I'm just going to miss you."

"Me too, but I gotta tell you, I won't miss taking cold showers." She gestured her head to the bathroom. "If anyone should be taking cold showers, it should be you and Finch." She laughed.

Evie fought to roll her eyes.

"Oh, please don't deny it."

"I'm not saying anything." Evie looked down and closed her eyes. She could feel her face turning ruddy.

"Gotcha!" Katie smiled. "You've got my seal of approval by the way, in case you wanted it. He's a keeper."

"Thanks, but I don't know how serious it is. He goes to his next location in two weeks," she said.

"So?"

"So," Evie repeated. "It'll be hard to date when he's gone," she said and paused. "If that's what we're doing," she added.

Katie twisted her lips to the side and waved her hand up in the air. "Y'all are definitely dating. You could make it work. Todd and I were going to continue to date while he was at Wake Forest."

Evie gave her a silent look.

"Well, we saw how well that worked out." She laughed, but Evie could tell it was forced. "Have you seen him?"

"No," Evie said. She hadn't seen him since Finch made him piss his pants. She hoped he hopped on a train or drove off into the sunset and would never come back to Haines again. Rumor had it that he was staying with his grandparents on the coast until he started school at Wake Forest. *Good riddance*, Evie thought.

"What about my father? Have you seen him again?" Katie asked.

"Not since that one time," she said. Katie knew about the run-in they had in town. "You know he still calls me Evelyn? The only other person that called me that was my mother."

"They were friends. He probably picked it up from her," Katie said.

"They weren't friends when we were kids," Evie said incredulously.

"Sure they were. I remember her coming over to the house a few times."

Evie leaned forward. "What do you mean?"

"I don't know. I was really little. I just remember her being over there."

"How come you never told me?" Evie asked.

"'Cause you never asked. It's not a big deal. Calm down, Evie." She let out a sigh. "Anytime your mother is brought up you have a shit fit, and it gets old real quick. Do you see me having a fit every time Todd's name is mentioned?"

"No," Evie agreed with a pout.

"I'm your best friend and I love you, but this shit with your mom has gotta stop."

Evie turned her head, looking out the window. She knew Katie was right. Her anger toward her mother had to go, but there were so many unanswered questions.

"You're right," she finally said.

"I know I'm right, Eves," she said. "I'm just saying, you've got yourself a daddy that thinks you hung the moon, and a boyfriend, or whatever you want to call him, who isn't far behind him in line. Appreciate what you've got, and stop thinking about the things that are out of your reach because you're never going to get a hold on them anyway," she said.

"Pregnancy has made you wise," Evie teased.

"I've just had to make a visit to shit city is all, and I don't want to drag you there with me."

***

They held hands, walking in silence and lost in their thoughts. "You're quiet tonight," Finch said.

"Just thinking," Evie said in a low voice.

"I saw the strain on your face," he kidded.

She formed a half-hearted smile.

"Oh man, I'm losing my touch."

"Who said you were funny to begin with?" She smirked.

He grabbed her by the waist and tickled her.

"Finch!" she squealed. "Stop!"

"No. Not until you admit that I'm the funniest person you've ever met!" He tickled her armpits, that spot on her neck he knew drove her crazy, and the right side of her stomach.

She giggled uncontrollably. "Stop it!"

"You heard my condition."

"Fine. You're the funniest person I've ever met," she said in between laughs.

He gave her a smug look.

"Don't be so smug. That was blackmail," she said.

"I can do it again," he said and gripped under her arms.

She playfully slapped his hand. "Cut it out!"

"Okay, I'll stop," he said with a mischievous grin.

"Hands in pockets, now!" she barked.

He pouted his lips and shoved his hands in his pockets. He nudged her with his shoulder and said, "So, you said you were thinking?"

"Yeah," she said.

"About?"

"A lot of things. My dad's really irritable lately, and I think it's because he's so worried about money. And I'm going to miss Katie, and then there's you," she said all in one breath, and paused, biting on her lip.

"What about me?"

She brought her finger to her mouth and chewed for a second. "You're leaving soon."

"In a couple of weeks," he said.

"I'm going to miss you," she admitted. There, she said it, and he could take it however he wanted.

"I'll miss you more," he said. "Evie." He breathed and cupped her face. "Just because I'm leaving doesn't mean we won't continue to talk."

"But how is it going to work?" She touched the surface of his hands and brought them down to her waist.

"There's this wonderful invention called the telephone, and let's not forget our friends at the United States Postal Service." He could tell she didn't appreciate the sarcasm. "Seriously, Evie, just enjoy what's going on right now and quit harping so much on the future. I've never met someone who worries as much as you."

"But," she started.

"I'm going to put everything I've got into this and make it work, whatever it is."

He brought her to him and kissed her, and her hands wandered up his shirt, feeling the smooth texture of his back. Her fingers roamed to his stomach, feeling the soft patch of hair that centered around his belly button. He trembled from her touch. "Evie," he murmured and kissed her again, drowning into her mouth.

***

Later that night, they lay in the grass staring up at the twinkling stars that lit up the opaque sky. "How far is that star?" Evie pointed to the sky.

"Don't know, but it shines so bright you'd think it was close by," he said and intertwined his fingers with her. He rubbed the surface of her hand with his thumb.

"The sun is a star," she said. She rarely paid attention in science class, but that was the one thing she remembered.

"You're like the sun," he said.

"How's that?"

"You brighten my day and give it life."

CHAPTER 22

Gray begged Evie to go to the carnival with him. A part of her felt guilty because the only reason she relented was so she could see Finch. She itched to see him, to have any contact with him, and the nights alone didn't seem like enough time for them to get to know each other.

She could tell at least ten random facts about Finch Mills to anyone who asked. She knew that he was allergic to milk, which she thought was ironic considering that she worked with cows day in and day out. And she knew that he didn't have a middle name. He loved peanut butter and would eat it straight from the jar. He slept lightly and could wake from any sound. She loved the small mole on the left side of his cheek, and if she were blindfolded, she could pinpoint its exact location.

If anyone asked Finch, he could tell them that Evie worried too much, so much that she gnawed her nails off and bit on her plump bottom lip until it bled. That she talked to the cattle like they were human beings, and that she loved mustard and would put it on any item of food she could. He knew that he loved her middle name as much as her first and would call her Evelyn Rose if she allowed him to.

"Let's walk for a change," Gray said. Evie thought to herself, *if he only knew! That's all I've been doing the past couple of weeks.* She noticed her shorts and pants were less snug, and if she kept at it, her clothes would be baggy by summer's end. Her appetite was nonexistent. Katie told her that's what happens when you fall in love, but Evie brushed her off and said it was the summer heat.

Gray peered up at the cloudless sky and then glanced at Evie. "It's a nice night, ain't it?"

"Yeah," she said. The weather was perfect – not too hot, not too cold, just right. It was nice enough to lay outside and watch the stars with Finch, she thought. Or maybe take a midnight swim. They hadn't been back to the pond since that one night, but she often thought of asking him if he'd want to join her again.

"Will you ride something with me?" he asked, and Evie thought that he sounded like a an anxious kid.

"I'm not much for rides, you know that," she said.

"Suit yourself, Debbie Downer." He nudged her and smiled. It was the first one she had seen on him in days.

"Have you been doing all right, Daddy?"

"Sure. Why?" He slowed his pace.

"You've just been cranky lately, and it's not like you."

He stopped and wrapped his arm around her and gave her a tight squeeze. Evie could feel the dampness of his shirt. He was already sweating, and they had barely begun their walk.

"I'm fine, Punkin. Really, I am." He plastered a wide grin. Evie knew not to question him anymore. If he wanted to tell her what was really the matter, he would. He let go of her and started moving. "You going to see Finch?"

"I'm sure I'll run into him," she said. Their visit to the carnival was a last-minute decision, and she didn't have time to tell Finch she'd be there.

"And I'm sure you'll make a point to," he said with a lopsided grin.

***

After spending five dollars of his hard earned cash only to come up empty handed, Gray decided the Ring Toss just wasn't his game. "Guess my aim ain't as good as it used to be." He wiped the sweat from his brow and frowned.

"That's okay." She patted him on the arm. "Good Lord, Daddy, you're sweating buckets!"

His clothes were drenched, and his hair was sopping wet. "Lawd have mercy, it's a scorcher," he said and wiped his forehead.

"You're soaked." She dried her hand off on her shirt.

"Men sweat, Punkin," he said. He did a quick nod and gestured with his head. "That fella of yours is coming this way."

She turned around and saw Finch approaching them.

"Hi," she said with a goofy grin.

"Hi," he said to her. "Hi, Mr. Barnes." He shook Gray's hand and didn't even flinch from the sweat.

"Hey, Finch," Gray said. His tone wasn't overly friendly, but it wasn't cold, either. "She decided to come with me tonight. Can't imagine what brought her here." He cocked an eyebrow.

Evie peered down and shook her head in embarrassment.

"It must be the rides. We know how much she loves them," Finch said.

Gray let out a laugh. "You know her well," he said. "I'm aiming to ride that ferris wheel. Evie, can I persuade you to change your mind?"

She shook her head vigorously.

"I take it that's still a no," he said. "See you later, Finch."

"Bye, Mr. Barnes," Finch said and brought his gaze back to Evie.

"Bye, Daddy," she said and then made a kissing sound and puckered up her lips to Finch.

"What? You wanna kiss right here? Right now? I knew you liked kissing me but..." Finch said with a half-grin.

"I was talking about you being a butt kisser," she said and

repeated the noise and puckered her lips again.

"You're cute when you do that. You look like a little hedgehog," he said and pinched her nose.

She touched her nose and grimaced. "You just pinched my nose."

"Yeah. So," he said.

She reached up to pinch his nose but his reflexes were too quick. She tried again and failed.

She sighed in frustration.

"I'm too fast for you, Evie."

"And annoying," she said.

"So, did you come with your dad tonight so you could see me?" He hooked his fingers in a belt loop of her denim shorts.

"No." Her cheeks glowed, and she couldn't stop the big smile from coming.

"You wanted to ride all the rides then? Or, maybe play some games?"

"Yep. That's it," she said with a sarcastic grin.

"So why aren't you on the ferris wheel with him then?"

She rolled her eyes.

"What?" he asked with a smirk.

"You know what. Besides I don't do heights, and he rides that dumb thing because he and my mother rode it together."

"Was your mom around when we started coming out here?"

"One summer," she said. "And it's the only ride she'd get on with him. He says he's over her, but why else would he make a point to get on it every year?"

"Because ferris wheels are fun. If you weren't such a chicken, I'd ride it with you."

"I'm not a chicken," she said defensively.

"When it comes to rides you are. It's nice up there." He gestured with his head. "You can see the entire farm."

"Are you spying on me from up there, Finch Mills?" she said, trying to be coy.

"Yes, and you're really boring," he said and fought a smile. He tugged on her hand and motioned for her to follow. "Come on. Let me win something for you."

***

Finch threw his last dart, popping the pink balloon to shreds. "That's the fifth one," Evie said. Even she couldn't deny that she was impressed. Finch had aim. He threw each dart and obliterated every balloon he aimed for.

"Hardly seems fair," the carny said with a huff and scowled at him.

"Aww come on, Mickey. I never play," Finch said.

"Still seems wrong," he said with a grunt and pursed his lips.

"Which one do you want?" Finch asked Evie, pointing up to the array of stuffed animals: rabbits, bears, and other cutesy animals that were far from fearless when they were stuffed with cotton.

"The koala bear is cute," she said.

"The cute but deadly bear it is," he said.

Mickey mumbled something to himself and reluctantly handed the bear to Finch, who then handed it to Evie.

"Thanks," she said, hugging it against her. It was soft and cuddly and the first gift she'd ever gotten from a guy who wasn't her dad.

"Want me to win you more? I've got every booth here beat," he said with excitement, not arrogantly. He wanted to win everything in the entire carnival and give it all to her.

"That's okay. I'm happy with the one," she said, looking down at the koala bear.

"You sure?" He asked in the same tone.

"Yep." She peered up at him with a smile and nodded reassuringly.

He took a hold of her hand as they ambled through the midway. Booths with games were on each side of them: lines of people tried to win a prize. Voices carried and sounded like an angry swarm of bees. Rock music from nearby rides overlapped each other.

"How do you hear yourself think?" Evie shouted to Finch.

"You get used to it," he said.

Evie's head was throbbing, and she wanted nothing more than to be on the other side of her property, staring up at the stars with Finch laying next to her. At least there they'd have peace and quiet. At least the stench of popcorn and funnel cakes wouldn't permeate the air.

They came to a dead stop, blocked by a large group of people who huddled near the ferris wheel. "What's going on?" she asked. The ferris wheel wasn't moving, and the looming crowd was growing.

"Don't know. Lemme go find out." He let go of her hand and pushed his way through the crowd.

Finch knew something was wrong. He could feel it in his gut, and his gut never lied to him. When his mom died, he knew. He felt a void, an emptiness he never experienced before, and a cold sensation came over him. And he knew before he was even told the dreadful news—she had passed.

The closer he got to the front of the huddle, the more his instincts told him that whatever it was, it wasn't good. He could read their faces: shock, uncertainty, fear. Those weren't good emotions. Those were omens.

He heard snippets of conversation, "He just collapsed," one person said, and another added, "They said he was holding onto his chest and then fell to the ground."

He shoved his way through the barricade of people, feeling a sense of urgency. Stoney was kneeling on the ground, bent over a man and pounding his fists against the man's chest. Finch jerked his head to the right and saw the face of that man laying on the ground. It was Gray, and his eyes were closed shut.

Finch's heart sped up, and he quickly flew to Gray. "What do we do?" he asked Stoney with desperation.

"Breathe air into him," Stoney said.

Finch bent over and opened Gray's mouth. He exhaled everything he had in him and came back up for a breath, seeing that Gray still lay motionless. Finch leaned over and breathed into him again. Nothing. Gray was lifeless.

Stoney shook his head and frowned at Finch. "He ain't gonna make it." He grabbed Gray's wrist and felt for a pulse. "Ain't got no pulse," he said with sadness.

Finch pushed Stoney out of his way and pounded against Gray's chest, beating him. "Come on!" he shouted. "Damn you, wake up!" He breathed into Gray's mouth and Stoney grasped onto Finch's arm.

"He's dead, Finch," he said. Finch fell back and squeezed his eyes shut.

He couldn't move, his body wanted to stay planted, but he knew he had to tell Evie, and it killed him to think of how much it was going to hurt her.

He struggled to get himself up off of the ground. His balance was off, and he swayed a little, fighting the shock of what just happened. He could feel tears coming and knew once he saw her and told her, it'd take everything he had in him to keep himself from losing it. He had to keep it together—for her sake.

He pushed himself through the shushed crowd of onlookers, seeking her. She was at the edge of the circle of people. He could see the top of her golden hair, but he knew she must have heard something because when he got a look at her, he saw absolute horror.

She was white as a ghost, paler than pale, and her mouth was gaped wide open. Her blue eyes were dead, and she wasn't moving. She wasn't doing anything. She was just standing there, staring into the unknown.

"Evie," he whispered to her.

She heard him but didn't respond.

"Evie, it's your dad." He was trying to be gentle, to say it in the most soothing tone he knew how. But he knew there was no easy way to tell her what he had to. There wasn't a magical way to tell someone that they had just lost their father. Bad news is just that – bad, and no matter how the news is delivered, it doesn't change the weight of its devastation.

He was conflicted, trying to decide what to do. Did he take her to him? Did he take her away from him so she wouldn't have to see the stark reality? She answered his internal questions and took a step forward, moving without any expression. He walked beside her, standing next to her as she inhaled a deep breath and peered down at her father.

Evie wailed. It was horrifying – the worst sound Finch Mills ever heard in his life—a myriad of emotions: heartbreak, shock, and regret all rolled into one guttural moan. She collapsed to the ground, flailing against Gray and choked by her uncontrollable sobs, crying into his chest. "Daddy," she murmured.

He wanted to shelter her from the pain, to take it all away. There was nothing he could say. No right words. Nothing that would make it better. He did the only thing he could. He knelt beside her and wrapped his arms around her.

CHAPTER 23

It was all a blur. One minute Evie was crying over her father's dead body, the next she was in her house curled up in a ball on the living room couch. She could still smell his aftershave lotion on the pillow. She didn't know if she should sniff it or throw it against the wall. Everything in that room reminded her of him: the plaque from The South Carolina Agriculture Association, the picture of him at the State Fair when he was just a kid standing next to his prize pig with a wide, toothy grin, and that awful Dolly Parton statue that she always hated because it was gaudy and cheap, but now all she could do when she saw it was start to cry.

The clock read eleven thirty P.M. She was fighting to keep her eyes open and couldn't remember what had transpired over the past few hours. There were conversations with police officers and a paramedic, but she didn't know what she said. She didn't even remember how she got home. It all happened so fast. She always heard people say that about death – that it comes quickly, faster than a blink of an eye, and as she lay on the living room couch, she realized the truth to that statement. She had just lost her father and would never get him back. Her heart sank at that thought, and she buried her head into the pillow. She wanted him back, oh God did she want him back in her life. A new never-felt-before feeling of emptiness consumed her as she quietly sobbed, wondering if the ache she felt at that moment would ever fade.

Their voices carried from the kitchen. She heard them mention her name more than once, and they weren't quiet about it, either.

Finch made his way into the living room and knelt in front of her. "Evie," he whispered. "Why don't you go on to sleep?"

"I can't," she croaked. Sleep? She couldn't sleep. She couldn't eat. She couldn't do anything except lay there.

"Try," he said, and she could hear the desperation in his voice.

"Katie?" she asked. Katie didn't know about her dad, and she needed her. She needed her best friend more than ever.

He jumped up and said, "I'll go get her." He wanted to do something. Anything. "Doris, Mouse, and Friedrich just got here."

So those were the voices, she thought. She couldn't put two and two together because her brain was a foggy mess. Any simple notion or thought was too much exertion at that point.

"I'll be right back." He went into the kitchen and came back with Mouse, Doris and Friedrich following.

Doris' thundering steps vibrated the end table. The glass lamp clattered against it. She bent down and peered into Evie's eyes. "Hey, hon," she said in a hushed voice, but even her hushed voice was loud. She patted her on the head, the way you would a small child. "I'm real sorry. Your daddy..." she started, and Finch shook his head, giving her the signal to shush.

"Can I get you something?" Doris asked.

"No," Evie answered.

Doris looked at Friedrich and Finch with helplessness. "I can make tea," Friedrich said.

"Tea, now there's a good idea," Doris said with wide eyes."Mama used to make me tea when I was blue."

Friedrich and Doris talked about the best way to make a cup of tea. Friedrich argued that tea should be strong with nothing added while Doris said a cup of tea was crap unless honey and cream were added.

"That is not tea," Friedrich said to her, and Doris smacked her lips in response.

Finch bent down and whispered to Evie, "I'll be right back. I'm going to get Katie."

"Okay," she murmured. She continue to lay on the couch with her eyes open, staring off in the distance.

Friedrich and Doris went to the kitchen to make a pot of tea. Mouse sat next to Evie. He fidgeted and shifted the way he sat, crossing one leg over the other. She could feel him moving on the couch. He was little and didn't weigh much, but his movement was obvious. Doris and Friedrich's voices grew louder from the kitchen, and Evie heard cabinet doors slamming and dishes clanking.

After several minutes, they each came back carrying two cups of tea.

Evie sat up, and Doris moved in front of Friedrich before he had time to hand her his cup of tea. "We figure you can drink the one you want." She handed the cup to Evie, and she cupped it with both hands, blowing on the surface before taking a sip.

She swallowed and said, "Thank you." It was sweet, really sweet, and all that did was remind her of Gray's sweet tooth. He would've loved that tea.

Friedrich stuck his cup in Evie's face and nodded with enthusiasm. "This will make you feel better. It is stronger," he said with confidence.

Evie peered at Mouse with uncertainty. He shrugged, and she traded cups with Friedrich, taking a sip of his strong black tea.

"Thanks," she said and handed him back the cup.

"You want mine, Honey Lamb?" Doris asked hopeful.

"No," she answered and dabbed her wet eyes. "Thank you," she said to them. "I just can't..." and Doris gave her an understanding nod and sat down across from her.

They all three stared at her, and under normal circumstances, Evie would feel compelled to be polite, to make small talk and offer them something to drink or eat. Gray had always preached manners. When company came over, he made sure to wear a clean shirt and offered whatever they had in the kitchen.

"Want me to draw you up a warm bath?" Doris offered, and Evie shook her head no. She tried to give her an appreciative smile.

"I don't have anyone left," Evie said. She felt the weight of what she said, and her knees buckled as she stood up.

Friedrich held her by the arm.

She lightly tapped him on the arm and said, "I'm okay." But she wasn't, and they knew that. "I'm going upstairs. Y'all can stay here tonight if you want. Help yourself to whatever I have," she said and slowly made her way up the steps and went to her room.

***

Katie climbed into Evie's bed and lay down beside her, spooning her while she sobbed into her pillow. Finch stood at the threshold, conflicted, feeling like he was intruding if he stayed but abandoning her if he left. It was a private moment between two best friends, and although he had very strong feelings for Evie, this wasn't his moment to share with her. He gently closed the door and headed down the stairs.

Doris was asleep in Gray's recliner: her mouth was wide open and her arms were folded against her chest. Mouse lay on one side of the couch while Friedrich lay on the other. Mouse snored, and the sound was reminiscent of a tractor or yard equipment. For someone so small, he had the lungs of a horse.

Friedrich woke the moment Finch entered the room. "How is

she?" he whispered to Finch.

"How you would suspect," he answered with a deep breath. He rubbed the back of his neck and exhaled. "This isn't going to be easy on her."

"Death never is, Finch."

"I mean her trying to run this place by herself."

"Certainly people in town can help," Friedrich said.

"I don't know, but it kills me to think we have to leave soon."

"Life has to go on, Finch. It can never stop its place in time just because there is heartache."

Finch patted him on his bicep and said with sarcasm, "You're getting all philosophical on me, Freddy."

He smacked his lips. "You know I don't like that nickname."

"You've called me worse," Finch said.

"That's because you deserved it."

"I can't argue with that."

"I am rarely wrong."

"All right already," Finch said. "You know, you guys don't have to stay here tonight, right?"

"We're not going anywhere. She is your special friend, and we are your family," he said.

***

When Finch lost his mother, several people in the carnival integrated themselves into his family. Without anyone left with a claim to his name, except a father who he rarely saw, friends like Doris, Friedrich, and Mouse were all Finch had.

Finch went through all the stages of grief, focusing more on anger than anything else. At the age of fifteen, when he felt as if the world was already against him, his path became filled with too many obstacles. It was easy to give in and be mad at everything that stood in his way.

But they wouldn't give up on him. His mother was too important to them, and Finch was just like a son, a nephew, a cousin. He was a part of their tight-knit circle.

Friedrich was the one that got through to him, who shared a personal story about his own life and upbringing that resonated with Finch and caused him rethink his anger. Friedrich came from a long line of gypsies who had migrated to Germany a hundred years before the Second World War. Once Hitler was in charge, most of his family was taken to concentration camps and eventually killed. When Finch heard, that at the young age of five, Friedrich lost everything and everyone and eventually overcame it, he knew he could handle his loss.

***

Of the entire group, Finch and Friedrich were the only ones who knew their way around a kitchen. Doris could boil water but that was about it, and Mouse usually ate food that didn't involve the use of a stove. Friedrich wasn't as skilled as Finch in the kitchen, but he knew enough of the basics to fix a decent meal. Finch detested crappy food—the kind he grew up on in the circuit—and he vowed to learn how to cook once he got his own place. Once he had his very own kitchen, he experimented with spices and ingredients and found he had a knack for cooking.

"I gotta do something, I can just stand here and watch y'all," Doris said.

"You can make the coffee," Finch said. He wiped his hands against his apron that read, "Kiss the Cook." He grabbed a nearby spatula and flipped the sausage patties over.

Friedrich whisked eggs together in a mixing bowl, and Doris

opened the pantry door searching for the coffee grounds. "She's got enough cans of food to get us through a nuclear holocaust," she said, pointing to the stacked shelves. They continued with their tasks, unaware of their noise level.

Katie entered the kitchen and inhaled with a smile. "Smells good," she said to them.

Finch turned in her direction and nodded. "Katie, this is Doris, Friedrich, and Mouse."

"Nice to meet y'all," she said to them.

They shook her hand, Friedrich a little too vigorously. Katie tried not to stare at him, but the tattoos caught her eye.

"Is Evie up?" Finch asked, plating the sausage and then scrambling the eggs in the frying pan.

"She is, but she didn't want to get out of bed," Katie answered with a frown.

"She's gotta eat," he said with concern. "Friedrich." He gestured to the spatula, and he took it from Finch's hands. Finch left the room and made his way up the stairs to Evie's room.

The door was slightly ajar, and he knocked before he entered. "Evie," he whispered and walked in.

She lay on her side, facing her bedroom window, the same window that had to be replaced a couple of weeks before. Finch moved around her bed and stooped down in front of her. Her face was red, and her eyes were puffy. "Evie," he said.

She blinked in recognition.

"You gotta eat something," he said. "We've made breakfast."

"I don't want it," she said.

He stroked the top of her head. "You gotta keep up your strength."

She rolled over on her other side. "I'm tired, Finch."

"We'll save you a plate," he said before he left. He stood at the threshold and looked at her. "Try to eat soon." He closed the door and walked down the steps. He knew she was strong, but everybody had their point, the imaginary line where they can't take it anymore and then they lose everything in them.

"She won't eat," he told them with a pained expression.

"Give her time. She'll come around. She has to," Katie said.

"What about all them cows?" Doris asked. "Ain't they got to be fed?"

"Yeah, I would think so. Guess we'll eat breakfast and try our hand at feeding them," he said with an edge of worry. "Katie, do you know anything about feeding cattle?"

"Not really. My dad has people work for him. I've never had much to do with them," she answered.

"We can figure it out. How difficult can it be to feed a cow?" Doris said, and Finch knew that those would be famous last words.

CHAPTER 24

Finch asked Katie to stay inside in case Evie needed her. He didn't want the risk of someone seeing her when it was so close to her leaving for Florida.

He stood inside the barn, next to Friedrich, Doris and Mouse, staring at the two ATVs. "I think we gotta get on these and scare the cattle into the barn." He scratched at his head.

"That's a lot of ground to cover," Doris said, and Mouse checked his watch.

"We have a show in three hours," he said to them. "I think we can get them fed by then."

Finch took a deep breath. "Guess Friedrich and me should get them in there, and you guys should get the food ready."

"What do they eat?" Doris asked.

Finch shrugged. "Grain I suppose. There's gotta be bags of it in the barn."

"Makes sense," she said. "How much do we put out?"

"I don't know." He shook his head. "Guess." Even he could hear the ridiculousness of it. That was like telling someone to fix one of the rides and guess to see if it would work. It'd be playing with fire, and that's exactly what they were doing with those damn cattle.

A flicker of worry crossed her face. "Okay, Honey Lamb. We'll take a shot at it," Doris said.

She and Mouse headed toward the feeding barn. Finch hopped on the ATV and motioned for Friedrich to follow his lead. They started up the engines and shot out of the barn. Finch reached the gate, and he unlatched it for them, remembering the importance of closing it behind him. They drove near the cattle, who seemed unfazed by the racket. Several obstinate heifers refused to budge and continued grazing.

Finch shouted to Friedrich, "We have to yell at them!"

Friedrich nodded and yelled, "Bewegung! Bewegung!"

The heifers continued grazing. "They aren't bilingual!" Finch shouted to him, and then he remembered the word that Evie had used that seemed to make the heifers bust tail. "Sug! Sug!" he yelled, waving his arm in the air. The heifers instantly moved, and Finch saw that that word, whatever it meant, was the secret weapon.

"Say 'Sug,'" he yelled to Friedrich, and they shouted the word at the heifers. The heifers responded with a quick step, moving toward the barn. Once a few fell into line, the rest followed, with only a couple left, either too dumb or too lazy to follow.

Finch drove the ATV, circling around the stubborn heifers and yelled with a growl "Sug!"

Friedrich did the same, and the loner heifers finally relented and moved toward the barn.

Finch breathed hard and heavy, taking just a moment to catch his breath. Friedrich's chest rose and then fell flat; sweat trickled down his forehead. They let the ATVs idle just long enough to get their wind back and then flew down the hill to the feeding barn.

The heifers were crammed in to the barn, lined up against the trough. Doris dragged the bag of grain, grunting from the effort. Friedrich grabbed the bag from her hands and lifted it over his shoulder, pouring the contents into the empty trough.

"Thanks, hon," she shouted over the mooing, hungry heifers.

Finch grabbed another bag and emptied it into the trough. The barn smelled like manure, and Finch felt a squish against his shoes. He looked down and saw he was standing in a pile of cow dung.

He grimaced and then moved forward. He'd have to worry about his shoes later. There was work to do and if those heifers weren't fed soon, they were going to have major problems.

***

The last of the heifers left the barn, and they bottle fed the calves. Mouse checked his watch. "We got less than an hour," he said to Doris and Friedrich. The bottom of his dress trousers was covered in cow dung, and his white shirt was coated in dirt.

Finch squeezed the back of his sore neck and cracked his back. His muscles ached, and it hurt to move. "I don't know how she does this every day," he said with a new admiration for Evie. She was tough and had guts, he knew that about her, but she had stamina too. If she could stand that job day after day, she was stronger than he thought.

They hopped on their ATVs and Mouse sat in front of Finch, while Doris tried to ride on the ATV with Friedrich. "This ain't gonna work, Honey Lamb," she told him. "Mouse you ride with me, and Friedrich will ride with you, Finch."

"Can you drive it?" Finch asked. He remembered his disastrous first time on the three wheeler.

"Sure," she said.

She straddled the machine, and Mouse sat in front of her. She moved forward several feet and then slammed on the brakes. Mouse gripped onto the handles and shot a nervous look. "Just scared is all," she shouted to Friedrich and Finch.

"Go slow!" Finch barked

She barely tapped her foot against the accelerator and moved at a snail's pace. Finch slowed to a near stop so he could stay beside her. "I said slow down, not stop, Granny!" he shouted at her.

She glared at him. "Piss-ant!" She pressed her foot against the accelerator and flew down the hill.

Finch and Friedrich lost sight of them and heard "Yeehaw!" and "Whee!"

After they made their way down hill, they met Doris and Mouse inside of the barn. Their ATV was turned off, and Doris made a face at Finch. "Guess I proved you wrong, didn't I?"

Finch turned his ATV off and decided not to respond.

"I ain't been this sore in a long time. Sure hate to walk back to the carnival," she said.

"I can't believe Kip is opening it today after what happened," Finch said.

"Money is money, Honey Lamb. All he cares about is making it," she said.

"Still. It seems disrespectful if you ask me," he said.

"Kip ain't one to worry about social etiquette," Doris said. "We better head back. You coming with us, or are you gonna stick around here for a while?"

"I'll catch up to you," he said.

Friedrich patted himself on the shoulders. "I think we did good today."

"Not bad for a bunch of carnies, huh?" Doris said.

"It's like those cows were taking pity on us," Mouse said. "Like they knew we didn't know our ass from our heads when it came to them."

"Animals can smell fear. I'm sure they can smell stupidity," Finch said. "Anyway, I think we did a decent job for a bunch of rubes." He smiled at his family.

"Rubes with talent," Doris said.

"She's still laying in bed, Finch," Katie said with a wrinkled brow. "I can't get her to come down and eat."

"She can't stay up there forever," he said. "I have to go to work, but I'll be back later."

"Okay," she answered. "Finch," she said to him on his way out the door. "I've been thinking about this a lot, and there's just no way I can get on that bus now. I can't leave her. We're all we have."

He breathed and peered down and looked up at her with an understanding expression. "I get it, Katie. I get it."

Business at the carnival was slow. Most townies felt it would be rude if they enjoyed themselves on Gray's property right after he had passed, and the only people who did come were those from other towns who didn't have a connection to Gray. Kip didn't understand that in the south, manners were as important as the good Lord's word, and frolicking on the man's land a day after he died was as bad as spitting on him in his coffin.

Word had gotten out quickly, and Cooper was one of the first people to arrive at Gray's house just as Finch had left that morning. Gray was his best friend, and after a major breakdown with Evie, he pulled himself together and resolved to help her get through it all. He knew that's what Gray would have wanted.

Katie begged Cooper to keep her presence there a secret. "Promise me you won't say a word," she said. She heard the rumors. Cooper's yap wasn't known for being Ft. Knox. He often spewed out more than he should.

He promised, swearing to God himself that he wouldn't tell a living soul. "Your daddy doesn't deserve you. Don't you worry, I won't tell anyone," he said. If anything, a small part of him wanted Nate McDaniels to suffer, to sweat it out, pondering where Katie could have gone. On top of that, Cooper just didn't think that he should have the right to tell his daughter what to do with her baby. It was hers, and looking into her desperate hazel eyes, he felt nothing but sympathy for her.

As people from Gray's church and old friends of his made their way to Evie's, intent on paying their respects, Katie hid herself up in the guest room, hating that she couldn't hold her best friend's hand while people expressed their sympathies.

"They can't know you're here, Katie," Evie said.

Evie managed to get out of bed. Katie combed her tangled hair and helped her get dressed. A shower helped but only temporarily. She crawled right back into bed as soon as her company left.

All of the visitors brought food, as was custom in a town like Haines. If someone passed away, especially someone like Gray Barnes whose family had lived there for generations, bringing food was a sign of respect. Casseroles and pies filled Evie's refrigerator. Cooper did most of the talking for her, seeing that she was struggling to sit through the painstaking process of hearing every single person say they were sorry for her loss.

She just wasn't cut out for that role, the new title she had inherited. She didn't want to be fatherless. She didn't want to farm the land by herself. She didn't want to be the lone survivor in the Barnes family, but she was all of those things. What she really wanted was to lay in her bed and forget it ever happened and then wake up, hearing her dad clatter around in the kitchen, causing a bunch of racket and burning toast and making nasty coffee. She wanted to hear him call her by her nickname: Punkin.

Finch knocked on the front door, and Cooper answered it, appraising him skeptically. "You the boy from the carnival?" He looked at him with a stern face, and Finch had to peer up to stare him square in the eye.

"Yes sir," Finch said.

"Gray told me you were sweet on Evie." He held an empty glass Coke bottle in his hand and spit chew into it.

"Can I come in?" he asked, and Cooper motioned for him to come inside. Finch wiped his feet against the welcome mat before entering.

"She's asleep." He moved his head up toward the ceiling. "Cooper Dobbins." He extended his hand, and Finch shook it.

"Finch Mills," he said.

"Gray said you had an odd name," Cooper said with twisted lips and then lowered his head reflectively for a moment. "He was my best friend," he said almost in a whisper.

"I'm sorry," Finch said.

"Ain't your fault, but thanks anyhow," he said and spit into the bottle again. "Katie said you tried saving him but he had already gone to Heaven."

Finch nodded with a frown, thinking back to that moment, and even though it was only the day before, it felt like years ago. "Mind if I go upstairs to check on her?" Finch asked.

"See if you can get her down here to eat. Miss Mable made her favorite: Coke cake. Tell her that and maybe she'll spring out of that bed of hers."

"I'll tell her," Finch said, before he climbed up the steps.

The door was cracked, and Finch pushed it open. The moonlight cast light into the dark room. Evie was curled up into a ball, hugging her pillow.

"Evie," he whispered.

She muttered, "Uh hmm."

He sat beside her on the bed. "Cooper says you haven't eaten."

Her eyes were closed, and she let out a soft sigh. "I don't want to."

"You have to. Someone brought a Coke cake." Finch was trying so hard; he'd drive across the state line if there was something specific she wanted, just so she'd eat.

She opened her eyes. "I'm not hungry," she said.

"Just try."

"Maybe tomorrow." She closed her eyes again and rolled on her side, her back facing him.

"Promise me you'll eat tomorrow," he said and received no response from her. He stared at her, thinking that as she lay there, she looked like a wounded animal. "Night, Evie," he finally said and shut the door behind him. He walked down the stairs, and Katie called after him.

"We're in here," she said, and he stepped into the kitchen.

Cooper and Katie were seated around the breakfast table, eating a slice of key lime pie. "Want some?" Cooper asked. Crumbs fell on his University of South Carolina sweatshirt, and whipped cream covered his bottom lip.

"Sure," Finch said.

Cooper cut him an ample slice and placed it on a plate, sliding it in front of him. Finch took a bite and thought he had reached heaven. People in this town could bake.

"She won't come down?" Katie said.

"No," Finch said in between bites. "She needs to eat."

"And get out of bed," Cooper added with a full mouth. "We're all sad, but having each other sure makes the grieving easier," he added.

Katie furrowed her brows. "Hopefully tomorrow she'll come around."

"Speaking of which, I'll be over first thing to help with the cows," Finch said.

Cooper let out a laugh. "You trying your hand at farming?"

"Trying is an understatement," Finch said. "Those cows just about killed us today."

"Cows aren't as stupid as everyone thinks," Cooper said. "I'll be here tomorrow to help you, or maybe I should say it the other way around." He formed a wry grin.

CHAPTER 25

Finch showed early in the morning, with Doris, Friedrich, Mouse, and even Stoney in tow. "You don't have to help," he told them all, but they plugged their ears and rolled their eyes at such a notion.

"We ain't gonna leave the poor girl stranded," Doris said to him.

Cooper waited for them on the front porch. He paced back and forth and spit chew into his glass Coke bottle. Brown liquid oozed its way toward the bottom.

"See you brought a crew," he said to them as they approached him.

"They wanted to help," Finch said. "This is Doris, Friedrich, Mouse and Stoney." He pointed, and they all smiled at Cooper.

He squinted, staring at them all. "Ain't y'all a peculiar lot," he said. He sighed and spit again. "Well... this oughta be good. Can't complain about free labor, though." He walked down the steps. "Y'all eat yet?"

"Yes," Finch answered for them.

"There's a million casseroles in the fridge if you get hungry," he said.

"Why do they bring food?" Finch asked. "And why casseroles?"

Cooper shrugged, and Doris cut in before he could try and explain. "When my Papa died, people in my town brought pound cakes, pies, casseroles, hams, and fried chicken. It's just what you do, Honey Lamb – to show respect."

Finch let what she said sink in. When his mom died, he wasn't offered a homemade pound cake or any other food for that matter. Sure, people hugged him and whispered their condolences, but his mom's funeral came and went. There wasn't any sense of formality – no offerings of food or visitations from family and friends – just a bunch of carnies standing around her casket at her funeral, and then off they went to go on with their lives.

He thought it was nice, and even though eating that much food is the last thing he would've wanted to do when his mom died, the gesture itself was what mattered.

"We would've done it for you, but we were on the circuit, and there ain't no way to cook," Doris explained.

Finch ignored her last statement. It had been so long, he had no interest in rehashing painful memories. "Is she up?" he asked Cooper.

Cooper blinked and tightened his lips. "Can't get her out of that bed."

Finch took a deep breath and frowned. "She can't keep this up..." his voice trailed off.

"Ain't much we can do to change that girl's mind. I remember one time her mama told her she had to wear a dress on her first day of school. I think she was six or seven." He scratched his stubbly chin, thinking. "She wouldn't budge. Refused to do it, and even after her mama got her in the dress, she had on a pair of jeans underneath." He laughed. "Gray said he had to hold his laugh the entire drive to school."

Finch laughed with him, picturing Evie dressed in a pair of jeans and a dress, pouting about it on her way to school.

"I'm sure she eventually won," Finch said.

"Oh yeah. Her mama fought a good fight, but in the end, she just gave up on her. Evie's always been her daddy's girl, and well, that mama of hers, she..." he hesitated. "I ain't gonna stand here and bad mouth the woman. She's done been gone for a long time." He looked at them all, tilting his head and his mouth was wide open. He stared more intently at Friedrich. "It's time we get a move on." He gestured for them to follow.

***

It didn't take quite as long as the day before. Cooper's experience and knack for dealing with cattle made things much more seamless, and once he started barking orders, they readily followed without question. Everyone had a job to do, and even though they were novices, their heart was in it. Stoney didn't even know the girl, but if Finch liked her a whole lot, as Doris told him he did, then he'd help out. "It just about killed me to hear the poor girl crying like that the night her daddy died," he told her.

Everyone but Finch and Cooper left once the task was done. They walked inside the house and found Katie sitting alone in the kitchen, eating a slice of lemon pound cake. "She won't come down." She shook her head and frowned.

"Let me see what I can do," Finch said and exited the room, heading up the stairs in a hurry.

He knocked on her door and didn't hear a response. He pushed the door open and saw she was in the same position as the night before. The room was dark and gloomy. He made his way to her window to open the curtains, letting the sunshine in, and Evie moaned from the shock of the bright light. She rolled over on her side and faced the door.

"Thought you were awake," he said and stood in front of her. "You can't keep laying here."

She kept her eyes closed.

"Listen to me, Evie Barnes. You've gotta quit wallowing and get up," he said and reached for her arm.

She jerked his hand off of her and glared at him.

"There's the look I know so well," he said.

"Go away, Finch!" she yelled with a cracked voice.

"No." He sat down beside her, and she attempted to roll on her other side but he stopped her. "You can't hide from me. You can't keep hiding from the world."

"I'm not hiding."

"Seems to me you are. Look at you," he said, staring down at her. "Your hair is a mess. You're in the same clothes you wore yesterday morning, and you stink!"

"Shut up and go away, Finch Mills!" He made her so mad, but deep down, she knew he was right.

"I get it, Evie. You know out of everyone, I'm someone who gets it. But, this..." he pointed to her, "has got to stop. You've got a farm to take care of. You've got responsibilities. We can't keep taking care of things for you," he said, feeling his gut wrench. He was talking harshly, but he knew it'd be the only way to get through to her.

"Then don't help. No one asked you to anyway," she said, and he could see her eyes were welling up with tears. If she started crying, he'd lose it right then and there.

"I know I sound like a real jerk," he said in a steady voice. "But you've got to get it together and quit feeling sorry for yourself."

"I lost my dad," she said, sobbing.

"I know," he said in a hushed tone. "But do you think he'd want you to lay around in bed all day?"

She waited to answer him. "No," she finally said, sniffling.

He pulled her up and into him, holding her tight. "Then start by getting up," he whispered.

She backed away from him, staring into his brown eyes. She

swiped a few tears. "It hurts. It hurts so bad, Finch."

"I know," he said, feeling his eyes starting to water. "But you're strong. You can do this. You have to." He kissed her on the cheek, tasting the saltiness of her tears. "If anyone can get through this, you can, Evie."

Her lips quivered and more tears trickled down her blemished face.

He pulled her to him again, allowing her to sob against his chest. He kissed the top of her greasy head of hair, telling her it was going to be all right, that everything was going to be all right.

She eventually let go and wiped at her face, giving him a slight grateful smile, so faint her lips barely curled, but he could see the trace of one, a flicker of her old self shining through.

"How about you take a shower and come down for some food?" he said and nudged her.

She nodded slowly.

"I'll be downstairs." He got up off of the bed and moved to the door.

"Finch," she said, and he turned around, facing her. "Your face isn't stupid at all." Her grin was wider, and a slight gleam shone in her sea blue eyes.

He smiled. "And yours is the smartest I've ever seen."

***

"We can't let all of that food go to waste," Evie said to Finch. "Tell them to come over tonight."

"You sure?" he asked.

"Positive." Feeding the people who helped take care of her farm was the least she could do. They had come over and helped without question, without an expectation of anything in return. They just did it because she needed the help, and Evie thought that even though the people in Haines showed they cared by coming over and offering her their condolences, the carnies showed heart.

Her long blond hair was braided, and she wore a wrinkle-free t-shirt and shorts—the first fresh articles of clothing she had on in days. She was determined to get out of the house and start with the funeral arrangements.

"I wish I could go with you," Katie said.

"If you did, there'd be talk, and then your dad would be up here in no time. I still think you should get on that bus," Evie said to Katie.

"There's no way I'm doing that, so you're better off dropping the subject," she said.

Evie turned her head and spoke to Finch. "Just bring them over tonight. We'll have the table set with a cornucopia of food."

Finch bent down, kissed her on the cheek and tugged on her braid. "Never seen you in one of these before, but I like it. Your face looks really intelligent, although," he smirked and paused, "you do have a Laura Ingalls look about you with it."

She scowled at him and then playfully hit him on his arm. "Get out of here before I change my mind."

***

The dining room table was set – Evie's grandmother's fine china was out, and the table was covered with her white lace table cloth. The table cloth and the china rarely made an appearance, and the last time Evie saw them was several Easters before. A silver candelabra was placed in the center of the table. Katie had spent most of the day cleaning the house to get everything ready, while Cooper went with Evie to the funeral home to plan Gray's funeral.

Cooper dropped Evie off at her house and promised her he'd be back later on for dinner. He had his own life to contend with, and Evie told him he didn't need to help her so much, but he refused to listen to her. She figured it would be the same way once Katie had a child. Being best friends with Katie for most of her life entitled her to a surrogate parenting role with her child. Cooper was like family, and with Gray gone, his role had more foundation to it.

She was amazed at how immaculate the place looked and praised Katie for working so hard. "Katie, you didn't have to," she said. As she trailed up the steps, she ran her fingers across the stair banister and noticed that not one speck of dust clung to it.

Dinner was served late to work around everyone's schedules. Business at the carnival picked back up. As it was with anything else, people remember when it's convenient for them. Gray had passed three days before, and most people thought that was plenty of time to show their respects and start enjoying the rides and spectacles again before the carnival left town.

Everyone had cleaned up for the evening. Friedrich wore a button-down black shirt and jeans. Mouse wore his usual dress slacks with a shirt and tie. He chose a gray plaid fedora for the occasion. Doris plastered on more make-up and didn't alter anything else, wearing the same pink frocks she normally did. Stoney wore the cleanest shirt and jeans he had.

Finch smoothed down his wild mane of hair and tugged on his shirt. Doris insisted that he run to the florist and buy a bouquet of flowers. He never bought a girl flowers before, and the florist recommended red roses, but he knew Evie wasn't a red rose girl. When he thought of her, he saw pink peonies.

"Those are beautiful," she said, taking them from his hands

and admiring them. This was the first time in her life that she had ever received flowers from a man; even her dad never bought her any. After she searched through the buffet and pulled out a glass vase, she carried them both to the kitchen, added water, and then brought them back to the living room. She took the candelabra off of the table, replaced it with the vase of flowers, and gave a satisfactory smile at them.

His face grew warm. "I didn't think you were a rose girl," he said.

"You did just fine, Finch Mills," she said. "Y'all grab your plates and come on back to the kitchen and serve yourselves." She motioned for them to follow her.

The kitchen counters were cluttered with casserole dishes, pie pans, a basket of fried chicken, and cake plates. Even the breakfast table was littered with dishes.

"Well... have at it." Evie swooped her hands forward.

They filled their plates. Cooper in particular towered his food, and Finch waited in the kitchen with Evie while she fixed her plate. "Did things go okay today?" he asked her.

"Yeah. As well as they could," she said. "The visitation is tomorrow, and the funeral is the day after that."

"Anything I can do?" he asked. He took the plate from her hands and carried it as they walked to the dining area.

"No," she said with a grateful smile. "You've done so much already."

***

If anyone had told Evie Barnes a month ago that she'd be sharing a meal with the folks she was surrounded by at that very moment, she'd tell them they were crazy. Trying times brought the strangest allies, the folks you'd never think would have your back, but all of a sudden you find them standing behind you supporting you so you don't fall. These people centered around her table were just that—support—especially Finch.

Evie knew it may not come to anything more than it was. He had to leave soon: his life was hectic, unpredictable, and hers was on a similar path. But her heart was wide open, and there was a special place just for him if he wanted it.

They all left, and Finch lingered, helping Evie and Katie clean the dishes. He couldn't keep his eyes off of Evie. The soap suds floated and found a resting spot on her cheek and the tip of her pointed chin. He gently flicked them off of her, and she gave him a lopsided grin. She could see he was tired and felt selfish for allowing him to do so much for her in the past few days.

Katie let out a loud yawn and stretched. "I'm going to bed." She hugged Evie good night and offered Finch an unexpected side hug before she left the room.

"She likes you," she said.

"Of course she does," he teased, and she shot him a look.

She dried the last dish and sat down at the breakfast table. Finch sat across from her and latched onto her hand, mindlessly stroking the surface.

"She's decided to stay?" Finch said more as a fact than a question.

"Yeah," she answered with a whisper.

"And?" He could read her like he could read his own reflection.

"I feel guilty. She has a chance to start over in Florida and now she'll be holed up here for who knows how long," she admitted. It felt good to get it off of her chest.

"She's choosing to stay, and I don't blame her."

She formed a surprised expression.

"You make sacrifices when you care deeply for someone," he said.

"But I feel like all I'm doing is taking from everyone, and I have nothing to offer except a bunch of damn casseroles."

"What you did for my friends was big, Evie. No one's ever invited us into their home before tonight. Most people take one look at Friedrich or Mouse and run the other way. You look them square in the eye on an equal level and treat them with dignity and respect. That's why they're helping," he said. "'Cause you treat them like they're human beings."

"I didn't know the reason why." She half-shrugged.

"When people are shown a little kindness, they want to pay it back." He squeezed her hand. "You don't notice it because you're not a judgmental person. I remember that first night at the skating rink and those punks were making fun of Mouse, and you kicked them out." He let out a laugh. "That's when I knew." He stared her in the eye.

She fought to catch her breath. "Knew what?" she barely uttered.

"That your face was definitely not stupid," he teased, and Evie's grin fell. "I know what you want me to say, and I'm not that guy, Evie. I don't dish out flowery words and poetic lyrics. You've got enough sense to know how I feel."

Her chin dipped down and her cheeks grew flushed.

"I don't expect those things," she said, still avoiding eye contact. "I know how you feel because I feel the same." She tilted her head up and looked at him, seeing his eyes dance and his lips curl up at her words. "Do you have to go?"

"It's my job, Evie, and I'll come back to visit once I'm done on the circuit."

"No." She shook her head. "Do you... want to stay here tonight?"

She caught him off guard, and he had to catch his breath. "Evie," he struggled to say, hearing the rasping in his own voice. "I don't think..."

"Not for *that*," she said, and a rush of color crept quickly across her face and ears. "Just to sleep." She finally made eye contact, and Finch could see the longing in her eyes. "I..." her voice trailed off. "The visitation is tomorrow," she said with an exhale. "And I..."

He laid his hand on her shoulder, letting her know that he knew what she meant, what she wanted to say. He'd had these same feelings years before. She was lonely, scared, desperate, a mixture of all three. It was one thing to lay in the grass together and stare up at the sky but laying in a bed with her was another. Even if the temptation and the yearning were there, oh man were they there, he'd let those feelings go. If she needed to be held, he'd hold her. If she needed to know he was there, he would be.

"Okay," he said with a faint smile, the kind that said, I'll do it, Evie; I'll do it for you.

She blinked her eyes, thanking him, and stood up to turn off the light. He trailed behind her as they made their way up the stair case, walking as quietly as they could. When they reached her room, Evie stopped and turned to face him. "It's messy," she said to him, apologizing for the shape her room was in.

He wanted to tell her it didn't matter because it didn't. Her life was in shambles—a dirty room wasn't a problem.

She opened the door and turned on the table side lamp, giving the room just enough dim light. "You can sit down if you want," she said, gesturing to the rocking chair.

The rocking chair had been hand crafted by Evie's grandfather years ago. It was made from oak, and had hand carved flowers adorning the top. Evie always admired the chair. Gray gave it to her when her grandfather passed.

Clothes were draped over the arms and piled in the middle of the seat. Finch scooped them to the side and sat down, trying to find a comfortable position, but he couldn't. Somehow his nerves got the best of him, and trying to make his head rule over everything else was like climbing a mountain blindfolded.

She rummaged through her dresser drawer, searching for pajamas. *Please not the lime green night shirt*, he thought.

Evie pulled out an Easter bunny pink night gown, one that was just as gaudy and ugly as the lime green frock he'd fantasized about her in too many times. "I'll be right back." She bundled it under her arms and tip toed out of the room.

He rocked back and forth, taking a look around the room. Evie wasn't much for decorating. A colorful patchwork quilt covered her white iron post bed. The pale pink walls were mostly bare with the exception of a couple of posters: Fleetwood Mac and Blondie. Finch got up from the chair. It continued to rock back and forth as he ambled toward her bookshelf.

The wooden bookshelf was painted white and had a few books on one shelf, most of which were written by Laura Ingalls Wilder. He laughed at the irony, and the image of the first time he saw her popped in his head. He remembered her reaction when he first called her 'Laura Ingalls.'

The rest of the bookshelf was filled with record albums. He combed through her collection, noticing that Evie had alphabetized them all by last name. He rolled his eyes when he reached the C's. "Shaun Cassidy. Really?" he muttered aloud.

He continued rummaging through her collection, noticing Evie's eclectic taste in music. Everything from Fleetwood Mac, The Eagles, to the soundtrack from *Willy Wonka and The Chocolate Factory*, and Miles Davis. He wondered if that's where her pet ox's name came from – the great jazz artist himself. He laughed again.

From what he could see, Evie didn't spend much time in her bedroom like most girls. There wasn't a vanity dresser covered with make-up and perfume or pictures of friends plastered all over the walls. The room was sparse but still managed to have a warm feeling about it. In his opinion, her room felt more like home than his apartment in Florida did.

She entered and closed the door behind her. Her fingers tugged on the fabric of her night gown. This one wasn't sheer. She had made sure of that when she checked herself in the bathroom light. If she couldn't see her floral undies, then Finch couldn't either. Still, when she saw his brown eyes lingering longer than normal, she wondered if she had chosen the wrong thing to wear.

She could wear a potato sack, a hideous burlap sack, and he'd still stare at her like he wanted to eat her for dinner. He came to his senses and looked in the other direction, directly at the bookshelf. "Shaun Cassidy?" he said with a grimace.

"Yeah. I had a crush on him when I was younger," she said, knowing that was less than a year ago.

"Your taste has improved," he teased.

"Maybe not. Maybe it's gotten worse." She picked up her pillow from her bed and threw it at him, hitting him smack dab in the face.

"You just asked for it." He toppled her to the bed and rested on his elbows, gazing down at her. She tried to catch her breath. Not from the heaviness of him. He made sure not to crush her and placed most of his weight on his arms. She could see the muscles bulging from the arms of his t-shirt and a small patch of his chest hair peaked through the neck line.

No. Her breaths were shallow because of his proximity to her. Him being on top of her and in her bed, that made her heart pound against her chest and her breath uneven and ragged.

He sniffed and crinkled his nose. He moved closer to her and sniffed again. "You use the strong stuff, huh?"

"What?" She instantly put her hand over her mouth, feeling self-conscious.

"Listerine. It's the stuff Stoney uses to ward off his cigarette and coffee stench."

"It kills germs," she defended, still covering her mouth. She had spent extra time flossing her teeth, brushing them longer than her standard minute, and finished with Listerine. Just in case they kissed, she wanted to ward off the remnants from dinner that evening.

"It kills everything. How could it not," he said and removed her hand from her mouth. He shifted his body so he was off of her and lay on his side, resting his elbow against the bed. He leaned closer to her, and their parted lips barely touched. "I've never tasted it before, though." He kissed her on the lips, his tongue lightly touching hers. If he got carried away, he'd lose any will power he had, and he swore to himself he'd keep it in his pants.

When he pulled away, he formed a soft smile. "It tastes a lot better than it smells."

She slid from underneath him and sat up against her pillow. "I've never had anyone up here," she admitted.

"And I've never tasted Listerine until tonight. It's a night of firsts for us both," he kidded. He wanted to lighten the mood. The air was thick with sexual tension, and Finch wasn't planning to go there. Not this night. Not until she was ready. He was giving Evie what she needed and that was all.

She folded the covers back and got underneath them, pulling them to her waist. "I'm too tired to think of a comeback." She let out a yawn.

"Hold up." He lay down beside her on top of the quilt. He had decided he wasn't going underneath those covers, nor was he shredding one piece of his clothing. He was even going to keep his shoes on for the love of all things holy. "You mean to tell me you put thought into those comebacks of yours?"

She pursed her lips and stuck her tongue out at him.

He let out a loud laugh and smiled.

"Good night, Finch," she said and turned off the light. She lay on her side, her back facing him. "Finch?" she said.

"Yeah?"

"How come you quit knife throwing?"

The room was silent, and she waited for him to respond.

"Finch?"

"The most random questions pop out of that mouth of yours," he said and paused for a moment. She could hear him breathing. "It reminded me too much of my mom, and it wasn't the same without her. I didn't enjoy it anymore."

"Oh," she answered reflectively. "How'd she die?"

She could hear him scratching the stubble on his chin. "The doctor said it was encephalitis. She got real sick all of a sudden, and there wasn't anything that could be done," he said, and the faint sounds of pain lingered in his statement. "You would've liked her."

She rolled over on her side, facing him, and searched for his hand. She laced her fingers in his, and said, "I know I would have. Thanks for staying with me tonight. It means a lot to me."

"Whatever you need, Evie." He wrapped his arms around her, knowing that for a light sleeper, he may just sleep soundly that night.

CHAPTER 26

A line wrapped around the outside of the funeral home and reached all the way to the paved brick sidewalk that faced Main Street. People had arrived early, as was custom, so they could pay their respects to Evie.

Most stood in front of Gray's casket, commenting on how good he looked, or what a great job the funeral director did. Evie never understood why people said such things. Dead was dead, and the person never looked good in that condition. Globs of make-up and a nice dress or suit didn't make a world of a difference in her opinion.

Others told jokes, stories about Gray that tickled their funny bones, and that brought a smile to Evie's face when she heard them. She shook so many hands that day, her wrist was limp and her voice cracked when she talked. She had uttered "thank you" too many times to count.

There were some who got caught up in the moment, and their tears wouldn't hold back. She tried to maintain her decorum, but sometimes it was just too much. Seeing grown men cry just about did her in.

Finch sat in the front pew for the entire two hours. Most of the carnies came by, paying their respects, tipping their hats in front of Gray's casket and muttering a few words to Evie. Most were general statements: a few who had met Gray told her how kind her daddy was, and what a smart businessman he was. She was thankful for their words.

Nate McDaniels and his wife, Julia, made an appearance. Of

all the hypocritical things, Evie thought, for him to show up at her daddy's visitation, but she knew he was more concerned about appearances. People from Haines shot him dirty looks and muttered things under their breaths. "He ain't here to offer his sympathy," they said with a scowl. "Sauntering in here like he and Gray were friends," they whispered. "He wouldn't have offered Gray a drink of water if his life depended on it," another said. They knew. They knew the man all too well. The McDaniels men were all the same.

As much as Evie wanted to spit on her hand before she shook his, her daddy brought her up better than that, and she wouldn't disrespect him at his own visitation. She unwillingly shook hands with Nate and received a faint hug from Katie's mom, whom Evie never had any qualms with. She just didn't have much respect for the weak woman.

He kept his comments to himself; Evie was thankful for that. She was likely to slug him if he said the wrong thing. The only thing he managed to ask was, "Have you heard from my Katie?" Evie shook her head no, and thought he had some nerve asking her about "his" Katie, but that was Nate McDaniels for you. At least he didn't put on the pretense that he was sorry about her daddy, because she knew deep down he couldn't care less. "We're real sorry for your loss," Julia added, and Evie acknowledged her with a quick nod and a faint smile. Nate yanked her by the arm and moved on.

The last of the line trickled to nothing, and Finch and Cooper were the only two that remained. Evie moved away from that dreadful casket and sat down next to Finch on the front pew. She took a hold of his hand and squeezed. "You didn't have to stay," she said.

"I'll drive you home," he replied, ignoring her last statement. As if he wouldn't stay. He'd spend the night on the pew if she wanted him to.

Evie looked up at Cooper and smiled. "I've never seen you in a real shirt before, Coop." He was wearing a white button down shirt tucked into a pair of dark Wranglers. His farmer's tan was prevalent, with a white strip showing where his cap normally was.

"It ain't nothing," he said, smoothing the wrinkles. "Y'all need a lift?"

"Finch is taking me home," she answered.

"I'll see you tomorrow then," he said. "They done a real good job on your daddy," he added quietly before he left the two of them alone.

"You mind waiting while I talk to him for a second?" Evie asked.

"Take all the time you need," Finch said. "You want me to wait outside?"

"No." She got up and walked to the open casket and whispered into it, peering down at her father. Finch couldn't hear what she was saying, nor did he want to. This was her time, and he felt like he was intruding being there. After a few minutes, she headed back to Finch, wiping a few tears from her eyes, and told him she was ready to leave.

***

The funeral was just as crowded as the visitation. People from Haines and neighboring towns came to pay their last respects. Evie met plenty of strangers, folks who told her how kind her daddy was and what he meant to them. "My husband died. He and your daddy went to school together. I was barely able to feed my kids, and we were fixin' to lose our house. Your daddy sold one of his cows and gave me the money. It was enough to get me on my feet. I told him I'd pay him back and he wouldn't hear of it," the older woman said. She squeezed Evie's hand and smiled. "He did it without expecting something in return. He said to me, 'You just repay it someone else.' And that's what I did."

Evie met others with similar stories. She never knew. Gray wasn't the type to boast, and she never thought to ask where some of the money went.

She counted her blessings, that the world had been kind enough to grace her with a father who had a heart of gold. But eighteen years didn't feel like enough time, because from the tales she heard that day, there were so many things about her father that she didn't know. And she wondered if she had known these things earlier, would she had clung to him because a man that good can't be ignored. A man with those qualities was like the sun on a cloudy day. But Evie realized that in life, most people don't come to their senses about a loved one until they're gone. Evie often heard Gray boast about his daddy, her grandfather, saying what a great man he was, and when he was alive, Gray didn't flock to him either.

"Thank you," she uttered to them. She was thankful to know that he touched so many lives and not just her own.

***

Finch stayed over for the night again. Evie asked him to, and he couldn't say no. He didn't want to say no, anyway. When he lay next to her, he slept like a log, and she felt so good to spoon with. Evie liked knowing he was there laying next to her. She liked the feel of his arms wrapped around her.

Katie raised an eyebrow when she saw Finch coming down the stairs, but Evie just shook her head and told her, "It isn't what you think."

Katie smirked. "Maybe not for long. Adam and Eve eventually ate the fruit, Evie. Y'all will too."

"He's leaving in less than a week," she said.

"That's just more time for y'all to skirt around the issue. I'd eat *that* fruit if it were offered to me," she said with a grin.

"We all know where that got you," she teased.

Katie playfully knuckled her on the arm. "Very funny."

"Ow. That hurt," Evie grimaced.

"Serves you right. I'm just saying if I were sleeping next to Mister Hunkster, I wouldn't be coming out of my bedroom so early in the morning."

"Mister Hunkster?" Evie repeated. "Where'd you come up with that?"

Katie pointed to her temple. "Right here. He's a hunk, dummy."

"Shush," Evie said to her as Finch entered the room, and the room was silent.

"That's not obvious or anything," Finch said with a laugh.

Evie grew quiet, and Katie said, "She's not real subtle sometimes. We were just talking about you." She grinned at Evie sardonically.

Evie kicked her under the breakfast table. Katie winced and then kicked her in return.

"Oh yeah. What were you saying?" Finch asked, and they both looked at him.

"Nothing much, really," Katie said.

"Okay," Finch said, knowing to leave well enough alone. Some things were better not broached, especially when it involved two women.

Finch checked his watch. "I gotta go," he said. He had work to do at the carnival, and Evie seemed to have things under control with the cows. "Walk me out," he said to her, pulling on her hand. "Please." Manners were important to Evie. Finch had learned pretty quickly that adding a few "pleases" and "thank yous" made a world of a difference with her.

She got up and followed him out the front door. They stood on the front porch. The sun had just risen, and there was still dew on the ground. Tripod hobbled to Finch and wagged his tail. Finch bent over and patted him on the head, cooing at him. Evie just shook her head in disbelief.

"What?" he asked her.

"I've had that dog half my life, and he is never *that* happy to see me. Animals like you," she said.

"Feed him some bacon, and he'll change his mind," he said.

"You give him bacon?"

"Yep," Finch said with a smile.

"No wonder." She laughed. "Here I thought something was wrong with me."

"Oh there's still something wrong with you," he said. He grabbed a handful of her hair and wrapped it around her ear until her ear was completely covered in her honey locks.

"Yeah," she said. "I've got the worst taste in guys."

"That was good and quick too," he praised her. "I'm impressed." He placed his hand under his chin and appraised her.

Before she could utter a weak comeback, he brought her to him and wrapped his arms around her. She could feel the warmth of him and took a whiff, smelling Pert shampoo and   cologne. She inched closer, kissing the part of his shirt where his heart was, feeling the soft texture of cotton and the rapidity of his heartbeat as it pulsated against her parted lips.

She stared up at him, and he leaned down to kiss her. And for that moment he forget where he was and where he was supposed to be, and how he was supposed to act, and gave into her.

CHAPTER 27

The fire and Gray's death had impacted business for a few days, but things were improving. Most townies were intent on getting their cheap thrill before the week was over. Locals from neighboring towns wanted a taste of the fun and were spending their money faster than it took them to earn it.

As the sun began to move its way down the afternoon sky, Finch found a shade tree and plopped down under it ready for a nap. Kip wouldn't notice – he was too busy counting his stack of bills and couldn't care less about Finch's whereabouts. The two had an ugly exchange of words after Gray died. Finch told him he was a heartless dick for opening the carnival the day after Gray's death and then proceeded to use a few more expletives to prove his point.

Finch was at a point where he didn't care anymore anyway. He had no passion for the job, and if Kip wanted to fire him, then so be it. His insecure side told him he'd struggle to find a job, and he should thank his lucky stars he had a weekly paycheck. Evie would tell him he was being a stupid head—another term she used a lot—for doubting himself. Finch marveled at her ability to find so many different ways to use the word "stupid."

He closed his eyes and pictured her – in her lime green night shirt and wearing those cowboy boots of hers. He swooped the thought to the side and tried to fall asleep.

***

"Finch! Finch!" Friedrich shook Finch's shoulders, jostling him awake.

Finch's eyes shot open.

"You have to come now. There's been an accident," he said,

yanking Finch off of the ground.

"What happened?" Finch asked, chasing Friedrich as he ran through the carnival. Friedrich didn't hear him, or chose not to respond. "Is it Evie?" he yelled. "Did something happen to Evie?" He couldn't stand the deafening silence.

An ambulance siren blared in the distance, and Finch looked at Friedrich with a horrified expression.

"No," Friedrich answered. "No, it's not her."

Finch breathed a sigh of relief. For that brief moment, he felt okay.

Crowds stood by helplessly as paramedics rushed to the scene. Finch watched as they worked to pull a man, woman and little boy out of a small carriage. He placed his hand over his mouth and looked at Friedrich with disbelief. The carriage was separated from the cluster of other carriages and no longer connected to the central beam of the ride. It was smashed into a metal gate, damaged beyond repair.

Their clothes were covered in blood; the little boy's Star Wars t-shirt was more red than blue, and he wailed in pain. "Mommy," he cried over and over again, and Finch's heart went out to him. The mother tried to soothe her son, but her eyes kept closing, and then she fell against her husband's shoulder and passed out.

The paramedics lay each of them on a gurney. The little boy was the worst off. His leg and arm were broken, and even someone as strong as Finch couldn't stomach the sight of that. He felt the sensation to vomit and tried to catch his breath. Never in all of his years of working on the circuit had he seen an accident like this.

On his watch, there had only been one other accident at Kip's carnival. A seatbelt malfunction that caused more of a scare than anything else. No one was really hurt – just a few scrapes and raised pulses, but no blood was shed. It was tame, child's play compared to this.

"How?" he said in a low voice to Friedrich.

Friedrich shook his head. "I don't know," he answered. "I was coming back from my show, and the next thing I know, that carriage flew up in the air and landed over there..." He placed his palm against his face and sighed. "This is awful."

"That thing was bolted on tight. I checked it this morning," he said. "I swear I did." He drew in a deep breath. His eyes darted back and forth, focusing on the lone carriage, and then back at the ride.

"I did," he repeated.

Friedrich placed his hand on Finch's shoulder and gave him a tight squeeze. "I know." He blinked. "I know."

They watched helplessly as two ambulances sped off of the property. Carnies walked around in a daze, staring at the scene in disbelief. Several townies lingered and continued to gawk at the accident, talking amongst themselves. "How could this happen?" they whispered. "I knew we shouldn't have come here," they said.

Friedrich and Finch were too stunned to move. Doris made her way to them and wrapped her arms around Friedrich's waist, speaking in a low voice to him. For once Finch couldn't hear her. Whatever she was saying to him, it was between the two of them only. Mouse took off his fedora, bowed his head and said a silent prayer.

Several police cars arrived. Their sirens echoed into the wind. All of the rides had been shut down when the tragedy occurred. No one knew what to do or what to say. They never had to deal with this type of accident and sought guidance from Kip for what to do. He offered no consolation, but paced the midway, muttering things to himself and waving his arms up in the air in a bout of frustration.

Time passed, and police officers cordoned off the area with yellow caution tape and searched for evidence in the enclosed area—something to tell them how this tragedy happened.

Kip approached Finch and said, "The sheriff is here, and he wants to have a word with you." He gulped and took a shallow breath. Finch could read Kip's face, and it told him this wasn't going to be an informal chit-chat.

Finch pointed to himself. "With me?"

"Yeah," Kip said with a frown.

Finch rubbed the back of his neck and gave Friedrich, Doris and Mouse a strange look.

"What's he want to talk to Finch for? He doesn't have anything to do with this," Doris said.

Kip didn't reply and gestured for Finch to follow him to his office. Finch passed by shocked townies and carnies and could feel their eyes on him. A few turned their lips down and scowled. Fingers were going to be pointed. Someone had to be blamed. This wasn't an act of God, and Finch had that sinking feeling he was the target.

The sheriff sat at Kip's desk, his deputy beside him. For a town as small as Haines, Finch was amazed at the number of police officers that were on the force. When he thought of towns that size, he pictured Andy Griffith and Don Knots.

The hair above Ford's thin lips was a poor excuse for a mustache. A small patch of black hair barely covered the area, and as sparse as it was, it looked more like a Hitler mustache. *Strike one for that guy*, Finch thought. Any one with an decent IQ would not replicate anything that had to do with Hitler.

His dark brown hair was cut short in an unflattering crew cut style. He had beady little brown eyes, and he had an obvious dandruff problem. White flakes adorned his shoulders. A dark blue police uniform was the man's worst enemy.

"Sit down," he said to Finch and spoke with a subtle lisp. It wasn't a barking order, but it wasn't an invitation either. He didn't introduce himself, nor did he offer to shake Finch's hand.

Finch did as he was told.

"Mr. Kierkin told me you're the one responsible for fixing the rides," he said. The "s" was especially prominent when he spoke. He narrowed his eyes to Finch.

"Yes."

"And did you inspect the scrambler ride today?"

"Once this morning and then later this afternoon."

"Where were you at four o'clock today?" he asked incredulously. He folded his hands and tapped his fingers against his chin. His fingernails needed to be cut and dirt could be seen in them.

"I was taking a nap."

"A nap?" he said with a smirk. "So you often sleep on the job?" He snickered and looked at his deputy. "Can you imagine us napping on the job?"

The deputy shook his head in disbelief and laughed along with him.

Finch thought it was like those lame interrogation scenes in the movies. Only no one was playing "good cop" in this instance. This guy was a bad cop, or at least an idiot; he could tell that just by looking at him.

"It's not uncommon for me to take a nap 'cause I work all hours of the day, and I'm not needed all the time," Finch said and turned to Kip for help. Kip cleared his throat and stayed silent. *Of all the times for Kip to lose his balls*, Finch thought.

"We're not needed all the time, either, but we don't nap when it's quiet at the station." He searched through his note pad and read carefully, then jotted something down. "A few witnesses say they saw you near the ride this afternoon. Conveniently right before the accident." He raised an eyebrow and waited for an answer.

"I told you I checked on the ride this afternoon before I took a nap," Finch said with exasperation.

"You're the only one that can fix the rides? Ain't that right, Mr. Kierkin?" Everyone turned to Kip, waiting for his response.

Kip cleared his throat again and fidgeted. "Yes," he finally answered.

Finch's face became crestfallen, and he tried to recover from the feeling of being kicked in the gut.

"I think it's best if we finish our questioning down at the station," the sheriff said.

***

He was escorted to the police cruiser. They rough handled him and shoved him into the back seat like a common criminal. All of the windows were rolled up. He sat in the car for fifteen minutes before they started up the engine. He caught a hint of a breeze from the driver's side window but not enough to cool him off. By the time Finch reached the station, he was drenched and on the verge of passing out.

They dragged him out of the car, using more force than necessary. Finch was used to disrespect. When they discovered he was a carny, the stigma that he was a derelict of society automatically stuck to him like glue. But in all of his twenty-two years of life, he had never been treated like he was a criminal.

He knew better than to say anything. If he uttered one word of disgust about the way they were treating him, they would do it again, only worse. He couldn't let them win. He refused to.

He sat in a cold, windowless room for a very long time. The colder the room got, the more he shivered. They hadn't handcuffed him. They followed the law where that was concerned, but they were testing him.

Another hour passed, and Finch paced the room back and forth, the concrete walls closed in on him. If he was claustrophobic, he'd be having a panic attack right about then.

But he wasn't, and the longer he was stuck in that confining room, the angrier he became. They had nothing on him. Someone seeing him by the ride didn't mean he broke the ride, and he wondered, *what the hell happened and who the hell did mess with it?* It had to be someone in the carnival, that much he knew.

The door opened, and the sheriff sauntered in holding a cup of water. He took a long hard sip and wiped his wet lips. Finch fought the thirst. He could feel the dryness in the back of his throat, and he swallowed, savoring what little bit of saliva he had left in him.

Sheriff Ford sat across from him and tapped his fingers against the scuffed wooden table. "You said you were napping?"

"Yes," Finch croaked.

He licked his lips and tapped his fingers again. Finch watched his beady eyes dart back and forth. He didn't have enough evidence. Finch knew it was only a matter of time until they had to let him go.

"When did you say you checked the ride?"

"It was in the afternoon, around two o'clock I think," Finch said with uncertainty. He never paid much attention to what time he checked the rides.

"Sure it wasn't four o'clock?"

"Yeah. I'm sure," Finch said with irritation.

"Don't get smart with me boy," he said and clenched his jaw. "We can keep you here all night if we want."

Finch sighed heavily.

The sheriff got up and left the room. Within a minute, one of the deputies entered and man handled Finch, jerking him from the chair. "Maybe spending some time in a jail cell will help you learn some respect," the deputy said.

CHAPTER 28

He sat on a cold concrete bench. He tried to lay down, but it was too narrow and not made for a guy of his build, or any build for that matter – even Evie would've struggled to lay on it. It was the only holding cell in the station, and he was the only person occupying it. Every now and again, a deputy came back there, stared at him for a few seconds, tapped his night stick on the jail cell bars, and then went back in the direction from which he came.

By this time, his throat was aching, and he was seriously parched. He needed something to drink, any liquid would suffice. He checked his watch. It was eight o'clock at night, and he wasn't going anywhere. He leaned back against the wall, pulled his knees up to his chest and let out a deep sigh. And then he dozed off.

Shouting woke him. He knew that voice all too well.

"You don't have any evidence!" she shouted.

He laughed and smiled to himself, thanking his lucky stars that she had come into his life.

A few more harsh phrases were said, along with a few curse word infused threats, and before Finch could blink, the door opened and a deputy walked his way holding a set of keys. He unlocked the door and motioned for Finch to get up and get out. Finch stood up and strolled down the corridor toward the door. At last. Freedom.

She wasn't alone. Stoney, Mouse, Doris, Friedrich, Cooper, and a man Finch had never seen before were huddled together in the station. Evie ran to Finch and hugged him. "You okay?" she asked. She let go and appraised him with a concerned face. "You look really bad."

"Just thirsty," he said; his voice was scratchy.

She glared at the sheriff and his deputies, and stepped over to the vending machine, dropping in one quarter and one dime to buy Finch a drink. Out came a bottle of Coke. She handed it to him, and said, "Here." She scowled at the sheriff.

Finch popped the cap off using the opener built into the machine and then guzzled the drink all in one vigorous swig.

"Finch, this is Spence Dobbins, Cooper's brother. He's an attorney," she said, introducing the man who faintly resembled Cooper.

Spence shook Finch's hand and smiled. Spence and Cooper had the same crooked grin, but not the same fashion sense. Spence was neat and polished; he wore a button down shirt with khaki pants. Cooper's choice for the evening was a tattered pair of sweat pants and a faded college t-shirt.

"Nice to meet you," Finch said.

"You too. Evie's told me all about you," he said. His southern accent was less prominent than Cooper's. He turned his attention to Sheriff Ford and said, "Well, if that will be all, I'd like to take my client home."

Ford gave a reluctant nod and pursed his lips. "That's all, Spence." The sheriff spit into his coffee mug and frowned.

"Thanks, Winton," Spence said with sarcasm. He gestured for them to follow him outside.

Evie took one last look at the sheriff and shook her head. Finch could tell she was about to give him a piece of her mind, and he took her by the hand and muttered under his breath, "Evie," he warned.

She held back and walked outside with the group. They stood in front of their trucks that littered the street. Spence's was the only new one out of the bunch.

"Honey Lamb, we were spitting fire at Kip for not having the balls to stand up for you," Doris said to Finch. "Like this is your fault."

Friedrich and Mouse nodded in agreement with her.

"Kip's a pussy," Stoney said. "Sorry," he said to Evie for his language.

"It was someone in the carnival," Finch said. "I had a lot of time to think in there, and it wouldn't make sense otherwise."

"But who?" Evie interrupted. "Who would be that mean?"

"People surprise you, Evie. That's why I was always telling you to let me walk with you at night. There's a lot of carnies that Kip hires who I wouldn't want to share a truck ride with," he said.

"I agree with you, Finch. It most likely was someone in your carnival, and if I were you all, I'd pay close attention and try and figure out who it is before you get to the next town," Spence said.

"Is that family all right?" Finch asked him.

"They're fine. The little boy has some broken bones, but considering the severity of what that accident could've been, they walked away relatively unscathed," he said.

"That's good. When I saw that boy..." Finch said with a wrinkled brow.

"Finch, it was unfortunate to meet you under these circumstances. You're free to leave town. The Sheriff knows he doesn't have enough evidence to arrest you," Spence said.

"We've got another week here," Finch replied.

Doris shook her head. "Maybe not, Honey Lamb. Kip's wavering about moving on. With what happened, he's worried ain't no one gonna come near the carnival now."

He looked at Evie. By the frown on her face, he could tell she had already thought of this.

"Well, if there's nothing else you need from me, I'm going home. Betsy has a chicken pot pie waiting for me," Spence said and rubbed his stomach.

"Think she'd want to share some of it with her brother-in-law?" Cooper asked.

"Yeah, why not, Coop," he said. He shook all of their hands and got in his truck.

Cooper turned to Evie, and she hugged him. "Thank you," she said.

"Ain't nothin'," he said and faced Finch. "You be careful out there. If you're right, it ain't safe for y'all. Just know you got some real friends here." He offered his hand, and Finch shook it.

"Thank you," Finch said.

Cooper hopped in his truck and drove off.

"I've got plenty of left overs if y'all are hungry. I know I am," Evie said. She hadn't eaten in several hours. Once she heard from Friedrich that they had taken Finch to the station, she called Cooper to see if Spence could help. "We'll have ourselves a real feast," she said.

"A feast sounds great. I know I'm starving," Doris said.

"I am famished," Friedrich agreed.

"Me too," Mouse chimed in.

"I could eat," Stoney said.

"Well, then, I guess it's settled. Y'all come on," Evie said with a laugh. She laced her fingers in Finch's. "You ride with me."

***

The radio played 1950s tunes, and a strong whoosh of air blew through the truck. The windows were rolled all the way down, and the cool outside air, along with the oscillating fan, made things comfortable.

"Evie, what you did, that was..." he struggled for words and finally settled on, "incredible."

"I didn't do anything really. Spence scared the shit out of the sheriff with all his legal jargon." She laughed. "Daddy didn't like Sheriff Ford. He said he had no scruples. I always thought it was 'cause he was Mr. McDaniels' cousin. Now I know why. Daddy was no dummy when it came to people."

"Are all the men dicks in Katie's family?"

"Yep. That's why she's got bad taste when it comes to men. I had a good father, and it shows," she said, and Finch appreciated the implied compliment. A girl like Evie thought he was worthy of her.

"She's just like my mother when it comes to choosing a guy," he said with a hint of sadness. "You'll have to make sure she doesn't get wrapped up in the first guy that shows her some attention after her baby is born."

"I know," Evie said quietly. "How'd you turn out to be such a good guy? I mean, you never had a father figure."

"I've had plenty of them, they're just not my biological father." He thought of Friedrich, Mouse, Stoney, and Rolf. "And, there's a time in a man's life when he has to decide if he's gonna be a man," he said. "I wasn't going to let the faults of others dictate the kind of person I wanted to be. It's like that with your mom, right?" He was delving deeper.

"Yeah," Evie answered honestly. "But I wasn't as perceptive as you. It took me a while to figure that out." She paused for a moment. "What's going to happen?"

He knew what she meant – what was going to happen between them. "I don't know," he answered her honestly.

"Me neither, and that worries me," she said and bit on her lip.

***

Evie brought down her Miles Davis record album and put it on the record player. Davis' jazz instrumentals filled the room as they sat around the dining room table. Their plates were full, and they continued to stuff themselves, piling their plates with seconds and thirds late into the night. It was well after midnight by the time they got up to leave. She would miss them when they left: Finch was a given, but Doris, Friedrich, Mouse, and even Stoney, had a tug on her heart, and knowing that they'd be gone made her feel the loss. Even though she had only known them for a short time, she felt like they were a part of her family—a family that she wished she could spend the holidays with. She'd cook Christmas dinner and decorate the living room with the largest tree she could find. She would stuff gifts under the tree for each one of them, and they would reminisce about old times. They would be the family she hadn't been a part of since she was a very young girl.

"Stay tonight," Evie whispered to Finch.

"Okay," he agreed, happy that she asked him to.

Evie gave them all a tight hug, even Stoney, who was resistant to the idea.

"Thought you weren't much for hugging?" Katie said to her.

She half-shrugged. "I regret that I never hugged Daddy enough, and I don't want to feel that way the rest of my life."

"Very profound, Eves," she said. "Freud would be proud."

***

It was early in the morning, and Finch and Evie lay in her bed.

Neither of them were tired, and both had the same intention: to talk themselves to sleep. It was easy for Evie. She had a million random questions stored that she'd been dying to ask Finch.

"If you could be any animal what would you be?" she asked.

He laughed, and said, "You and your questions. I guess I'd be a bird. I could fly anywhere I wanted, and I wouldn't have a lot of natural enemies. What about you?"

"I don't know," she said.

"But you asked the question."

She thought for a moment. "Probably a lion. They kick butt, and everyone is scared of them," she said.

"And they sleep all the time," he added. "You wouldn't want to be a cow?" he teased.

"Hell no," she said emphatically. "All they do is poop, pee, and eat," she said.

"Like most animals," he kidded and took a hold of her hand. He wanted to hug her, give her a solid noogie, and kiss her on the lips.

"What makes you laugh?" she asked him.

"That's easy," he said. "You."

"Why? I'm not funny."

"Sure you are. You just don't know it." He pinched the tip of her nose. "What makes you laugh?"

"Everything, really. My dad used to make me laugh," she said in a serious tone and was silent for a moment. "But I haven't laughed as hard as I did when when you fell onto that pile of shit." She giggled.

"Yeah. Yeah. I gave you a good laugh that night. Okay, next question."

"What makes you cry?" she asked.

"Hmm..." he pondered for a moment. "I don't cry a lot, Evie."

"Because you're a guy? That's stupid."

"No, I try not to let things affect me," he said and rubbed his chin. "I cried when Mom died, when some idiot townie beat Mouse to a pulp," he shuddered and added, "and when your dad died."

"My dad? You didn't really know him."

"It wasn't because of him; it was because of you," he explained. "I knew exactly what you were going through, and there wasn't anything I could do to make your pain go away," he admitted.

Evie leaned forward and kissed him on the corner of his mouth, feeling his pointed hairs against her lips, and she knew she would cherish the meaning behind that statement for the rest of her life.

CHAPTER 29

The sun rose too early, or it seemed that way to Finch and Evie. They had tried to stay awake as long as they could, but they had only gotten a couple of hours of sleep, Evie more than Finch.

"Morning," Evie said, smiling. Finch's chocolate tresses were tussled, and he gave her a tired grin.

He waved his hand in front of his face. A shadow of stubble hinted above his lips and on his chin. "Pew," he said with a scrunched face.

Evie brought her hand up to her mouth.

"I just got a whiff of manure," he said.

Evie quickly removed her hand from her face. Her bedroom window was wide open, and the echoes of cows mooing pervaded the room.

"You are on a farm, you know?" She laughed at him as he plugged his nose.

"How do you stand it?" he said in a nasally tone.

"After a while you stop smelling it," she said. She sat up in bed and yawned. It was still dawn, and the sky was various shades of orange overlapping each other.

He rolled on his side and lay his head on her stomach, hearing the sounds of hunger gurgling toward the surface. "There's a monster in there."

"I bet yours sounds the same," she said, pushing him off of her.

He lay on his back with his head propped against a pillow and pointed to his stomach. "No way. See for yourself," he said with confidence.

Evie glared at him and scooted down, laying her head on his

stomach, feeling the flatness of it against her ear and cheek. She peeked up at him, and he gave her a self-contented look. "See," he said. "No monster."

She twisted her lips and shot him a dirty look. He chuckled quietly and played with her hair. "I'm gonna miss that look."

She frowned at his words.

"And...I'd love to kiss you right now, but between the manure and our garlic breaths, it wouldn't be very romantic," he said.

"Well, maybe we should brush our teeth and use some Listerine so we can spend the next half hour making out?" She raised an eyebrow and gave him an impish grin.

He jumped out of bed in a hurry and pulled her up, taking a hold of her hand. "It takes a minute to brush our teeth and gargle with mouthwash. That gives us twenty-nine minutes. Come on."

Evie giggled as she followed him to the bathroom.

***

As he headed back to the carnival, he whistled and then inwardly ridiculed himself for it. Serial killers whistled, he thought. But he was so happy and wondered how he could feel this way when he was going to have to say goodbye to Evie in a week. After a twenty-nine minute make-out session that resulted in a shirt being removed (Finch's), he was feeling the aftermath of it. His cheeks were still red, and he felt warm, even though the sun's rays hadn't had their impact yet.

Finch was an expert when it came to smells, and he was just as keen with voices. He could hear someone and know exactly who they were even if he was blindfolded. To him, Evie's voice was like a sultry melody that shouted with joy one moment and then teased him relentlessly with an array of seducing pitches the next.

He continued his way through the maze of tents and slowed his pace when he heard a muffled conversation. As he moved closer, he heard a deep-pitched twangy voice that instantly brought him back to the night he went out for dinner with Evie. The tone of his voice was all too familiar. Then, a heavily accented Russian spoke, and a cold chill instantly ran up Finch's spine.

He peered around the corner of the tent. His instincts were right; they were never wrong anyway. Like when he just knew about his mother's ex-boyfriend Don. Don was too much charm – a red flag for Finch. No one in the world was that nice, and when he found his mom with empty pockets and a bloodied lip, he wasn't surprised. There had been a long line of "Don's" in Finch's mother's short-lived life.

"That accident didn't scare enough people. I want this carnival gone, and I don't care what you have to do to make that happen," Nate McDaniels said to Dmitri.

Dmitri cowered and frowned. "I'm not doing anything else. That boy was hurt. He could've been killed. I just won't," he cried.

"You can and you will," Nate threatened. "If you and that wife of yours want my baby, you'll do it! I need you to come through or our deal is off," he demanded. "I don't care what you've got to do. Just make sure that no one wants to come to this carnival or else you'll never get your hands on my baby!" Nate left in a huff.

Finch couldn't move, and his hands shook. He gritted his teeth and tried to see straight, but all he could see was red. He breathed heavy and hard and tried to calm himself, to get his anger in check, but all he wanted to do was storm over to Dmitri and punch him square in his jaw. Once for hurting that kid. Twice for the shit he put him through. And a third time for screwing with Evie's money.

She was banking on profit from the carnival, and that accident could ruin things.

"Fucking traitor," he muttered. Before he took a step forward, he watched Dmitri shake violently as he slumped to the ground and cried. A moment of sympathy overcame Finch, and he stopped himself from doing something he knew he'd regret later. It took him months to overcome the guilt he had when he fought Tony Marello, all because Tony called his mom a slut. Finch knew it was true—she slept with anyone who would tell her he loved her—but hearing it from some snot-nosed kid pissed him off, and he swung violently at Tony, breaking his nose and jaw. It was a moment of triumph followed by months of regret. He didn't want to repeat the same mistake now. He spun on his heels and turned in the other direction, heading toward Friedrich's tent.

***

After he told Friedrich what he saw and heard, Friedrich decided they needed to confront Dmitri. "We must discover his reasoning before we do anything," Friedrich said.

Dmitri was planted in the same spot. His long, boney legs were bent, and his face was buried in his hands.

"Dmitri," Friedrich said in a stern tone.

Dmitri looked up at Finch. His pale angular face was flushed, and his ice blue eyes were damp with tears.

"We need to talk," Friedrich said.

He ran his long fingers through his dirty blond hair. "I cannot talk right now," Dmitri muttered.

"You can talk," Friedrich said, lifting him off of the ground.

Friedrich held onto Dmitri's arm as they made their way back to his tent. Once inside, he shoved Dmitri down on his cot and stood

before him. He narrowed his eyes on Dmitri and said, "Confess."
He nodded his head once and added, "We already know what you
have done; we just don't know why you have disgraced us."

Dmitri looked down at the ground.

"Why?" Friedrich said.

Dmitri didn't respond and gave a hiccuped cry. Finch stood
next to Friedrich, his arms folded against his chest. He watched as
Dmitri's wet eyes darted back and forth.

"Why'd you do it?" Finch asked. "It doesn't make sense."

He brought his gaze to their incredulous stares and inhaled. "I
was desperate," he said. "Olga and I cannot have a baby, and Mr.
McDaniels promised us one."

Finch already suspected whose baby he had promised, but he
decided to ask anyway. "Whose baby?"

"He said his daughter was with child and was giving the baby up
for adoption," he answered.

"That's not true. She's pregnant all right, but she isn't giving her
baby up," Finch said.

Dmitri looked at him with surprise. "He promised us," he said.

"And you believed him?" Finch said with exasperation. "You're
going to have to start from the beginning so I can see where your
stupidity began." He sat down across from him.

He swallowed. "Olga and I were eating at The Diner. She
likes the milkshakes, and we go there frequently," he explained.
"There was a young couple—they could not have been much older
than you—sitting in the booth next to us, and they had the most
beautiful baby. Olga could not take her eyes off of him. She is so
good with children, you see," he said with a faint smile. "Babies like
her, and this child was smitten with her."

Finch thought of the few kids that were in the carnival, and how they naturally latched themselves onto Olga. She was a kind woman and had a natural affinity to children.

"Olga asked if she could hold him, and they allowed her while they paid the bill. She held him, and her face lit up. It always does when she is around children. She even got him to laugh with her funny faces," he said with a chuckle and then frowned. "That's when we met Mr. McDaniels. He knew the young couple, and they introduced us to him. He seemed like a nice man and was very interested in our work here at the carnival."

"Humph," Finch said, and Friedrich rested his elbow on the chest of drawers as he leaned against it.

"The couple told us we should have a child since Olga was good with their baby. Ryan was his name," he said, scratching at his chin in recollection. "That's when Olga started to cry. She couldn't help it, and the young couple had no idea what they had said or done, but Olga couldn't hold Ryan anymore. It was just too painful for her." He wiped at his eyes. "She excused herself to the restroom, and I apologized for her and told them that she was tired. It was a poor excuse for a lie, and I know they knew the real reason," he said.

"How does McDaniels come into this?" Finch asked.

Dmitri fidgeted and breathed heavily. "He approached me the next day after one of my shows. He was so persuasive and told me he could give us a baby, our very own baby, if I caused problems around here."

"And you just did it without question?" Finch said with irritation.

"Have you ever wanted anything you couldn't have? Have you ever loved someone so much that their wants go above yours? Olga wants a child more than anything, and I cannot give her one," he said.

"I've never wanted to hurt others to give someone I love what they want," Finch said to him with a tinge of disgust.

"You have not loved strongly then," Dmitri said. "I would do anything to make Olga happy, and what he promised me would give her that."

"Did you cause the fire?" Friedrich asked.

Dmitri sighed and finally answered. "Yes."

Finch stood upright and got in Dmitri's face. "You son of a bitch! That fire could've killed Mouse. You know he still coughs? His lungs will probably never be the same."

Friedrich placed his hand on Finch's shoulder. "Finch," he warned, and Finch backed away from Dmitri, still breathing heavily.

"I know, and I'm sorry for that," Dmitri said.

"Not sorry enough. You could've killed someone with that accident," Finch spat. "That little boy had broken bones!"

"I know. I know," Dmitri cried. "And I'm sorry. That's why I told Mr. McDaniels I won't do anything else. I won't. I won't. Believe me, I won't," he pleaded.

"Once Kip hears this, your days here are done," Finch said.

"I know," Dmitri said remorsefully. "I understand."

"You disgust me," Finch snapped. "Your idea of love is screwed up. If you loved your wife, you would've thought of how this will hurt her once she discovers that you're a crook, a man who'll hurt anyone to give her what she wants. Any decent woman wouldn't love a man like that."

"She'll forgive me. She'll understand," Dmitri cried.

"We need to talk to Kip," Friedrich said, pulling Dmitri off of the cot. He didn't fight him and followed along with his head held low.

CHAPTER 30

Kip's response surprised Finch. "We'll keep this quiet and move on," Kip said. "If we turn you in, word will spread that we've got people like you in our carnival, and no one will trust us."

"What about the fact that he broke the law? That he could've killed that kid? That he started a fire that could've killed people? Doris, Mouse, and Friedrich were in that tent," Finch said.

"I'll make sure he doesn't get a job anywhere else, but Finch, if we keep reminding people of what happened, no one is gonna want us here or in any other town. It's best if we let him go quietly," he said.

"It's all about money with you, isn't it?" Finch spat. "Aren't other people's lives worth anything or is money just too important to you?"

"They weren't seriously injured, Finch," he said. "I'm a business owner, and this is a business. If we don't make money, you don't get paid."

"Fuck the pay! This isn't justice," Finch said, shaking his head. "It's wrong, Kip. You know it's wrong. He should pay for what he's done."

"This is the way life works, Finch. Take it or leave it; it's what I've decided," Kip said without a hint of remorse. He narrowed his eyes to Dmitri. "It's best if you and Olga pack up and leave immediately."

Dmitri nodded solemnly and scooted out of the room. Kip turned to his assistant, who was known to most people as Gar but his real name was Garrett. "Better follow him and make sure there ain't no trouble."

Gar nodded and exited the tent.

Finch breathed heavily.

"Young people always look at the world through rose-colored glasses. Life ain't flowers and bunny rabbits, Finch." He opened his business ledger and peered down it. He picked up a pencil and made a note. "If there's nothing else you need, I have work to do, and so do you."

Finch stormed out with Friedrich in tow. "That rotten, good for nothing, son of a bitch!" Fitch spat. "It's not right, Friedrich."

Friedrich sighed through his nose. "No, it's not, but there is nothing we can do about it. Dmitri will have to live with the shame, and once Olga discovers what he's done, she will not forgive him."

"It's still not right, and Kip's just trying to save his own ass," he said.

"Kip has always been this way. He thinks with his wallet, not his heart," Friedrich said. He touched Finch on the shoulder, and Finch flinched. "You need to calm that awful temper of yours and think about the bigger problem at hand."

"Evie," he sighed when he said it. "McDaniels is intent on messing things up for her, and I don't know why."

Friedrich turned his head in all directions. "Look around," he said. "This is beautiful land."

***

Evie fed the last of the heifers and locked the fence. Miles nudged her, chewing on the tail end of her tattered t-shirt. She was wearing one of Gray's old t-shirts and figured if anyone saw her, they'd remark how much of a resemblance the two had. Her in her overalls, trucker hat, and Gray's *Moonpies Aren't Edible* t-shirt.

She cupped her hand over her eyes and scanned the property. All this time she wanted nothing to do with the work, and now it was all she could think about. She was intent on saving her father's land – land that was now in her delicate hands. She was glad that her parents had officially divorced some years back, because if they hadn't, she'd be in a war with her mother over that land, and she knew without a shadow of a doubt her mother would sell it to the highest bidder.

She trekked the property, allowing the warm breeze from the west to run through her hair. She stared up at the sun, and the rays bounced off her face.

Katie was inside making lunch. Evie laughed at the irony – Katie becoming domesticated, a better version of what Evie had tried to be for her father. And Evie was thankful, having someone to cook and clean for once in her life was a gift—a small but welcome gift.

She had tried one final time to persuade Katie to get on that bus. It had come and gone, but she told her she could come up with the funds after the heifers were sold. Katie wouldn't hear of it. "No way am I leaving, so just drop it!"

Evie took the hint and let the subject drop. She'd bring it up again when the timing was right, if it ever was. It seemed to Evie that there was never such a thing – right timing. After losing Gray, she learned that in life there was no such thing as proper timing. Shit happened, and you had to do the things you wanted before it was too late.

It was near afternoon. Evie rolled up her pant legs. She was a sight – covered in dirt and grime and smelling like the outdoors. Her daddy would be proud, seeing her working her tail off. She relished the thought and looked up into the blue sky. "See Daddy, you taught me right," she whispered and then brought her gaze back to the property.

She wrinkled her brow and cupped her hand over her eyes, watching a trail of cars coming toward her driveway. Tripod barked incessantly at them. Evie ran in haste toward her house as two police cruisers and Nate McDaniels' obscene truck, as Evie often referred to it, parked in a single file line, blocking her driveway.

Sheriff Ford and a deputy got out of their cars, followed by Nate and one of his workers. Evie often referred to his workers as TinMan goons, because they did anything he said without question – like they didn't have a heart.

"Whatcha need Sheriff?" she asked.

"Evelyn, you need to shut that carnival down!" Nate interrupted, charging toward them. He inched his way between the two of them and leaned over Evie.

"I can't shut them down," she said. "And I wouldn't if I could anyway."

He pursed his lips. "They're a danger to this community!"

Evie refrained from rolling her eyes, trying to appear as mature as she could. "It was an accident. Accidents happen," she said.

"That boy is in the hospital, and I've spoken to his parents. They're thinking of pressing charges," he snapped. "You'd be smart if you closed it. No one in this town is going to step within a mile of this dangerous property."

"My property isn't dangerous, and why are you meddling when it's not your business? Why don't you go back home and concern yourself with your own problems," she said, moving away from him and stepping onto the porch. "If that's all you're wanting, then I think it's best y'all get off my land now. I've got work to do." She folded her arms against her chest and raised an eyebrow in defiance. She felt her father's strength coming through her and let out a soft satisfied smile.

"We'll be back with the whole damn town, then you'll see. You've got yourself a liability, Evelyn," he said, refusing to budge. Sheriff Ford tapped him on the arm, but he jerked it away from him and remained where he was.

The front door opened, and Katie walked out and stepped onto the porch, making her way down the steps. Evie looked at her with surprise and said with a concerned tone, "Katie." But Katie ignored her and kept on moving toward her father.

"This is private property," Katie said to her dad. "Go on home to Mom and leave us alone."

"Katie," he breathed. "I've been looking all over for you." Nate looked down at her, and she covered the bump in her stomach protectively. His mood shifted, and he furrowed his brows. "You're coming with me." He grabbed her by the arm. Katie fought him, trying to break herself free.

Evie dashed down the steps and ran toward them. "Get your hands off of her!" she shouted. Nate had a strong hold of Katie and tried dragging her with him.

"Sheriff!" Evie screamed. "He can't do this! She's an adult!"

"She's my daughter, and I can make her come with me if I want," Nate said as Katie shouted at him to let go of her.

Sheriff Ford moved their way and lay his hands on an irate Nate. "Sorry Nate, but Evie's right. Katie's eighteen and can come and go as she pleases. In the eyes of the law, she's an adult."

Nate looked down at his upset daughter and a look of realization filled him. The sheriff unlatched Nate's grip on Katie. She rubbed the red sore spot with her other hand and took a step back from him. She covered her mouth with her hand and shook her head at her father. Tears fell from her eyes.

"She's an adult, Nate. She can choose to live here if she wants," Sheriff Ford said delicately. "You can't make her go with you."

Nate fixed his gaze on Katie's. "You're not coming with me?"

"No," Katie said. "I'm protecting me and my child. From *you*."

He clenched his hand into a fist and brought it to his forehead and frowned. "Your mother," he said. It was his one last defense, and Katie could sense the manipulation behind it.

"If she wants to see me, she's welcome here, but I'm not leaving," she said and latched onto Evie's free hand. "I'm staying right here where I belong. Go on home and don't look back because I'm not coming home, you hear?"

"And she can stay here for as long as she wants," Evie added. They stood side-by-side and locked their arms, squeezing each other's hands.

"Thank you, friend," Katie whispered to Evie.

"That carnival is done!" Nate shouted. "You'll see. This town isn't so forgiving." He took one last look at Katie before he hopped into his truck and backed out of the driveway.

"He's right about that carnival, Evie. It's best if those folks packed up their bags and never came back here," Sheriff Ford said.

"They didn't do anything," Evie defended. "They're not to blame!"

The sheriff gave her a skeptical look. "It's still best if their kind weren't here no more." He strutted to his car and left.

Katie collapsed onto the top step, with Evie still holding onto her hand. "You okay?" Evie asked.

"Yeah," she breathed. "That was the hardest thing I've ever done."

"Well... you're fixin' to have a kid, which will be even harder. I'd say this was good practice."

"You don't even like kids," Katie said, wiping her tears.

"I'll like yours," Evie said. "If he's anything like you, I'll like him just fine." Evie said with a reassuring smile.

***

It was late in the night, and Evie still hadn't seen Finch. She paced the front porch, sat for a minute on the swing, then got up again just to pace.

Katie peered out the window and shouted, "Eves, quit being a worry wart and just walk on down there!"

"Fine!" she said with resolve. "I'll be back," Evie hollered and walked down the steps and toward the open field.

August was just around the corner, she could feel it. The air was stifling hot, and beads of sweat formed on her neck and forehead. August in the upstate was the worst of summer – hot and no reprieve in sight until fall decided to slowly inch its way in.

She tugged on her braid, fiddling with it, and tried to keep her fingers out of her mouth. Since Finch told her that biting her nails was equivalent to eating cockroaches, she'd all but given up the habit. "How is it like eating cockroaches?" she said to him.

"'Cause your hands touch everything, and roaches crawl over everything," he said to her, and that instantly made her see a cockroach anytime her fingernails were near her lips.

He was coming her way – she could see his silhouette – a build and shape she'd grown to know so well. He increased his pace to meet up with her, and the two of them held onto each other.

"Where've you been?" she asked him.

"Evie," he murmured. He cupped her chin and brought her to him, kissing her on the lips.

"You still," she said, and kissed him, "didn't," another kiss, "answer my question."

He laughed and hugged her again.

"It's not good, Evie," he said with a frown.

She brought her palm to his cheek, running her fingers against his stubble. "What is it?"

He took her hand and kissed it, then laced his fingers in hers. He took a deep breath and exhaled. "We're leaving," he finally said.

Evie's face was downcast. "Oh," she said.

"The town isn't so keen on our presence, and Kip decided it's best to head out tomorrow," he said.

She huffed. "It was McDaniels wasn't it?"

He nodded. "How'd you know?"

"That sorry ass was on my property today 'causing a ruckus," she said.

"Seems like he was causing a ruckus all over town," he said, enjoying Evie's choice of words. "Stoney went to town to get some supplies, and McDaniels was seen talking to several people about how dangerous the carnival was. Stoney said it looked like half the town was on his side."

"Why would they believe anything he has to say? Half of them don't even like him," she said with disgust.

"You start talking about kids being hurt, you change your tune," he said. "I don't know if we'll be back next year. Stoney said he couldn't even get service today in town. They wouldn't even take his money." He gave her a look of disbelief. "McDaniels is dangerous," he said more seriously. "Evie, you need to watch out for him."

She read the warning in his eyes. "He's not a good man, but I don't think he'd do anything to hurt me."

"I mean it, Evie. He's the reason there was an accident at the carnival," he said.

"What?" She widened her eyes.

"He offered up Katie's baby to Dmitri, our juggler, if he'd mess things up. Dmitri caused the fire and the accident," he said, and she let out a gasp. "I'm worried he's not done with his vendetta. He wants your land, Evie, and he wants it bad enough he'll do anything. I think he's the one who had those kids leave your gate open. He's dangerous."

"That's just crazy talk. You make this all sound like a soap opera," she said, trying to feign indifference, but deep down she was scared at the prospect that Nate was a man capable of doing such a thing.

"I'm being dead serious," he said with a stern voice. "You've gotta be careful around him. I sure as hell don't like leaving you with him around."

"This is too much," she said, closing her eyes and exhaling. "You're telling me he caused the accident?"

"Yes. That's what I'm saying. You need to be careful." He looked at her seriously.

She thought about what he said and tried to keep herself from fidgeting. She bit on her lip and chewed, and she shut her eyes for a brief second. She let out a long-winded sigh and nearly whispered, "This isn't good."

He rubbed his hands on her chin and said, "No, Evie, it's not.

Promise me you'll be careful."

She stared him in the eyes and blinked. "I promise," she said. "You could stay, you know. You could stay here. With me."

"Evie," he said quietly. "As much as I want to, I can't. What would I do? Live off of you, taking care of your cows? That's not right. I have a job with the carnival," he said, but even he wondered why he said those words. A job? It was just a job, a job he didn't care about. A job where he didn't respect his boss and dreaded what he did. A job that meant nothing to him, not like Evie, not the way she made him feel – the way she gave him hope for a better life.

"You wouldn't be living off me. I'd put you to work," she said with a hopeful grin. "Just consider it. The offer is there..." her voice trailed off.

He'd think about it every minute of the day, but he wouldn't tell her that. He didn't want to get her hopes up that he would change his mind. But he wasn't about to freeload off of her, to take what was hers and make it his. That's what it would feel like, and he didn't know if he could stand to look himself in the mirror if he did.

"Wanna go for a swim?" she asked.

"You and your subject changing." He let out a loud, hearty laugh.

"I can't deal with all this melodrama right now. It's been a shit storm of a summer. First with Katie, then my daddy," she sucked her cheeks in and took a breath and frowned, "then I hear that Mr. McDaniels is in cahoots with the Devil, and now you're leaving."

"Cahoots with the Devil?" he repeated with a laugh.

"Yeah. So." A wrinkle formed on the bridge of her nose.

"So, you were saying you wanted to go swimming?" He tugged on her braid and wrapped it around her neck creating a scarf.

She flicked his hand away and frowned at him.

"And now you're mad," he said.

"No," she pouted.

"You sure?" He leaned closer to her and peered into her blue eyes.

"So, do you want to?"

"Wanna what?"

"Swim," she said with frustration.

"In the pond?" He made a face.

"Do you see a swimming pool?" she said sarcastically.

"I guess I can swim with you," he said, trying to sound like it was the worst invitation he'd ever gotten.

"If you don't want to." She shrugged. "I just thought since you were leaving we could spend some more time together, and it's so hot out," she said, taking a few steps forward.

He ran to catch up to her, wrapped his hands around her waist and whispered in her ear. "I just wanna be with you, even if it's in that nasty pond of yours." He kissed her on the neck and smiled.

CHAPTER 31

Evie kicked off her boots and stuck her big toe in the water. "Feels good," she said.

Finch bent over to unlace his shoes and rolled up his jeans. He walked to the water's edge and placed his left foot in. "It's nice."

"It's more than nice," she said. "Turn the other way."

He formed a confused expression.

She motioned with her hands. "Don't peek." She placed her hands on his arms and tried moving him. "A little help would be nice."

He spun on his heels so he was facing the opposite direction.

"Okay." She breathed. "Don't turn around. I mean it," she barked.

She pulled her t-shirt above her head and unbuttoned her shorts, tugging the zipper all the way down.

Finch swallowed. "What are you doing, Evie?"

"I can't swim with all this stuff on, Finch," she answered.

He heard something fall to the ground and felt a piece of fabric graze his ankle. He closed his eyes and tried to think about anything: math equations, ducks in migration, the last mission to space, anything that would get his mind off what was standing right behind him.

"You done yet?" his voice cracked as he said it.

He heard a splash. "Yeah. It feels good. Come on in," she said with a giggle.

He turned around and looked down at the ground and saw a pile of clothes. Her clothes.

"Come on!" she shouted.

"Okay. If I couldn't peek, you can't either," he said. "Turn around, Evie!"

She shot him a look and begrudgingly swam the other way, facing the other side of her property.

He tore off his jeans and t-shirt, and then finally, his underwear. He heard another giggle and peered over his shoulder.

"I see your hiney. It's all white and shiny," she sang.

"Quit peeking," he said, feeling her eyes burning on his backside. "And how old are you anyway?" he shouted. "That's a song five-year-olds sing!"

"You've got yourself a Coppertone tan line, Finch." She laughed again.

He covered his front side with both of his hands as he made his way through the water and swam to Evie.

"You cheated." He splashed water at her. "You weren't supposed to look."

"You flaunted it like you wanted me to," she said with an impish grin. "No reason to get all cheeky." She laughed at her pun.

"You're a riot. " He rolled his eyes, and then ran his fingers across her shoulders, yanking on her bra strap. "What's this?"

A trail of goosebumps formed from her neck to her shoulders. "My bra. Women wear them you know."

"I know what a bra is. Why are you wearing it?"

"I didn't say I was skinny dipping." She flashed him a big grin.

"You little sneak," he said and grabbed her by the waist, feeling her bare stomach, and then dunked her under water.

She came back up for air. "That wasn't nice." She scowled at him and splashed water in his face.

"You just wanted to see me. All of me." He cocked an eyebrow and smirked. "Admit it."

"There's that dumb smirk," she complained. "As if I'd want to see all of you." Even she could hear the lilt in her voice. That was a bold faced lie. She liked his muscular chest well enough the night before. She sure as hell didn't mind a peek at the rest of him. Any girl with half-sense would agree.

He gave her an incredulous look.

"You liked my chest well enough last night," he said. It's like he was reading her thoughts.

"No, your chest is stupid," she said, failing again at a witty response. Once she saw the trail of hair from Finch's chest down to his navel she couldn't help but run her fingers along it, feeling the soft dark brown hairs brush against her fingertips.

Without saying another word, Finch swam up to her and placed his hands on her shoulders. He leaned in close and kissed her gently on her wet lips. "Eventually you're gonna have to get out of this water," he teased and waggled his brows.

"And?"

He tapped his index finger against his wet chin and smiled. "And... I can swim faster than you." He started swimming toward the shore with Evie trailing behind him, trying hard to keep up.

Finch raced out of the water, grabbed Evie's and his clothes off of the ground in one swoop and ran behind a nearby Blue Cypress tree.

Evie swam to the shore and saw her clothes were missing once she got out. "Finch!" She quickly ran back into the water.

He laughed as he put the rest of his dry clothes on. He shook his wet hair and walked from behind the tree.

"Looking for these?" He held her clothes in his hand.

"Give them back," she said, standing in the pond. The water hit her mid chest.

"Why should I?"

"Give them back or else," she threatened.

"Seems to me like you're in no position to threaten me," he teased.

"Fine. If that's the way you want it," she said in a huff and stomped out of the water, facing him.

He tried to dart his eyes in another direction but couldn't help but stare at the beautiful sight in front of him: Evie in her bra and underwear, sopping wet.

He cleared his throat and caught himself ogling. At her. He was gawking shamelessly and he couldn't make his eyes stop.

"You see something you like?" she said being coy and grabbed her clothes from his hand before he had time to comment. "Close that mouth of yours, Finch, or else you'll end up eating some horseflies." Her hips swayed as she sauntered behind the tree and got dressed.

It took her a while to get her clothes on, and Finch appreciated the break. He needed to compose himself. He smoothed his hair; pulled up his loose jeans, and every few seconds peered at that darn tree. She had just done the unexpected, but that's what he liked about Evie – that she made things interesting.

She came out fully clothed and with a look on her face that read "Ha, got you, dummy!" She stuck her tongue in her cheek and smiled. "You closed your mouth," she said as she approached him.

He sighed and formed a soft grin. "Come here." He stuck his fingers in her belt loops and brought her to him. He placed his palms on the soft damp skin of her cheeks and said, "You've got quite the mouth on you, you know that?"

"Ditto," she said.

He placed his hand on her lower back. "I'd like to kiss that mouth of yours," he said, breathing into her. His lips met hers, and she willingly surrendered, letting their tongues inter mingle as she felt his lips pressing harder against hers.

She let go and looked at him, flustered. Her chest rose and then fell flat, and he could hear the sounds of her heavy breaths expelling from her mouth as she pointed her finger at him and said, "You have to stop doing that."

"Ditto," he kidded and kissed her at the nape of her neck and whispered in her ear, "serves you right."

She backed away. "For what?"

"For being you," he said.

She playfully hit him on the arm. "What about you?"

"What about me?"

"You started it with your dreamy eyes and expert kissing," she said.

"Expert kissing?" he repeated and patted his chest with a confident grin. "Dreamy eyes, huh?"

"Don't get smug," she said.

"Can't help it. You all but told me I am the best kisser you've ever known and that my eyes are beautiful," he said.

"I said nothing of the sort," she said with frustration. "Quit putting words in my mouth."

He placed his hands on her hips and said with a wide smile, "Oh Evie, you make my heart smile."

"Hearts can't smile," she argued.

"Mine can, and you're the cause of it."

Evie pulled the lid off of the cake stand and cut two slices of Coke cake. "Katie's trying her hand at baking," she said, placing the slices on plates. She slid a plate his way.

He bit into his slice and smiled. "It's good."

Evie agreed and handed him a bottle of Coke. "Here. To wash it down with," she said.

He took a sip and swallowed.

"Have you thought more about what I said?" she asked.

"What? That I'm an expert kisser or that my eyes are dreamy?"

She shot him a look.

"I've thought about it, and Evie, as much as I want to stay, it wouldn't be right for me to live off of you."

"You wouldn't be living off of me. I told you I'd put you to work," she said.

He sighed. "And where would I stay? Here? The town would talk."

"Who cares what the town says. And when did you become a nanny panny?"

"Nanny panny?" he repeated and gave her a peculiar look. "You mean, namby pamby?"

"Namby pamby, nanny panny, either way, you're acting like one if you're worrying about what the town thinks."

He lay his hand on hers. "I just don't want people saying bad things about you. Me I can handle, you, you're a different story."

"I can handle a few bad choice words, Finch. You think I didn't hear people talking when my mom left, or when Daddy came up with some of his hair brained schemes? I'm tougher than you think," she said. "Besides, you make it sound scandalous. You'd just be staying here, not like we'd be shacking up."

"You're my girlfriend, Evie, what else would you call it?"

Evie formed a slight smile hearing him call her his girlfriend.

"People in a town this size in the middle of the Bible belt aren't going to see it any other way," he said.

"They're all..."

"Stupid heads," he interrupted, finishing her sentence. He laughed and then his lips cast down. "You're just stretching, reaching for a way to make me stay, and believe me, a huge part of me wants to forget everything, all my responsibilities and the life I know, and take you up on your offer. But I can't," he said.

"You can't because you're afraid," she said, and he couldn't argue that. "I am too, you know," she whispered. "Every single day since my daddy's been gone."

"You're tough, Evie. I've never met anyone stronger than you."

"The offer still stands."

"And my answer is still the same. Can't we drop this topic for tonight and just enjoy each other with the time we've got left?"

Evie looked up at the clock, seeing the hands steadily moving. Time was closing in on them, and she knew Finch was as pig-headed as she was. She wasn't going to talk him into anything. "Okay," she finally agreed.

***

Finch rose early. He stood over Evie, watching her sleep peacefully, and felt a sharp pain to his heart. He'd miss this, this feeling of bliss that life had given him this summer. Never before in his life had he ever been so content, so happy. He poked her gently and whispered, "I have to go."

She opened her eyes and peeked out the window, seeing the sun hadn't even risen yet. "Right now?"

"We've gotta take everything down, and it'll take a while," he said.

She sat up and peered up at him. "At least have breakfast with me." She yawned and stretched her arms high above her head.

"Okay," he agreed. "But then I have to go."

"Pour more lemon juice on that paper cut will you," she said sarcastically.

***

They finished their breakfast, and Katie had woken early to join them. "Promise you'll not forget about us farm girls," she said to him.

"I could never forget about you farm girls," he said.

She gave him a tight side hug and patted him on the back. "You're a good egg, Finch Mills," she said.

He gave her a warm smile. "Take care of yourself and that baby of yours."

"I'll walk you out," Evie said to him.

They made their way out to the front porch, and the sun had just started to rise above the horizon. Patches of orange and blue filled the skyline, and a rooster's crow echoed into the morning air.

Tripod hobbled to Finch, begging for a pat, and he bent down to pet him a few times. Then he stood up, looking at Evie. She was fighting back tears and promised herself she wouldn't be a sniffling mess when he left.

"I'll call you, and I'll write as often as I can," he said, holding her.

"And you'll come back when you're done on the circuit, right?"

"Yep," he said with a reassuring nod.

She looked up at him and wrapped her arms around his neck. "Kiss me soft before you go."

"Only namby pamby's kiss soft, Evie," he said, mocking her.

"Fine. Kiss me hard before you go," she said in a challenging tone.

"You asked for it," he said.

His lips smashed against her parted lips, and he brought her closer to him, kissing her violently with a sense of urgency. It was careless, reckless, and messy, and Evie yearned for more. She wanted more of him. When he would try to pull away, she tugged on his shirt, moving him back to her, and she kissed him harder and with more passion, her hands roaming all over him.

He reluctantly pulled away from her and took each of her hands, kissing her on the finger tips. "Evie," he said as if drugged. "You can't kiss me like that and expect me to leave."

She lay her head against his chest and wrapped her arms around him. "Then don't."

"I have to," he said, and it hurt to say those words. He let go of her and looked down into her blue eyes.

She swore she wouldn't cry, and so help her, she was trying, but her damn eyes were welling up with tears faster than a flash flood.

"Don't cry," he said, and he ached to see her so sad.

"I'm not," she lied, sniffling. "I've just got something in my eyes."

He laughed with a sad expression and brought her to him, kissing her on the forehead and then letting her go. "I'll call you when we're set up. Promise."

CHAPTER 32

As the days passed, Evie attempted to go back to her old routine. She got up at the crack of dawn to take care of the pregnant heifers and then the calves and spent the rest of her time trying to occupy herself by taking care of the property. She repaired what she could without resources, funds or people.

She felt the void – her daddy was gone, and Finch, and that carnival that she used to hate. Now she missed it. She'd give anything to smell a funnel cake or hear that annoying music.

The town hadn't been so kind, and McDaniels had his way, inciting some lemmings in his quest to make sure the carnival left Haines as soon as possible. She received her cash payment from Kip – it was less than she anticipated, but with the fire and the accident, business had come to a near dead stop.

"Don't know if we'll be back next year," he told Evie.

"I figured," she said, sticking the stack of bills in the front pocket of her overalls.

"Maybe being gone a year will make people forget," he said.

"Maybe so," she said.

"We'll give it some time and see how it goes…" his voice trailed off, and he offered no further promises.

But she knew—they were probably gone for good which meant no more extra income and more importantly, no more Finch. He called her his girlfriend and promised to write and to call, and so far his word was good as gold. Each night at precisely the same time – nine thirty – he called her, and they talked as long as he had dimes, and he had a stack of them.

"I wrote you a letter today," he told her one night.

"Oh yeah, what'd it say?" She lay on her couch with her right leg crossed over the left, and the phone cord stretched all the way from the kitchen to the living room.

"You'll have to wait to see," he said.

She sighed. "I wish I could write you."

"I don't stay in a town long enough, Evie," he said sadly. He wished he could receive letters from her, but with his vagabond lifestyle, he'd never receive them. "What would you say? If you wrote me?"

"I don't know," she said.

"Sure you do. What would you say?" He leaned against the glass in the phone booth, trying to stay dry. It was raining buckets outside, but that didn't stop him from driving to that phone booth in the crappy town where the carnival was.

"I guess I'd say Dear Finch," she started.

"And?" He smiled at the anticipation.

"This is embarrassing," she admitted, blushing.

"It shouldn't be."

"Well... it is. Maybe if I had it written I could just read it?"

"Then do it. Tomorrow night. Read me the letter you can't send," he said.

She bit on her lip and breathed. "I can't promise you anything good."

"I can't wait to hear it," he said.

***

He called her the next night a few minutes late, explaining that he got stuck behind an old driver who he guessed couldn't see too well at night considering that he swerved the entire time and kept slamming on his brakes.

"So," he started, dying to hear what she would say. He had thought about it all day. All damn day.

She blushed again. "You have to promise not to laugh," she said.

"I can't do that," he said. "You make me laugh."

"But this isn't funny," she said.

"But your Evieism's make me laugh," he defended.

"Finch," she whined.

"Okay. I promise." He crossed his fingers as he said it.

"Dear Finch," she started.

"That has a nice ring to it," he interrupted.

"Shh," she said. "Are you going to let me read this or not?"

"Go on."

She held the notebook paper in her shaking hand, unsure why she was so nervous. "Dear Finch," she repeated. "I woke up this morning, thinking it was time to clean Daddy's room. I've had the door closed for a while, and thought if I kept it that way, he wouldn't be gone. But the more I kept passing that shut door, the more my heart hurt. It just reminded me he was gone." She cleared her throat, feeling the tears forming.

"It took me a few hours to get up the nerve to open the door, and once I did, I shut it as quickly as I had opened it and walked away," she said. "It took me a while, but I came back to his room, and finally resolved to open the door and go on inside. Everything was the same – his bed was unmade, his dirty clothes were in a laundry basket near the door, and I could smell him, Finch. Like he was there."

Finch didn't say anything. The operator interrupted requesting another dime be put in and Finch added two just to shut her up.

"And I just sat there, smelling him, and seeing everything in that room that was a part of him, and I couldn't do it. I just couldn't do it," she said with a strained voice. "Katie came in and saw me crying, and she knew just what to say and do because best friends are like soul sisters – she just knew. And we took things real slow. I changed his sheets and remade his bed, and washed his dirty clothes. But I couldn't get rid of anything. Not yet, anyway. It would just seem wrong, but you know what's strange?"

"What?" he asked quietly, forgetting that she was reading from her letter.

"It helped. It really helped to go in there and do what I did," she said and continued. "That was how I spent most of my day with the exception of thinking about you. You cross my mind at the most peculiar times, Finch Mills. When I'm cleaning dishes, or bottle feeding the calves, or riding on my ATV. I see your face everywhere. I'm not going to spend the rest of this letter writing how much I miss you because I think you know. If I'm seeing you outside of my dreams, then you know. Love, Evie," she said and took a deep breath. She lay the letter in her lap and then sat on her shaking hands.

"I liked that Evie Barnes," he said with a wide smile. He placed his hand to his chest, feeling his heart beating quicker. "I liked that a lot."

***

Evie received Finch's letter the next day. She ripped the envelope open and ran up the stairs, closing the door behind her to read it in private. She knew she was being silly, like those school girls with crushes, but this was more than a crush, it was something deeper and more profound, grown-up and delightful. She put a Kiss album on the record player and pointed the needle to the song, "Beth," one of Finch's favorites. She bought the record after Finch left town and played it every night just to think of him.

She lay down on her bed, propping herself up against the pillow, and unfolded the notebook paper.

Dear Evie,

I'm in some town (can't even remember the name it's that unmemorable) outside of Greensboro, North Carolina, and one of the largest cigarette factories is a few miles away. You know how I love the smell of cigarette smoke. All the carnies are having a field day, and the stench of cigarette smoke is everywhere. Everyone here smokes, even the kids. I swear I saw a toddler holding a cigarette. I want to get out of this dive, but we've got a few more days here.

I woke up this morning and realized something - I miss hearing the cows. They grew on me. Who thought a "citified" guy like me would say such a thing? I know you're probably glaring at me now. You know I always say these things on purpose because it's so much fun to get a rise out of you. Your face turns beet red and that little nose of yours scrunches up.

I miss you, Evie. There, I said it. Take it how you want, but I miss you more than you'll ever know, and sometimes I kick myself and call myself a "stupid head" for not staying there with you because you're all I ever think about. Well... you and those cows of yours.

I'll talk to you tonight. Same time. Nine thirty at night has become my favorite time of day.

Finch

Evie reread the letter three more times before she folded it into a neat square and placed it in her top dresser drawer, safe and sound. Within a couple of weeks, her dresser drawer was lined with identical squares – each and every one of them was from Finch.

Every night after he called her, he wrote her a letter. Each letter became a confessional, him expressing himself in a way Evie had never seen or heard. He never promised her flowers and poetry or words of love. But he implied that and more in his letters to her.

"I saw peonies today and thought of you." Or, "I saw this quote by John Barrymore, whoever that is, and thought of you – 'Happiness often sneaks through a door you didn't know you left open.'"

She lit up like a firefly when she read statements like those. They were words he'd never tell her, things he had never dared to say, but give him a pen and paper and he was an open book. He was a covert romantic, and Evie relished the surprise of this side of Finch each time she opened a new letter.

***

It was nine thirty at night, and the phone rang more than once in Evie's house. Katie rushed to answer it before it rang a fourth time. "Hello," she said, trying to catch her breath.

"Hi Katie," Finch said. Cars honked their horns and car engines revved up in the background.

"Sounds like you're on a race track," Katie said.

"Just outside of Knoxville, Tennessee. I thought this state was known for Jack Daniels and country music. But everyone around here just likes to go cruising," he said.

Katie let out a forced giggle and then became quiet.

"So how've you been?"

"I'm, I'm good," she said, fumbling for words.

"You sure?" he asked.

"Yeah."

"Is Evie there?"

Katie hesitated.

"Katie?"

"Um, no she's not here," she answered with a slight stutter.

"Where is she?" he asked.

"She's with Cooper and Spence," she said.

"At this time of night?"

Silence.

"Katie, what's going on?"

"It's not good, Finch."

CHAPTER 33

Finch pressed the receiver closer to him. "Tell me, Katie. What is it?" he said with a note of concern.

"She wouldn't want me telling you," she said.

"Telling me what?"

Silence.

"Katie?" he sounded desperate, and Katie couldn't stand to hear him like that.

"She's about to lose the farm, Finch," she said.

"What?" He fell back against the glass in the phone booth. "How?"

"She wasn't going to tell me, either. She didn't want any of us to know," she explained. "I went to town to run some errands and ran into my dad. We had a pretty nasty exchange of words, and he basically hinted that Evie's land was gonna be his soon." She paused and sighed through her nose. "I didn't know what he meant by that, and when I got up enough nerve to tell him he had lost his mind, he said it'd only be a matter of time till I crawled back home because I wouldn't have anywhere else to go. Because her land would be his." She shuddered, thinking back to that moment.

"Katie, I'm sorry," Finch said.

"It's okay, Finch. It's okay," she said reassuringly. "I've come to terms with him..."

Finch waited for her to continue.

"When I came home, I went straight to Evie to ask her what the hell my dad was talking about. Losing the farm? It didn't make sense, and you know what, Finch? She just lost it right there and then." Katie sniffled, and Finch's eyes filled with tears. "She's been keeping this burden on those bony shoulders of hers all by herself, trying to take care of it on her own."

"How, Katie? How?" He rubbed the back of his neck. "How is she losing the farm?"

"Evie got notice from the bank that Mr. Gray had taken out a loan against the property," she said.

Finch felt his knees buckling. He knew what was coming next.

"And she owes five thousand dollars by the end of this week or the bank is going to repossess the farm. I think Mr. Gray was banking on making enough money this summer to pay it off but he was too far in debt, Finch," she cried as she said it. "Evie's planning to sell off all the heifers and calves but that won't cover everything she owes. She won't be able to pay any of her other bills if she doesn't have any cattle." She wiped her tears from her face and sucked in some air.

Finch dried the damp spots on his face with the palm of his hand. "She can't do that," he whispered.

"She has to. It's the only way to satisfy the bank right now," she said. "She's talking to Cooper and Spence about different options. Cooper says he doesn't want her to sell off her cattle, but she doesn't see any other way. She loves this land, Finch."

"I know," he said.

"If she loses it, it'll crush her, Finch."

The operator interrupted, "Deposit another dime please."

"I have to go, Katie," he said.

"I'll tell Evie you called," she tried to calm her quivering voice.

"It's going to be all right, Katie," he said. "Don't let Evie sell those cattle. You hear? No matter what, don't let her."

And the line went dead.

Finch walked in Kip's tent without knocking. Kip sighed heavily and scolded, "It says knock." He pointed to the make-shift sign that dangled above the entrance.

"If I did, you wouldn't have let me in," Finch said.

"What do you want, Finch?" he said with exasperation. The two didn't see eye-to-eye about how the situation with Dmitri was handled, and since that time, there had been nothing but tension between them.

"I need to know what circuit David Mills is on," he said.

"Why?" Kip pushed his papers to the side and stared up at him. "And what makes you think I know where he is."

"It's none of your business why I need to know," Finch said. "And I know damn well you know where he is. You carnival owners talk, and I'm sure you've heard which crappy carnival was dumb enough to take his sorry ass."

"After all this time, you want to talk to your father?"

Finch looked at his wrist watch and then back at Kip. "I'd like to leave tonight."

He paused and pursed his lips. "He's in Memphis," he finally answered. "With Wes Wheaton's Carnival."

Finch made a face. "He's sinking lower than I thought," he said.

He left without a goodbye. Just a scribbled note folded on Stoney's chest telling him he was borrowing his truck and wouldn't be back for a while. It was pitch black outside. The roads were isolated, and only the moon and stars above provided any glimmer of light. Stoney's old truck shifted hard into third gear, and Finch could hear rocks and gravel flying up as he sped through the night.

***

He drove into the early morning. He rode without a compass, just on instinct alone. Wes Wheaton's Carnival was a cheap imitation of Kip's, one of *those* kind, as Kip would refer to it. But Finch knew that Kip didn't have the right to judge anymore. He lost that privilege when he allowed Dmitri to leave unscathed and without any repercussions for what he had done.

He pulled into a make-shift parking lot, turned the engine off, and sat there for a while, tapping his fingers against the weathered steering wheel. A few carnies were up, getting ready to start their day. The land wasn't pretty, not like Evie's, and trash was everywhere. Trash cans were overflowing with paper cups, plates, and other crap, and Finch got a whiff of rotting food when he opened the truck door.

He searched through the carnival. He peeked at feet under trailers, and into tents tattered with holes and ripped seams, rides that looked as old as the Earth, and employees that looked hard— hard in life with stories that wouldn't be pleasant to hear. Some people wore their lives on their sleeves, and he could see a mile long trail of stories that would make anyone squeamish if they sat down to tell them.

An older woman with smeared lip stick and mascara, showing too much cleavage and more than enough leg, approached him. She licked her lips and tried to smile seductively, but with her yellow teeth and tangled up hair, it just wasn't sexy. It was pathetic. And maybe her charms or overt offers of a quick roll in the hay would work on a rube or a horny guy desperate for some action, but they didn't work on Finch. His heart belonged somewhere else, and he just stared at the woman feeling sorry for her.

"Where you going, handsome?" she said. Her voice was husky,

and it was obvious from the stench and sound of her that she smoked more than a pack a day.

"I'm looking for David Mills," he said.

"David? Whatcha want with him?" She lay her hands on him.

"Do you know where he is?" He brushed her hand off of his arm.

"Maybe I do. Maybe I don't," she teased. "You his kin? You're the spittin' image of him, just a younger, more delicious version."

"I don't have time for this," he said with irritation.

She shot him a dirty look. "You're no fun, are you?" she said with a huff. "He's over there." She pointed to a nearby tent.

He went on his way and stood outside that tent, taking a few deep breaths before he entered.

David and a woman lay stark naked on a blanket, and when Finch got a closer look at the woman's face he realized she had to have been Evie's age or not much older.

"David!" he yelled.

David's chest rose and fell flat, and he snored heavily.

Finch kicked him on his side and shouted his name again. "David!"

David jerked upright and looked at Finch with a dazed expression. He rubbed his bloodshot eyes and took a closer look at him and scrunched his face. "Finch?"

Finch heard the uncertainty in his voice.

"David," he answered with annoyance. The man was his father but couldn't recognize his own son.

"What are you doing here?" He looked down at his exposed groin and then heaved himself up, and searched for his pants.

Finch threw David's jeans at him, and answered, "I need to

speak with you, but I'm not doing it in here with that naked girl." He pointed aggressively. "Get dressed and meet me outside," he barked.

Finch waited outside, pacing. He could hear David moving around inside the tent, searching for his things. The girl muttered something, her high-pitched voice made her sound even younger than she looked, and when she uttered, "Come back to bed, Davey," Finch felt the strong urge to throw up.

David exited the tent, wearing jeans, a faded black t-shirt and a pair of scuffed up boots. Looking at him, Finch could see the resemblance – the same brown eyes and dimpled chin. But David was showing signs of wear and tear – salt and peppered hair and lines around his eyes and on his forehead. The stubble on his face was almost all white.

"You robbing cradles now?" Finch said with disgust.

"She's your age," he said, which wasn't much of a defense in Finch's eyes. "Is it your birthday or something?"

"No, it's not my birthday," Finch said with irritation. "You think I'd come here to celebrate that occasion with you?"

"Probably not," he answered. "So, what are you doing here?" He ran his fingers through his greasy hair and tried to offer a smile.

"I need something from you," Finch said. He wasn't going to do small talk with the man. There was no reason to. He didn't care what the man had been up to, where he had been, or what he had going on in his life.

"Okay," David said with a questioning tone.

"I've never asked you for anything. You know that, and I wouldn't ask for this unless I really needed it."

"What do you need, son?"

Finch held his hand up. "First off, you don't get to call me 'son,' just like I'll never call you 'Dad.' It seems a bit late for terms of endearment, doesn't it?"

"If I'm giving you something I'd think I'd have the right to call you whatever I damn well please," he said, and Finch shot him a look of disdain.

"Don't," he said, shaking his head. "I didn't drive all the way here to fight with you. Just try not to be a dick for once."

David grew quiet and softened his tone. "What do you want?"

"I won't ever ask you for anything else in my entire life, and it kills me to ask you for this. But I need it, and what you're gonna give me is something you should've given Mom all of those years she struggled to make ends meet. You give me this, maybe you can live with yourself for not being there," Finch said.

"I know I've never been a father to you," David started.

"It doesn't matter now," Finch interrupted. "I'm not here to hash up old painful memories. I need you to do this one thing for me and you won't ever hear from me. Ever. I promise."

***

"What do you mean you're leaving?" Doris asked Finch as he packed the last of his things into a duffle bag.

"I can't stay here and work for a man like Kip. And this.... it's just not in me anymore," he said to her, zipping up the bag.

She placed her hand on his shoulder. "I think love has more to do with it," she said.

His cheeks turned a slight shade of pink.

She hit him on the arm. "You love her," she said, exaggerating the word "love."

"Do you have enough money to pay off the bank?" Friedrich asked.

"No," he said. "David gave me what he had, and I had some saved, but it still won't cover the full amount. I'm thinking the bank will work with us."

"Ain't no bank gonna work with anyone when it comes to money being owed," she said.

"Your optimism is so encouraging," Finch said.

"How much more do you need?" she asked, ignoring his quip.

"One thousand three hundred and fifty-six dollars and twenty cents," he said.

"Guess who has one thousand, three hundred and fifty-six dollar and twenty cents?" She waggled her painted in brows. "Us." She pointed to Friedrich and her.

"Don't forget about me," Mouse added.

"I can't take your money," Finch said.

"She means a lot to you, doesn't she, Honey Lamb?"

Finch nodded.

"Well, you mean a lot to us. I think between the three of us," she widened her arms and pointed to Friedrich and Mouse, "we can come up with the rest of that money."

"No. It's your money," Finch argued.

"It's ours to do what we want with, and besides, I don't want to work here anymore."

"Me neither," Friedrich said.

"That goes for me, as well," Mouse added.

"You're all leaving the carnival?" Finch said incredulously.

"Been wanting to leave it for a long time. I just needed a reason to do so, and Kip's been itching to fire us anyway. We can just beat him to the punch," Doris answered. "You think Evie's got room for us on that farm of hers?"

CHAPTER 34

Evie grunted as she shoved one of the stubborn heifers up the wooden platform and into the semi-truck trailer. She, Katie, and Cooper had already loaded close to fifty heifers. She was worn out, feeling the strain of a day's hard work. Her muscles ached, and she was drenched with sweat. The morning sun was beating down hard on her, and the cattle weren't cooperating.

"They're being so damn stubborn," she complained to Cooper.

He gave her a look. "They can sense your mood," he said. He was right, she was irritable. "You're cranky."

She sighed, rubbing the back of her neck. "I'm just tired," she lied.

"You know how I feel about this," he said.

She had sought Cooper and Spence's advice, even though she had already made up her mind. Once she told Cooper she intended to sell the heifers, he had argued with her for days trying to persuade her to change her mind.

He was adamantly against the idea. "That's your livelihood, and once they're sold, you'll have nothing – just acres and acres of land with no money coming in," he said to her when she told him.

She owed too much money to the bank, and Mr. Phillips, the loan officer from Haines First Trust, had told her that if it wasn't paid within the week, they'd take the property.

"You'll probably have to sell half of the property next year just to stay afloat. You won't have any revenue coming in once those heifers and calves are sold," Spence had warned her.

"I know," she said with deep breath. "But what else can I do? If you can think of something else, tell me," she said with desperation.

"I'd give you the money if I had it," Cooper said. "Gray never said anything. I figured y'all were livin' as best as you could with what you had, but I didn't know things were this bad."

"Me neither, Coop. I think Daddy was hoping the carnival would bring extra income, and he'd talk his way out of this mess, but Mr. Phillips won't hear me out. He says this has been going on for a while," she had said to Cooper.

She felt like her life was flashing before her eyes. All her life she complained about farming, and now that it was going to be out of her reach, she couldn't imagine herself doing anything else.

"What else can I do?" she shouted at Cooper as they stood in front of the loaded truck. The scent of manure permeated the air. The cows mooed and whined behind them. Their big heads tried to get through the open space in the iron gate. "Where am I going to get that kind of money?" She looked up at the sky and then back at him and Katie. "You see it falling? There isn't a tree around here that grows cash, so what else can I do?" she snapped.

Cooper spit into his bottle. "Like I say, cranky."

Katie stifled a laugh.

"I don't know how y'all can think anything about this is funny," she said.

"We don't, Eves. This is heartbreaking, but if we don't laugh, we'll start to cry and how's that gonna help you?" Katie said.

"I can't deal with mushy right now," Evie said to her. "If you're going to get all hormonal on me just go inside."

Katie and Cooper both gave her a look.

"Sorry," she mumbled and rubbed her right arm. "That last heifer about killed my arm."

"You need to talk softer to them," Cooper said. "You keep yelling at them like that, they're going to be like this all day, and I'm too old to be pushin' pregnant heifers."

"Maybe you need to rest a minute," Katie said to her. "To cool off."

"I need to get going so we can get done," she said. She pulled the keys out of her pocket and jingled them. "You coming with me, Cooper?"

"I guess," he muttered. "Not like I have much choice," he added.

They locked the gate and made their way to the front of the truck. Evie climbed into the driver's side, and Cooper sat down beside her. She started up the truck and the engine chugged. The cattle moved around in the back – she could hear their hooves hitting the metal floor, and their cries as she shifted into second gear, and the truck moved along the gravel road.

She continued to the entrance to her property and slowed down. She squinted her eyes and leaned forward, peering closely out the windshield. "Who is that?"

The gate was blocked by an old familiar pick up truck. She braked and shut the engine off. She glanced again and opened her mouth in surprise. "That looks like..." her voice trailed off, and she swung her door open, jumping out of the truck. The cattle were startled. They all let out a chorus of moos. Evie kicked up her pace and ran to the old truck.

He opened the driver's side, got out, and made his way to Evie in a hurry.

He lifted her off of the ground and wrapped his arms around her. "Evie." He nearly sang her name with happiness.

"Finch," she said and kissed him on the dimple of his chin. "I missed you so much."

"Not as much as I missed you," he said and lowered her to the ground. He placed his hands on hers and looked down at her. "You're a sight for sore, tired eyes."

She could see the bags under his brown eyes and dark shadows surrounding them. "You look beat," she said.

"I am. I've been driving all night," he said.

"He drives like a maniac," Stoney added. His head popped out the passenger side window.

"Try sitting in the back," Doris yelled.

"He is fortunate the Smokeys weren't out," Friedrich added, his voice calling from the back of the truck.

"We could've ended up in jail as fast as he was going," Mouse shouted.

Evie laughed and squeezed his hands. "You trying to be the Bandit?"

"Can't be the Bandit without Frog," he said.

"I never understood why he called her that," Evie said.

He shrugged. "People always give pet names to people they love, Laura Ingalls." He smiled down at her.

"They sure do, Jerk Face," she replied with a wide grin.

Doris, Friedrich, Mouse, and Stoney got out of the truck and walked over to Evie and Finch.

Evie looked down with a puzzled expression at the suitcases they were holding. "What are y'all doing here?" she asked them all.

"I think Finch should answer that question," Doris said.

She turned to Finch and gave a questioning look.

"Katie told me," he said, staring down into her eyes.

She frowned and said, "I didn't want you to know."

"Why, Evie?"

"It's not your problem," she said.

"Anything that's your problem becomes mine too," he said.

"And then it becomes ours too, Honey Lamb," Doris chimed in, and they all nodded in agreement.

"There's nothing you can do," Evie said to him with a wrinkled brow.

"Well, Evie, it brings me great pleasure to tell you that for once you are not right." He flashed a smile. "Can I say that one more time just for self-satisfaction?"

"What's going on?"

"We paid the bank this morning. That Mr. Phillips was all too eager to take our money. Seems like the first time someone's been happy to take anything from the likes of us, but when it's money, people can change their minds pretty fast," he said. "So you can back that truck up and let those cattle roam this land."

"What? How? Finch?"

He gave her a sincere smile. "We put our funds together, and I finally got my father to pay child support," he said.

"You got money from your dad?" she said.

"We put up our share, and he paid the rest. It's the least he could do."

"I can't take y'all's money," she said, shaking her head. "I just can't. And you got money from him?" she said in disbelief, trying to wrap her mind around their generosity.

"Well, it's too late for that," he said with a chuckle.

"Finch, I'll never be able to repay y'all." Tears fell from her eyes. "Any of y'all."

"Aww, who cares about that," he said. "Remember when I told you sometimes people just give 'cause they want to."

"But it's so much," she said. "It's too much."

"You can't measure love, Evie."

"You love me?" she said with a tone of hope.

"Duh, and I sure as hell hope you love me or else I look like a real idiot right now."

"I love you, Finch Mills," she said with certainty.

"Well, you're stuck with me if you'll have me."

"I wouldn't have it any other way." She smiled and giggled to herself. "Finch the farmer. It has a nice ring to it."

Doris, Friedrich, Mouse, and Stoney cleared their throats in unison.

"Oh," he breathed, "There's something else I forgot to mention." He scrunched up his face. "Can you fit three old carnies in that other house of yours? It seems that you're stuck with my family too if you'll have them."

"Old! Who you calling old?" Doris scoffed.

"Three? I'm counting four," Evie said.

"I'm only visiting," Stoney interrupted. "It gets too cold here for my old creaky bones. I'm gonna plant myself in the sunshine state."

"I'll take any baggage that comes with you," Evie said with a laugh, and hugged him tight. "Looks like we've got some unpacking to do."

"Kiss her, Finch!" Doris shouted. "Like they do in the movies."

Finch raised an eyebrow and peered down at Evie.

"Kiss me hard, Finch," Evie said.

"Okay," he said and rested his palm behind her neck, peering down into her eyes. "But this time I'm not going anywhere."

THE END

THE HEARTS OF HAINES SERIES CONTINUES

Check out the sequel, _Like All Things Beautiful_

In this sequel to _Kiss Me Hard Before You Go_, Evie Barnes is living day-to-day, trying to keep her father's land and his cattle business afloat. She is adjusting to his absence and to living with Finch and the rest of the carnies, which is creating quite a stir amongst the locals in Haines.

As Finch and the others learn a new way of life that doesn't involve the carnival, they're dealing with prejudice from almost everyone in town. A string of suspicious incidents occur, prompting all fingers to point the blame at them.

Just when Evie and Finch learn to deal with the mountain of obstacles facing them, the unexpected happens, causing them to question if their relationship can survive it all.

OTHER BOOKS BY THIS AUTHOR:

The Summer I Learned to Dive.

Since the time she was a little girl, eighteen-year-old Finley "Finn" Hemmings has always lived her life according to a plan, focused and driven with no time for the average young adult's carefree experiences. On the night of her high school graduation, things take a dramatic turn when she discovers that her mother has been keeping a secret from her—a secret that causes Finn to do something she had never done before—veer off her plan. In the middle of the night, Finn packs her bags and travels by bus to Graceville, SC seeking the truth. In Graceville, Finn has experiences that change her life forever; a summer of love, forgiveness and revelations. She learns to take chances, to take the plunge and to dive right in to what life has to offer.

The Year I Almost Drowned.

In this continuation of "The Summer I Learned to Dive," nineteen-year old Finley "Finn" Hemmings is living in Graceville, South Carolina with her grandparents. She's getting to know the family that she was separated from for the last sixteen years. Finn and Jesse's relationship seems to be going strong until they're forced to deal with obstacles that throw them off-track. As Finn prepares to leave for college, she has to say goodbye to the town, her friends and family, and the way of life that she has grown to love.

At college, Finn tries to acclimate to a new setting, but quickly falls into an old pattern. Just as things start to become normal and Finn begins to fit in, something unexpected happens that takes her back to Graceville where she is forced to deal with one challenge after another. Her world nearly collapses, and she finds herself struggling to keep from drowning. Through it all, Finn discovers the power of love and friendship. She learns what it means to follow her heart and to stay true to what she wants, even if what she wants isn't what she originally planned.

The Days Lost.

On the heels of her high school graduation, Ellie Morales is spending her summer vacation in the mountains of Western North Carolina with her dad and brother, Jonah. Having lost their mother only months earlier, all of them are trying to cope with the loss in their own way. Part routine, part escape, running is Ellie's way of dealing with her grief. Shortly after sunrise each morning, Ellie and her dog, Bosco, set out for a lengthy run on the path that passes by her house and leads deep into the woods of the Blue Ridge Mountains. One fateful morning, Ellie is lead off of the trail and discovers a secret that will change her life, as well as the lives of the family she meets, forever. One member of this mysterious family is Sam Gantry, who seems unlike any guy she's ever known. This meeting sparks a series of events, causing Ellie to question everything she's ever known and believed. The more she learns about Sam and his family, the more she wants to help him find the missing puzzle pieces.

ABOUT THE AUTHOR

Shannon McCrimmon was born and raised in Central Florida. She earned a Master's Degree in Counseling from Rollins College. In 2008, she moved to the upstate of South Carolina. It was the move to the upstate that inspired her to write novels. Shannon lives in Greenville, South Carolina with her husband and toy poodle.

Did you enjoy *Kiss Me Hard Before You Go?* Please consider supporting the author by writing a review on Amazon.com or Goodreads.com.

Interested in learning more about my upcoming projects? Sign up to receive my newsletter at http://bit.ly/Ma0iSJ Become a fan at www.facebook.com/shannonmccrimmonauthor or follow me on twitter@smccrimmon1

ACKNOWLEDGEMENTS

Chris, thank you for all of your support, your constructive criticism, your brainstorming sessions, your honest feedback, your brilliant and creative mind, and your unconditional love. You are my rock! Laurin Baker, thank you for your support, your honesty, and your eye for detail. You are an awesome editor, and I appreciate you constantly holding my hand and encouraging me throughout the writing process. Wendy Neuman Wilken and Betty Jones, thank you for beta reading this book. Your comments were so helpful and made this book even better. I appreciate you! Gordon, Sheila, Grayson, and Kennedi Lee, thank you for opening up your beautiful farm to me and teaching me everything I've ever needed to know about cattle. You are an amazing family, and I'm proud to call you my friends. Special thanks to Jeanette Padilla Ritz and her daughter for naming Miles. To my family and friends, thank you for all of your support, encouragement and love. I'm lucky to have you all in my life. To my readers, thank you so much for reading the words I've written. It means the world to me.

Made in the USA
Monee, IL
12 May 2021